About the au~~~

Anthony Zeid was born in Nottingham, and now lives in the Isle of Wight, where his work first took him. As well as many years as a manager in the hotel and hospitality industries, he has also been involved in politics. He holds a law degree, and now has a passion for writing. Having a keen interest in nature and wildlife, he is an avid animal lover.

THE DAY LIKE ANY OTHER

Anthony V. Zeid. LLB (Hons)

THE DAY LIKE ANY OTHER

Vanguard Press

A CIP catalogue record for this title is
available from the British Library.

ISBN 978-1-80016-024-8

*Vanguard Press is an imprint of
Pegasus Elliot MacKenzie Publishers Ltd.*
www.pegasuspublishers.com

First Published in 2020

**Vanguard Press
Sheraton House Castle Park
Cambridge England**

Printed & Bound in Great Britain

Dedication

I dedicate this book to my mother and father, of who I was so lucky and privileged to be born too and brought up by. And all of our dogs who made up such an important part of our family, both from a child through to my adulthood; and my very special boy, Zephyr.

Acknowledgements

I would like to acknowledge the genius and work of Albert Einstein, which I believe has led to a greater understanding of all creation which surrounds us, and which we are all so a part of.

I would also like to acknowledge my fiancée, Julie, whose both outer, and inner beauty were a source of inspiration to me during the writing of this book.

Chapter 1

The hands of the modern grandfather clock, clad in light oak, moved slowly but surely across its face as seven chimes ushered in a new early dawn...

It was a day like any other, the alarm went off, and Tony woke up to another working day. He got up, went to the bathroom, dressed and went downstairs, where he was greeted, as always, by Zephyr, who was his dog and closest, most loved companion. Zephyr was a cross Alsatian; crossed with what, he didn't really know. Big, strikingly beautiful, and extremely intelligent, Tony had always noticed the inescapable and quite extraordinary abilities he possessed, often thinking he was some kind of a throwback to the wolf, as apart from his black and tan colouring, his looks, expressions, stance and mannerisms had often suggested this. He got a couple of Zephyr's biscuits from the cupboard, put them in his bowl and stroked him. "Won't be long," he said, as he did every morning, then left the house to go to work.

Tony is a lawyer, and before this he had had a very successful career as a hotel manager, most of which he considered to be the best years of his life so far. His former job had held everything he could want for many years. All of life was there, especially for an energetic, ambitious and red-blooded young man. He had managed many large hotels, hopping all over the country at times, and Zephyr had been at his side for all of that time before they finally returned to the Isle of Wight, where they still live now and where Tony had come back to run the hotel he had first managed there.

Towards the latter part of his career, things had started to feel monotonous, mainly because he had been doing it for so long; he'd been in hotel management since his very early twenties. He'd also been involved in politics, had chaired two local political parties which he had previously belonged to, and had finally been elected as a member of

Ryde town council on the island. Tony's interests had also started to broaden during that time. He had qualified to become an operator in the passenger service industry by gaining the necessary qualification – Certificate of Professional Competence – and had acquired the licence to operate, purchased a 52-seat vehicle, and ran his coach business for a time while still running an 80-bedroom hotel.

He finally sold his coach and came out of that business when he decided he didn't have enough capital finance to really take it forward, but considered what he'd been able to do quite an achievement. When still in his old job though, it had become increasingly apparent to him that he really needed a change, to do something different. He had been a star player in his company, achieving Hotel of the Year at one point, and been a troubleshooter, but it recent times he'd felt he was falling out of favour, and in turn he was falling out of love with them, so to speak. With the benefit of hindsight, he'd now come to realise this to be a natural parting of their relationship after a very productive run.

Eventually he made the very brash move of leaving his employment to work full time on starting his own travel business, and he soon became aware that it was an error of judgement. The business didn't take off, leaving him unemployed and in a very difficult situation. It was hard to find other employment in the middle of a recession, however he managed to eventually find a job working for a company who had recently invested in a property which they were wanting to restore to its former glory as a hotel, restaurant and bar. By putting all of his management, leadership, hospitality and catering skills to their maximum use, it wasn't long before he was running the operation.

During the time he spent there he began studying for an academic degree, which was something he had wanted to do for a long time, and he now felt he had the opportunity. He decided on law, mainly because of the prestige it holds in any walk of life, and in any case he liked the idea of actually entering the law profession. After graduating with his law degree, he went on to study the legal practice course whilst doing pro bono work, mainly at the local Citizens Advice centre to get some of his work hours in the profession which would enable him to practice.

Finally gaining a position within a high street firm of solicitors, where he'd now been for the last two years as a legal executive, he mainly worked in the areas of conveyancing and contract law. Tony enjoyed his work, and the firm were generally pleased with him. His previous profession and life experiences had stood him in good stead for the law profession, and he was now building a pretty good reputation with his clients, who had mainly spoken highly of him to the senior partners. As a result, he was largely left to his own devices, which suited him immensely. Still, he often missed the heady days of his old career, but had come to realise you just can't have it all ways, and nothing lasts forever.

As he walked into the practice, a modernised, airy building on the high street with double-fronted windows, he was met by the Head Legal Secretary, Mrs Calthorpe. "Oh Christ," he thought to himself. A bristly woman who'd always been there, and always would, Tony thought she acted as though the practice would never survive without her, so hard faced was she; he'd argued with her more than once when she'd tried to scrutinise his work.

"Morning, Tony," she said, condescendingly.

"Morning", he replied with a forced smile. Just then, Chloe, her assistant, arrived and walked behind the desk, a vivacious and fairly attractive younger woman, but so shallow she made a trickling stream look deep, he'd observed. He had actually thought of asking her out at one time, but when he found out what she was really like he felt he didn't want to be bored to death.

So another day of drawing up contracts and dealing with property conveyance had begun. As he sat in his office, checking his list for the morning, there was a knock at the door, which he recognised only too well. His first client had arrived early, the double-hyphenated Mr Urskin-Brown, and he'd come to find out the search results Tony had carried out on his latest project. A large property owner in the area, all through inherited family money, he was in the business of buying up old run-down houses and turning them into multi box-size flats in order to squeeze as much rental income from them as he could, and mainly from the most vulnerable in society – the poor, people who had found themselves on hard times, those dependent on benefits, and so on. He even acted as though he was somehow being benevolent by his endeavours; yes, Tony really hated the bastard, he'd always thought to himself.

The rest of the morning passed quickly and he broke for lunch, went back to his house to feed Zephyr, as he always did, then let him out into the garden for a while, after which he would have his own lunch before it was time to go back for the afternoon. The last client of the day was one of his much preferred. After being with the firm for about a year he'd managed to agree with the partners to do some pro bono work. Apart from it usually being the most interesting, he felt he'd been fortunate in life to have been able to do all that he'd done, so he felt that to be some help to others that needed it was only fair. He was seeing a Ms Lattimer, a bit eccentric but he liked her more for it. She ran a local animal rescue charity, definitely his favourite cause, and one which he would spend many an hour of his free time on.

He finished at around five thirty p.m., went straight back to the house as usual and was welcomed back by Zephyr. "There we are, boy, the rest of the day to ourselves," he said as soon as he walked through the door. This was both Tony and Zephyr's favourite time of the day. He got changed into his jeans and T-shirt, made himself a strong cup of tea and gave Zephyr another couple of biscuits. They went to the living room and Tony put the radio on. As they sat there, a track came on which reminded him of his dear mother, Diana, who he was very close to and who had passed on a few years ago now. Her passing had hit him very hard at the time, but eventually, because they had both always believed in a life beyond this one, in time he saw beyond his grief to realise she was there.

As well as often thinking of his mother, Tony would frequently think of his dad, Sam, who had passed when he was only in his teens, but who was still so fresh in his mind. Tony was the only child of Sam and Diana, and he loved them both dearly, as he knew they did him; he considered himself the luckiest man alive to have had them as parents. Never could he know better people, in fact when he'd speak of them, he would say he'd have loved them as much had he not even been their son. They were a constant reminder to him of everything that was good and decent, in a world which he often considered to be increasingly corrupt, selfish and fast being void of any morals.

A strike of the clock on the half hour reminded him it was time for what they did every evening. "Well, Zeph, time for our walk, boy," Tony said. In his younger years, as well as working hard on his career he had also played hard, a real party animal at times and a one for the ladies! But now in his mid-forties he'd grown out of all that, and grown ever closer to the joys of nature, far preferring a walk with Zephyr to being in some bar or nightclub.

At one time he'd like to think of himself as living a James Bond lifestyle, he'd loved to travel, usually on his own, getting into all sorts of adventures with all sorts of people. Now, largely due to this previous lifestyle, he found himself unmarried and with no children; many opportunities he'd had to marry in the past but had considered himself not ready. He realised it had taken him a long time to grow up in this way, and had begun in a small way to regret this thing he'd not done so far, sometimes thinking that if he'd settled down earlier, he would in some way have been even more successful in life. But then, as the saying goes, 'you can't have your cake and eat it', he'd realise. Besides, he was still very young for his years and probably resembling someone in their mid-thirties – fit, strong and very energetic, he always thought there was plenty of time.

He clipped Zephyr's lead on, grabbed his jacket and keys and they started out for their walk. They would drive down to a secluded part of the island by a river where there were fields and a wood; it was midsummer, and when they arrived it was now a beautiful evening with not another soul around. As they got out of the car, Zephyr started to frolic with joy. Walking along a grass bank, Tony threw Zephyr's ball and the odd stick for him. He would always smile to himself as he watched him run – no one had ever named anything more aptly, the meaning of the word 'zephyr' being a trade wind of the sea, which he so closely resembled. He ran like the wind, with his ears and fur swept back and his tendrils trailing behind his legs. As they walked on, Tony looked out on all the beauty around him. He wasn't a religious man by any means, and he hated judgementalism, but ever since he could remember, he'd had an absolute and unshakeable belief in God. In relation to nature, his philosophy was that it was all part of an ongoing development of creation, and should be enjoyed, cared for and respected by man, something he wished much of the rest of the world shared with him.

Around halfway through their walk, just as they were passing by the woods, something caught Zephyr's attention; he suddenly bolted towards an opening in the trees and swiftly passed through it. "Zephyr, Zephyr!" Tony shouted, running after him, thinking he must have seen a fox or some other wild animal. He shot through the opening in pursuit but couldn't see him and started to worry. The woods were large and Tony must have been running for around a hundred metres, constantly shouting his name.

After a time, he reached the other side of the woods and could now see more daylight. He stepped out into an open deserted field to finally find Zephyr, sitting, looking outward onto the field. "There you are, please god, what are you doing?" Tony said as he looked at him intently. Zephyr looked back at him, then back towards the field. As he followed Zephyr's gaze, he couldn't believe what he was now looking at. There, straight in front of them, was what could only be described as some sort of... object.

"My... god," Tony said as he stood motionless. This thing was huge, spherical in shape, as tall as a ten-storey building and as wide as a football pitch. Opaque in appearance, it had a strange translucent quality, and seemed to be pulsating. Tony could feel a slight tremor through the ground and went to grab Zephyr. "Come away," he said, then, silently and without warning, an opening appeared in the huge object. Before Tony could take hold of Zephyr's collar, he swiftly started to run towards the opening. "Zephyr, no!" Tony shouted desperately, but there was no stopping him, he was headed straight for it.

Having no choice but to follow him, they both ran up a ramp, straight into the opening and were met by a blank wall. Tony turned around to look outward to the field, intending to grab Zephyr and get the hell out of there when suddenly the opening closed in front of them, seamlessly, enclosing them within. Tony looked around him into the pale grey light of the chamber they were now trapped in, at the bare walls which had the same appearance.

He ran at what had been the entrance, ferociously kicking and thumping the door which now held them, but it soon became obvious to him this wasn't going to achieve anything. When he stopped, he looked back at Zephyr. "You all right?' he said in a hushed voice. Zephyr seemed very much at ease, which told Tony they were not in imminent danger for now, although he was understandably still on extreme alert to their situation.

Suddenly, two fairly wide flat beams of what looked like ultraviolet light extended down from the ceiling, hitting them both simultaneously, moving up and down as though to scan them. There was no pain, or even discomfort, just a slight tingling sensation; this lasted for just a few seconds, after which Zephyr shook himself. Tony reached out to touch him: "OK, boy," he said reassuringly. "Right, let's find a way out of here!" He started to run his hand along the walls and tap them. The material they were made of felt like nothing he had touched before, it had a strange almost silky feel to it, but at the same time seemed like the hardest, most solid substance he'd ever felt; it was warm, and in some way felt... Alive. "What the hell is this place," he said to himself.

Tony started to explore the wall which had closed on them, again tapping it to see if he could discover some sort of obscured device which would open it, but no joy. Then feeling a brief rush of air behind him, he turned to find the inner wall had opened. "Oh great," he thought. "Just what I didn't want!" He stepped towards the opening whilst Zephyr stood looking cautiously at what had now appeared before them. Tony stepped through to discover a long, curving corridor to the right of him; he pondered on whether he should explore where this led to. It was against his better judgement that he decided he should go ahead, but he hoped 'this' might lead to a way out. Besides, anything was better than being trapped in that chamber, he thought.

"Come on, boy," he said to Zephyr. They made their way down the corridor; it was bathed in a pale version of that same ultraviolet light they'd seen in the chamber; it had a sort of sterile smell to it, like a hospital, and a strange sound of... silence. Tony had his eyes everywhere, constantly looking for some sort of means of escape, but the corridor itself seemed to be completely sealed. Walking further on, it occurred to him they might be being watched, although he couldn't see any CCTV cameras. He had by now realised that this whole thing

17

was obviously some kind of highly secured unit. But even so, the fact he'd never been aware of the existence of something the size and nature of this place, was a growing mystery to him. Nevertheless, he was hoping to catch the attention of a surveillance device, so that someone could come and let them out. But, just at that moment, a voice suddenly spoke.

"Hello, Tony." It seemed to come from every direction. The voice was female, it sounded formal but in some way had an understanding tone to it.. He was at first startled, but then gathered himself within a few seconds when Zephyr let out a deep bark. "We are sorry you and your friend have been inconvenienced," the voice went on to say.

"We... we are sorry!' Tony said in reply. "Who are 'we'"

"We will reveal ourselves to you all in good time," said the voice. "But for now, you are our guests here."

Thinking this was beginning to feel a bit sinister. "No that's OK, just let us out the way we came in, and we'll be on our way," Tony replied.

"That... will not be possible," replied the voice.

As he looked around him in almost disbelief. "What do you mean not possible, we're your prisoners then!" Tony said in a raised voice.

"We do not mean or intend for you to feel like that, Tony, but it is true that you will be here with us for quite some time, and will not be able to leave until certain events have been concluded," the voice ended by saying.

Tony looked up and shouted again. "Look, I don't know who the hell you are, or what you're talking about, but this is not right, and I'm telling you to let us go, you bastards!" He was really starting to get angry, as he often could. Zephyr was for the first time starting to get slightly distressed, but Tony knew this was only because of the way he was acting. He put his hand out to him and spoke reassuringly and, for the sake of Zephyr, calmed himself down.

The voice spoke again: "Tony, will you both please walk on a little further". Now knowing there was no point going back, Tony reluctantly continued. They reached what seemed to be the end of the corridor and were facing another wall, but this time with what looked like an ordinary conventional door. "Please go through, Tony," said the voice.

Approaching and putting his hand on the handle apprehensively, he opened it.

As he and Zephyr stepped in, Tony was shocked to see a room with living accommodations; austere but functional and modern; everything in there looked completely new and untouched. The voice spoke. "We want you and your friend to be comfortable and feel as at home as possible during your time with us."

"What the hell are we doing here?" replied Tony.

"We will speak again tomorrow," the voice ended by saying.

In the ensuing silence, Tony realised the conversation with the voice was over, at least for now anyway. "That's what she thinks – we'll be long gone by then!" he said to Zephyr. Seeing that there were other doors to the area, curiosity temporarily got the better of him and he began to look around. There was a wash room, a place that resembled a cooking and food storage area – which was open plan to the living area – and through another door a room with a bed and closed storage units. "This is crazy," he thought as he walked back into the living area. Tony stood silently for a few moments. Now that he had time to gather his thoughts, he was in disbelief about the events which had occurred in the last hour, and the situation he now found himself in. Zephyr sat looking at him knowingly, as he too seemed to sense the strangeness of their situation and surroundings.

As he looked around the room again, Tony remembered there was a very large oval-shaped window, which stretched from floor to ceiling on the right-hand side wall, where the living room area met the kitchen area. He and Zephyr walked over to it; Tony was pleased and almost relieved to see that it looked onto the outside world. They could see the field, the woods and the sky in front of them. It was now dusk and the sun was setting on a beautiful evening.

Then...Suddenly the walls and floor started to gently vibrate, it felt as though the whole room was alive! Then, to Tony's horror, he noticed that what ever they were in had started to slowly lift from the ground. "My god, we're moving," he said. Zephyr became agitated and started to bark. "OK, Zeph. OK, boy," Tony said, trying to calm him down. Still standing at the window, they watched the ground and woods getting smaller as they continued to ascend at an increasing rate. Within less than thirty seconds they were so high that Tony could make out the circumference of the Earth. He looked upwards and could now see the stars above him; within a few more seconds Tony could see they were now leaving Earth's atmosphere as they passed through the thin blue border line of the sky. He grabbed Zephyr and moved them back from the window, thinking they were in imminent danger, but what surrounded them remained stable, as they continued to move... through space.

Chapter 2

As he stood there, in a split-second Tony realised his sinister suspicions had been confirmed. He hadn't even wanted to admit it to himself because he'd thought it impossible, but everything he had experienced over the last hour or so had had an unearthly feel about it; the events of the last two minutes finally punctuating that they were on an alien space vessel of some kind, and the craft had now started to revolve.

Tony moved cautiously back towards the window. He could see his native world getting smaller with every revolution; they were now moving at such a speed that the planet became the size of a small shining speck in the vastness of space within just a few seconds. As Earth disappeared, Tony now watched the Sun start to almost halve in size with each subsequent revolution, before becoming the size of an average star in the sky in less than a minute. When the revolutions of the vessel finally stopped, Tony felt a sharp and powerful jolt as it adopted a fixed position and continued to hurtle through space at a rate which he could only imagine.

He stood at the window in almost disbelief, but in awe at the incredible sight of what was now deep space; he and Zephyr looked at each other, and Tony suddenly started to laugh in incredulity. "My god, Zeph," he said, in the absence of anything else to say. Zephyr had that knowing expression on his face, stood up and placed his paws on Tony's chest. Tony put the side of his face against his. "My god," he finally repeated, as he continued to stare-into space. As the events of the last few minutes started to catch up with him, Tony began to gather himself. He ran over to the door which they'd come in through. It was locked. His thoughts then turned to the fact that not only were they now millions of miles from Earth, but what about their home, their life, and ultimately, what was to become of them?

A cold shudder ran right through him, but after half an hour or so he shook his off concerns and decided the only thing for him to do for now was keep a grip on reality, take care of their immediate needs – survival. The first priority was food. Remembering it would now normally be Zephyr's time for dinner, he looked round into the kitchen area at what looked like a set of enclosed compartments. "Come on, boy, let's see what we've got in here. They've thought of everything else, they must have thought of food, I hope!" he said as he cautiously walked over.

Touching the front of the first compartment, he was briefly taken aback as it automatically slid open. It looked and felt like ordinary stainless steel, and as it revealed its contents, Tony could see an abundance of plain, see-through pouches, each containing what looked like a selection of cooking condiments; dried herbs and spices.

He continued to open the rest of them to find they contained all the usual kitchen utensils, until he finally got to the one which he hoped would be allocated for Zephyr.

The compartment contained several vacuum-packed, see-through pouches, each containing a substance which looked very similar to Zephyr's normal food; another see- through box-like object contained something that closely resembled his biscuits. "This is definitely yours then," he said to Zephyr, but with this there came a sinister realisation: "They know, how did they know what kind of food to provide. My god, it's as though they've been watching, observing us," he said to himself.

Thinking they wouldn't have gone to all this trouble just to poison them, he fed Zephyr, and then took a look inside what he figured was a large upright freezer unit. He always ate his main meal just before going to bed, which was a habit left over from his hotel management days, when his working day would end late in the evening. For the sake of convenience this would mainly consist of re-heating ready-made meals.

As he rifled through each compartment, he saw what he was now pretty much expecting, a wide selection of frozen meals, all encased in trays which were made of the same see-through materials as Zephyr's pouches. But one thing both shocked him, and sent a shiver down his spine. There, on its own in the bottom compartment, was a single bottle; Tony liked to have a couple of glasses of whisky last thing every evening before eating – he called it his 'libation' at the end of a long busy day. "My god, they even know that," he thought. He closed the freezer door, deciding not have his libation tonight. As much as he felt he could use a drink right now, he knew he could hardly afford to relax!

There was what he thought might be some kind of remote control hand set on the table next to a chair in the living room section; Tony took it over to what looked like a TV screen and pressed the 'on' button. As he scrolled through a menu, there appeared on the screen whole banks of hundreds of TV and film recordings. "Oh, maybe I'll watch Star Trek," he joked to himself, but he didn't exactly feel like watching television either and turned it off. "Tea, my god, let's see if they've even provided that," he thought.

He went back to the kitchen area, found something that contained what looked like tea bags, got what he thought was milk from a fridge; still at the forefront of his mind how crazy this all was, he made himself a good strong cup. "Mmm, not bad," he thought. Zephyr was by now making himself at home and laying on a rug with his legs stretched out. "I'd do well to learn from you, boy," Tony said with a wry smile. Zephyr sat up and looked over as though to assure him that again they were in no immediate danger at the moment. Tony tried out the chair which was next to Zephyr's rug. They both sat there in silence. Tony sipped his tea as he warily gazed out of the window and watched the stars in the distance pass by as their excursion through space continued, the reality of where they actually were dawning on him again and again like a shockwave.

Eventually, although still not feeling hungry, Tony did himself some dinner, thinking it no good not to eat. Besides, curiosity got the better of him and he had to find out what the things they'd provided tasted like! He filled a bowl of water for Zephyr and was now starting to feel tired; he'd decided to sleep on a couch in the living room area as Zephyr was getting used to his rug, went to the bedroom and grabbed a quilt. Before turning in he once again stood at the huge window to take a last look out, still in almost disbelief. "Lights," he thought. "Was there some kind of switch?" He spotted a dial on the wall, cautiously touched and started to turn it, and the lights began to dim to a very comfortable level for sleep. Tony sat down on the couch and reached out to stroke Zephyr. "Night, boy," he said. They both laid down and before long were fast asleep; it had been a 'very' long day!

Tony woke up after an uneasy night's sleep, his body clock telling him it should now be morning. The events of the previous day came quickly flooding back to him. He looked at his watch, the time was five thirty a.m., 'Earth time' that is. As he rose from the sofa, Zephyr stood up and had a long stretch. Tony stood up and went over to the dial to raise the light level. As he turned the disc, he noticed the lights were providing a kind of daylight atmosphere. This felt strange, but it was good to experience the natural feel of it. Not having even undressed last night, he went to the kitchen and gave Zephyr his morning biscuits; as he did this he suddenly realised Zephyr would need to go out for the usual reasons! Knowing he would never do this in the room unless he was desperate, Tony was just about to try to take him out through the door when the voice suddenly returned. "Good morning, Tony. I see you have both slept."

"Yes, yes, and whoever or whatever you are, Zephyr needs to go out, I mean go somewhere else, to do what he needs to do."

"Yes I know, Tony," the voice replied. Tony heard a click as the door to the room unlocked. "Walk through the entrance and follow my directions." They went through into the corridor. The voice, now about ten metres ahead, directed them along the corridor until they came to a connecting passage on the right-hand side about fifty metres from their accommodation. "Turn this way," the voice said. The passage was only around ten metres long and led to what looked like a set of large sliding doors. "Press the wall on the right-hand side with the palm of your hand, Tony," said the voice. As he pushed against the wall, the doors began to slowly slide open, and what they revealed was almost breathtaking.

Tony looked on in wonder at what appeared to be an ecologically natural environment, a large area of grass, around fifty metres in length and thirty metres in width, with trees, bushes and even the sound of birds singing! Zephyr walked cautiously onto the grass, finding the nearest bush to relieve himself. Tony stepped into the environment and walked up to one of the trees which also appeared to be real, and in full leaf. As he looked up and around, he was just able to catch sight of a couple of groups of birds high in the trees. They looked like sparrows and blackbirds. He watched in fascination as they flew from tree to tree, before eventually throwing a fallen branch for Zephyr, who swiftly retrieved it.

They both enjoyed stretching their legs. He'd now looked at and felt the grass trees and bushes, and as far as he could tell, they were all absolutely real, but because they were enclosed and the air must be manufactured in some way, Tony could still sense and smell the artificial nature of it all, like grass under an enclosed tent. After they'd spent about thirty minutes in the enclosure, they walked back through the doors. Tony placed his hand on the wall. "How the hell did they do this?" he said to himself as the doors closed behind them.

When they got back to their accommodation, he went to the bathroom, where there were all the personal items he needed: toothbrush and paste, shower gel, soap, shaving gel and razor. As there were no brand names on these things, he could only assume his capturers had manufactured this stuff themselves, but the food remained a complete mystery to him! He had a shower and shave and went to the set of drawers in the bedroom, where sure enough there were clean sets of clothes. Putting on a pair of jeans and a polo shirt, which fitted him almost perfectly, he went back into the kitchen to make himself another strong tea. Walking over to the window in the living area, he looked out onto the stars, by now thinking to himself that whoever these alien beings, whose hands he was now in were, and for whatever reasons they wanted them there for, they did seem to be relatively benevolent, at least for now anyway.

As he continued to watch the stars in the distance sweep by the window, an ominous thought suddenly dawned on him. "We're probably travelling at the speed of light, or even faster! That means we're also travelling into the future. My god, of course, there's no going back for us, not to our time anyway. If we do ever get back then everything, everyone we knew would be gone, long since in the past." Tony looked down at the floor and felt a brief moment of sadness, then looked round at Zephyr and smiled. "Well… they were all mainly colleagues and associations anyway. As long as we're together, that's the only important thing, we've always got each other," he said as he knelt down to stroke him.

Later on, he decided he would just think about the here and now for the moment. "OK, let's see if we've got radio, Zeph." He grabbed the remote and went over to the TV, turning it on and scrolling through a radio menu he'd found; it contained months of recordings of previous programmes. He switched to his usual channel and sat down, now beginning to feel a bit more at ease in his new environment. He didn't yet know exactly how long they were going to be there, but started to think about what he would do with his days throughout the duration. Vitally active and having always possessed a huge amount of energy, he knew he would need to devise himself a busy daily schedule, otherwise he'd go crazy with boredom and his energy levels would go through the ceiling.

As he pondered over this problem, he couldn't help but once again summon the ironic thoughts about his situation, and what had occurred over just the last 24 hours. Yesterday morning he was on his way to his office on a normal working day; this morning he was millions of miles out in space on some alien ship, sitting in a room thinking about what he was going to do all day! He had to laugh to himself.

After fixing himself some cereal for breakfast, Tony looked around to see if there was anything to read. There was no bookcase so he looked in all the compartments and drawers in every room – nothing. "Well, they didn't think of that," he said to himself. He flicked through the TV menu. "Huh, just all the usual daytime crap," he thought. "They must have set the program options to the relevant time of day. They really do mean for everything to be as realistic as possible for us, don't they, huh," he said to Zephyr.

As he glanced over to a desktop and chair, he suddenly noticed something which resembled a kind of laptop computer; an embossed sign just read 'Information Station'. Sitting down to flip the top open, it automatically came to life. It had a keyboard but the startup screen looked unlike any other he was so familiar with; there was just one large disk-shaped icon in the centre of the screen. He double-clicked on a pad just under the keyboard and a toolbar to type in quickly popped up. He fast got the hang of it as he typed in a series of commands, bringing up the widest range of subjects he could bring to mind; it became increasingly clear that this piece of equipment contained the sum total of human knowledge. "My god, they must have even downloaded the complete internet back on Earth!" he said to himself. A look at his watch told him it was now lunchtime. "Time for your dinner, boy," he said. Zephyr knew exactly what that meant and moved eagerly into the kitchen. He fed him the usual amount, which he woofed down swiftly.

In the absence of anything else to do, Tony decided they should attempt to go back to the natural environment again to get some exercise. "Come on, Zeph, let's get back to the 'park'," he joked. They walked through the door into the corridor; making their way back to the sliding doors, Tony realised they must now have full access to the route and the area. Again he placed the palm of his hand on the wall. As the doors opened in the same way, he noticed it was now warmer in there, as though to reflect the time of day. They spent about an hour in there this time. Tony found a good piece of branch and threw it a few times for Zephyr, as always enjoying watching him running like the wind. He also ran around the area a few times himself to work off some built up energy. "OK, back to our apartment, Zeph," he joked again.

When they got back, Zephyr laid on his rug and slipped into his afternoon snooze. As they had been up since five thirty a.m., Tony also felt quite tired. He looked at Zephyr. "Good idea," he thought, closed his eyes and went off himself for half an hour. As they woke, Zephyr got up, had another good stretch and went to his bowl for water, and Tony went to make himself another tea. He thought to himself how well they were both adjusting to their new situation and environment, although grudgingly, as far as he was concerned.

Just then, the voice spoke. "Now you've both had more time to get settled, it's time we spoke again, Tony." Zephyr let out a deep bark. Tony looked up in the direction of the voice.

"You know, I wish you would stop doing that!"

"Doing what?" said the voice.

"Sneaking up on me without warning and just speaking to me unexpectedly, it's getting really annoying!" His comment was met with silence. "OK, so what do you want to talk about then? Tony said.

The voice started to speak again: "Tony, I want to talk about the time you are going to spend here with us. I am sure you have many questions, but the first thing I want to reaffirm is that we mean you and

Zephyr no harm during your time here, you have my absolute assurance of that."

"How long will I be here?" Tony replied.

"The journey will take about four of your calendar months," the voice confirmed.

"Four months! At the speed we're moving, how far will that take us?" he asked.

"I need to know what you would like during your time here," the voice retorted, as though to avoid his question.

There was a silence whilst Tony contemplated what it was that he would need to occupy him, and what it was going to be like to be there for such a protracted period of time. He began by replying: "If we were not out here, in space, I would escape in that amount of time, you can be sure of that!" he said aggressively. "Anyway, as you're asking, I need physical and mental exercise, things to keep me busy every day."

"I am aware of that, Tony. We have an exercise area for you, and perhaps you would like to study something."

Tony cut in. "How do you know so much about me anyway? Everything in this place – you know what I eat, what I drink, that I need to keep busy... what else do you know?"

"Have a think about it, Tony, about what you would like to study. I will take you to the exercise facility tomorrow, but for now, try to enjoy the rest of the day," the voice replied.

'Oh, that's it for the day then, is it?" Tony shouted. "End of conversation again. Well in future, we'll talk when I want to as well. Do you hear me? Do you?" Tony's words were met with silence again. Now feeling annoyed and frustrated, he stomped around his accommodation a few times in a rage, only finally calming himself down because he could see Zephyr getting concerned. Taking a long deep breath as he once again contemplated the length of time they were going to be captive there, he began to have added thoughts of where they were actually destined for, and what would await them... when they arrived.

Later on, Tony decided the best thing for them both was to spend a normal night and do as they always did. He flicked through the TV menu again and mapped out the programmes he'd watch that evening;

decided what he was going to have for dinner; and took Zephyr back to the park for their usual evening walk. On returning to the apartment, Tony put on the first TV programme. For sheer amusement, he chose *The Sky at Night*!, laughing to himself and joking to Zephyr: "This has just gotta be done, boy." His heart warmed at Zephyr wagging his tail.

He also decided he would have his libation that night, after all he was pretty satisfied by now that they were in no imminent danger, and felt as though he could finally do with some relaxation. He took the bottle of whisky from out of the freezer and an appropriate glass from a cupboard and sat down in the chair. As he poured himself a strong one and looked over at Zephyr, who was now comfortable on his rug, he lifted his glass. "Cheers, Zeph," he said, as he often did at the end of a busy day. They sat there as though they were spending a normal evening at home; Tony was more relaxed than he'd been since this whole unbelievable event happened. If there was one thing about he and Zephyr, they were extremely adaptable. They'd had to be many times in the past, and now as always, and if it were possible, given where they now were, things began to feel more like a home from home!

Tony thought about what he wanted to study. When he was studying for his law degree, natural science had also appealed to him. This encompassed both the study of nature on Earth, and astronomy. "How appropriate!" he thought. After he'd had his dinner, he got the quilt from the bedroom again and they bedded down for the second night of their journey.

Chapter 3

When they woke the next morning, and after Tony gave Zephyr his usual biscuits, they went straight to the park for half an hour. Tony got the sense they were beginning to settle into a routine; this had always been important to them, and could only be a good thing. When they got back to their apartment, he decided he wanted to talk to the voice. "Hey, are you there? Hello, voice, hello! he called out sarcastically.

After a short time, the voice answered. "What is it, Tony?

"Oh, you do reply when you're called then!" Tony said. "Well you said you'd show me the gym."

"Yes, follow me in the usual way," the voice directed. He signalled Zephyr to come along with him; there was no way he was leaving him there on his own. They followed the voice along the corridor in the same direction, past the entrance to the park and then on another thirty metres to an opening with a short corridor, like the entrance to the park. Tony put his hand on the wall in the same way and the doors opened.

"Wow!" he said. As he stood there, a smile came over his face. He stepped into what was a very large area with fantastic gym equipment, and there was even a pool, about twenty metres in length and ten in width. He turned and looked up in the direction of the voice he'd been following. "Thanks, this is great. Oh, and by the way, natural science," he said.

"What?" the voice replied.

"Natural science, I want to study natural science and astronomy," he ended by saying. Tony took off his shirt, got onto the running machine, turned it on and started to jog. After about three minutes he turned to look at Zephyr, who was looking at him as if to say "what the hell are you doing that for?" Tony began to laugh, so much in the end he had to stop. He eventually carried on for a while longer, before switching to the rowing machine.

After finishing his land exercises, he decided to give the pool a try, felt the water, which was very well heated, and went to get ready to dive in. He suddenly realised he had no trunks, then smiled to himself as he realised that it hardly mattered here! He then had to think twice when he remembered they could be being watched. "Hey, well, they're aliens anyway. Probably won't even know what they're looking at, who cares!" he thought to himself. He stripped his remaining clothes off and took a running dive in. He was really in his element now; in his teens he'd swum as a sport. The water felt so good as he swam a good few lengths, almost forgetting where he was.

When they eventually left the gym, he was feeling all the better and they made their way back to the apartment. As they approached the door to their accommodation, Tony noticed what looked like a cardboard box to the side of it, and picked it up before they went back in. Sitting at the table in the living area, he opened the box to reveal its contents. "Wow," he said as he looked over at Zephyr. The box was packed full of university-style study books that he recognised all too well, each one with a plain cover, with the words 'Natural Sciences 1-2-3' and so on printed respectively on the front. "My god, what ever these things are, they certainly keep their word," he said to himself.

Later on that day, after he'd completed around four hours of study, he thought it was time for him and Zephyr to get some more exercise and go back to the park area. As they walked around, Tony had a good think about everything, looking up at the birds singing and flying around in the trees… "I want answers," he said to himself.
When they got back to the apartment, Tony called out to speak to the voice again.

"Yes, Tony," the voice said immediately and in an attentive way. "Are you pleased with your study materials?"

"Yes, yes I am, but never mind that for now – it's time for some answers," said Tony.

"What do you want to know?" the voice replied in an inquisitive yet authoritative manner.

Tony suddenly felt strange. It dawned on him at that moment that he felt much like a child as he stood there, feeling the way you do when your parents have left you in the care of an institution for a while, like a school. He quickly shook off this feeling from his childhood and began to speak. "Let me talk through what I do know so far. Three days ago you abducted us, and took us into space at what is probably the speed of light or even faster. Going to where and for what purpose I know not what, or why," he said as he continued. "You have treated us well, very well, I cannot deny, but I now want to know 'where' we are going and for 'what' purpose'. I want to know what will happen to my house, my life that I've left behind; I have to pay the mortgage and bills, if you know what that even means? And finally, I do know something of Einstein's theory of relativity, and as far as I can tell, even if you did take me back to Earth, then everything I knew would be history. I would be in the future where I won't belong."

There was silence for a while after Tony had finished speaking. The voice then replied: "These are all very valid questions which we know you must be wanting the answers to, Tony."

"Well!" said Tony.

The voice continued: "Your questions will all be answered when matters are completed, Tony. You will be released from us, just as I said when we first spoke, but for now I can say no more, I am sorry. Please know though that your house and other matters concerning your life back there are all fine, they are being taken care of."

"What do you mean by that!" Tony asked, but once again he was speaking only to a silent room. The voice had gone, and the conversation had now left Tony with even more questions than before, let alone with no real answers. What did the voice mean about his house and matters being taken care of – had they put an imposter in his place that looked and sounded the same as him? Was this all part of a greater conspiracy – were they doing this to other people in some kind of plot to take over our planet? Do they keep the abducted separate? And if so, were there or had there been others like him on the ship? This, along with many other wild thoughts, went through his mind until he decided not to let his imagination get the better of him.

He looked at Zephyr, who still appeared completely unperturbed by the whole thing. Tony smiled at him then laughed to himself. "Please god for you bringing me back to earth, Zeph," laughing again at the pun he'd just inadvertently made. "Well, boy, we're stuck with the situation for now, so we'll just have to carry on as we are. Don't worry though,

I'll make sure we'll be all right in the end. We've always been a great team and I know we'll get through all this." Later, they went back to the park again, spent their night in the usual way, then bedded down ready for another day of their continuing journey.

In the morning, they carried on with what was now their normal routine: the park, the gym, Tony's studies, and the park again. As the days passed, they continued with these daily activities. Tony was increasingly preparing himself for what might meet them, and wherever it was they were going. With the time spent in the gym he was becoming fitter than he'd been for some time; he was also progressing with his studies and finding natural and astrological science of great interest. At the same time, he found it ironic that the subject of Earth's science might not be of any use to him, where he was going; whereas in astronomy he could experience much more than he'd been studying so far by just looking out of his window! Yes, he could see far more in reality just now than any professor on the subject had ever imagined, he thought.

As he had so much time on his hands, he decided to put his chef's skills and qualifications and the excellent facilities of the kitchen area to good use. He would ask the voice for a list of fresh food every couple of days which, to his continued amazement, he would find outside his door in the morning, along with Zephyr's food replenishments, and a bottle of his whisky from time to time. He would prepare a different dish every afternoon, ready to eat it that night, and he'd add a bit more than he needed so Zephyr could have a share. He also made a makeshift calendar, which started from the date they found themselves on the ship, so that he wouldn't lose track of time. As the weeks went by, he would strike off each day as it passed, and they were now going into their fifth week.

One night, as they sat in the living room, Tony was looking out of the window, thinking about the incredible technology the ship must have, and how advanced these beings who were piloting and navigating it must be. He decided he would try to explore more of the ship, particularly the technology which powered it. The thought of this excited him and appealed to his adventurous nature. "Yes!" he said to himself. He turned to look at Zephyr, smiled and winked at him. "Yeah!

That's what we'll do," he thought.

The next day, he decided to try his luck. He wanted to see how far he could push it, how far they'd be allowed to explore the ship outside of the usual areas. So, after their last trip to the park that evening, instead of turning left when they came out of the corridor to go back to the accommodation, they turned the other way, walking about another fifty metres up the main corridor, and passing the point where Tony thought they'd first entered the ship. They eventually came to a point that veered off to the right from the main corridor, sloping in an upward direction. Tony thought this looked promising. Not only might it take them to a higher level of the ship, by the look of it, it would take them much further inward than they'd been before.

They walked cautiously in and Tony began to wonder how far they'd get before the voice would interrupt them or some obstruction be placed in their way, but to his surprise none of this happened and they carried on freely. As they continued, he began to come across a series of strange looking signs, none of which he either recognised or understood. The corridor had started to curve to the point where Tony could only see around two metres ahead of himself. He began to walk more cautiously, and increasingly started to feel more excited and apprehensive with every step, until… he stopped in his tracks when he was suddenly met with a blank wall. Standing there, feeling a mixture of being gutted and stupid, he heard just two words from the voice that he did understand: "Dead end."

"Very funny, very bloody funny!" he said as he looked up and around. "Come on, Zeph," he said, as they started to make their way back down. When they got back, he still felt annoyed to begin with, but eventually had to smile to himself about it all when he realised they had anticipated he'd do something like this. He also had to admit it was pretty naive of him to think he would be allowed to enter and see any of the working technology of the ship. He was about to switch on the TV for the night, when suddenly the voice spoke.

"Did you find your exploration interesting, Tony?

"Oh, fascinating," Tony answered sarcastically.

"No need for this, Tony," said the voice. "We realised you would eventually want to see some of the inner workings of the ship – you had only to ask."

"Really?" Tony replied.

"Indeed. I am sure you will find it interesting… come with me." Tony and Zephyr followed the voice down the corridor, again passing the point where they'd entered the ship, and passing the point they turned into earlier. They carried on until Tony thought they were probably on the other side of the ship; they were then told to stop… The voice continued: "Place your hand onto the wall to the right of you." The wall was to the inner part of the ship and was perfectly seamless.

"Here?" Tony asked.

"Correct," the voice confirmed. As he placed the palm of his hand on the wall, he immediately stood back as a very thin line began to appear, splitting the wall horizontally. It omitted a pure piercing white light. The line then started to slowly widen at an even and equal rate; when fully opened it left a space about the size of a double doorway.

Tony stood in awe at what he could now fully see before him. The size and sight of… whatever it was… was breathtaking. Housed within a void at least one third of the size of the ship, the object was a huge globe, supported by equally huge girders which encompassed it. There was no real noise, just a low hum, the light within it more pure and bright than he'd ever seen before, yet he could look straight into it without hurting his eyes. Spectrums of ultraviolet light with varying intensities – the same he'd seen when they first boarded the ship – encircled it; there were six in total. A series of strange spherical objects were orbiting around it in all directions, and at great speed, leaving a streak of light behind them, each seeming to appear from nowhere and disappear into nothingness.

Tony could feel a kind of energy emitting from the object, the like of which he'd never before experienced. He felt exhilarated, and had a strange sense of well-being. He looked down at Zephyr to see him with his eyes closed and face pointed towards the object, as though in enjoyment, looking and acting the way he does when he's enjoying the first of the spring sun on his face after the winter.

As he continued to stand and look in marvel at the phenomenon, he realised he was not looking at any kind of technology as he knew it – the thought suddenly occurred to him that it looked like some sort of supermassive atom. But God knows what it was and how it worked, he thought to himself. He turned to look up in the direction of the voice. "Thank you, thank you… but I don't suppose you're going to tell me anything about it, or how it works, are you?" he ended by saying.

The wall then closed in front of him, he didn't get an answer, the voice had gone. As they made their way back along the long corridor, Tony continued to feel a profound sense of well-being, both physically and mentally. When they returned to their accommodation, he could see that Zephyr was exceptionally lively, and he himself felt energised in a very positive way. The more he thought about what they'd just witnessed, the more he felt that it seemed as much a force of nature as extremely advanced technology, but still he had no way of knowing. Nevertheless, the event had left him with a sense of almost childlike wonder.

Chapter 4

In the two weeks that followed, Tony had now begun to feel cooped up. Even with the more than adequate facilities they'd been provided with, he hated confinement, and a sense of cabin fever had now started to set in. Episodes of frustration and aggression were emerging within him, and he could tell Zephyr was able to sense this. He tried hard to conceal these tendencies as best he could by stepping up his exercise regime. The voice had said the journey would take around four months, and so Tony realised they were now coming up to the halfway point. Instead of a sense of dread at what might lay before them, he now found himself longing to reach their destination, just so that he could break out of the confines of the ship. But nothing could prepare him for what was about to happen...

Early one morning, as they got back from their walk in the park area, Tony glanced out of the window to look at his usual view, when something unusual caught his eye. He went over to the window to take a closer look; there, in the distance, was a very dark spot in space. It appeared to be the same size as one of the many far distant stars, but was so distinctive in appearance that it stood out starkly against what, to Tony, had become the normal sight of space. As the hours passed, he could see that this strange object was becoming slightly larger. He also realised this was not because it was growing in size – they were heading directly towards it.

Another day had passed and whatever it was now appeared to be three times the size. Tony was able to see a ring of what looked like some kind of substance around it. As they got ever nearer, the true massive scope and scale of the object became more and more apparent. Now able to see the apparition in full detail, he took a step back and a deep breath. "My god, it's a black hole, and we're headed straight for it," he said to himself. Tony grabbed Zephyr, who was already looking intensely at the extraordinary sight of this huge gaping hole in space. As they continued to plunge towards it, all Tony could do was observe this breathtaking phenomenon. The hole itself was darker than anything he'd ever imagined, but most incredible of all was the sight around the circumference; he could see what looked like a mix of matter, light, and somehow the very fabric of space itself being sucked into the abyss. More vast than was imaginable, he could hardly believe he was seeing it through his own eyes.

Tony gathered himself, and with no more time to think, he moved himself and Zephyr further back from the window. They were approaching at what seemed like a thirty-degree angle, and were just seconds away from going in. The ship had now started to shake and tremble, making a sound like thunder that went with it; Zephyr began to growl and bark. Tony held him tightly, saying "All right boy, all right." Suddenly there was a huge surge of momentum and they were thrown to the other side of the room; there was a highly powerful tremor now pulsating through the ship. Tony managed to get back on his feet and Zephyr steadied himself. The ship swayed heavily from side to side but they managed to make their way back over to the window area. He looked directly down into the blackness, but to his amazement they hadn't actually gone in, instead they were orbiting around the circumference, just above everything that was being sucked in. It was an incredible sight to see all the matter and light up close, going in and literally disappearing into the dark void.

They circled around the edge at an unimaginable speed; everything was now a blur and Tony suddenly felt much heavier. Going around another three to four times, suddenly the ship began to elevate upwards. They were thrown across the room again, and were now both pinned to the floor, completely unable to move. Tony looked out of the window from across the room, then, after a few seconds, the ship seemed to break away from the black hole's formidable grip as they were catapulted back into space at an even more phenomenal speed. Still pinned to the floor, Tony could see the stars out of the window passing by so fast that a long tail of light trailed behind them. To his relief, he began to feel the weight of gravity start to ease and. Both were now able to get up from the floor. He turned round to check Zephyr, who seemed a bit shaken but was otherwise OK. The tremors and noise had subsided and everything had returned to more near normal.

Tony walked back over to the window. When he looked out, everything seemed different, apart from the effect on the appearance of the stars in the distance. There were strange spectrums of light that would flash by the window and then disappear. "What the hell is going on?" he said. He looked back at the black hole as it grew increasingly smaller, then... there was a flash of intense light and a piercing noise, before they became completely enveloped by a complete darkness. It was as though they'd entered into a black corridor. Tony could no longer see space or the stars, in fact he couldn't see anything. They seemed to be in a kind of... nothingness... it was totally silent... Around ten seconds passed, then what looked like a few random strings of light flashed by the window. Finally, they re-emerged into normal space.

Tony and Zephyr looked at each other. Zephyr shook himself and Tony took a long deep breath. He looked out into space with a great sense of relief; the stars were now passing by at their normal rate. He looked back around the room, at the furniture and other items which were strewn across the floor, then looked up at the ceiling and called for the voice. "What the hell was that all about?" he said angrily. A few seconds went by before the voice spoke...

"Sorry about any distress caused, Tony."

"Sorry! Sorry!" he shouted. "What was it? Something to break up the journey, to break the monotony!" he ended by saying.

"No need for sarcasm, Tony," the voice replied.

"Sarcasm? You nearly ran us into a black hole! And you accuse me of sarcasm. And what happened just now? What was that after we, please god, broke away?"

"It couldn't be helped, Tony. Anyway, everything is fine now, all is as it should be..."

"Really? Well I'm so pleased 'you' think so. Back on course for wherever out there, are we?" he shouted again, but there was no reply. Tony took another deep breath. "Right, let's get this place back together, Zeph."

As he was clearing up, putting everything back in place and just feeling relieved he and Zephyr had survived the ominous events, he began to realise that it seemed to have alleviated his pent-up aggression and cabin fever, for now at least anyway. After they'd had a period of recovery, later that day they went to the park area. Tony looked up at the trees in full leaf and listened to the birds whilst Zephyr ran around; how he now longed for them to be back on Earth and be at the place they'd take their walk every evening.

It was beginning to feel like a long time since that fateful day they first laid eyes on the ship, which had now been their prison for the last two months, a long time since he had breathed and smelt real fresh air, since he'd felt like a free man, with all the liberties which come with that freedom.

That evening, as they sat listening to the radio, Tony got up and walked over to the window, and gazed out at the sight of space, which had now so oddly become part of his normal familiar surroundings. As he did so, he couldn't help but contemplate the vastness of creation, and the meaning of existence within it. "So many questions," he thought. He looked back at Zephyr, and the song 'What a Wonderful World' by Louis Armstrong came into his mind. "Maybe a near-death experience gives you a new perspective on things," he said to himself. He smiled at Zephyr, and when they laid down to sleep that night, for the first time since their captivity, he felt a sense of peace.

The next day, during his studies of natural science, Tony went to a section on black holes. He read about the existence of the nearest one to Earth as being calculated at just over one and a half thousand light years away. If this was the one they'd just encountered, then he realised they would be around three thousand light years from home by the end of their journey. It also meant that they had been travelling at many times the speed of light. "My god, how advanced these beings must be to have been able to harness such power," he thought to himself.

In the weeks that followed, Tony became more focused on preparing for their arrival at where or what they were being taken to. He tried to think of as many given scenarios as he could. If he was being taken to their world, it was obviously going to be as advanced as anyone could imagine. Maybe they were planning to put them in some kind of zoo, as specimens, one human, one animal, as they would class them, kept in an environment like the one they were in now, so that visitors could come to observe their behaviour and the relationship between them? The thought of this filled him with horror, horror to think they would try to force them to live out the rest of their lives like this. He would spend hours thinking about ways in which he could use his resourcefulness and intelligence to escape from this situation, so they could somehow live as fugitives on the alien planet – if it was habitable, that is –or even use his legal knowledge and training to reason with them, in ways he could argue valid and persuasive points as to why they should let them go.

He'd also considered his capturers could be like a kind of Roman Empire of the galaxy, and were taking him to fight against beings from other worlds in some kind of gladiatorial ring for their amusement. So, in the time he had left, he would also step up his daily gym regime. The thought of all these situations in truth seemed crazy to him, but he was determined to try to be as ready as possible for the worst of all possibilities. At the same time, if some terrible fate *was* about to befall them, then Tony wanted to make the most of their time left on the ship. He took Zephyr to the park more often – where they would spend longer periods of time, giving him a good run – and would pack food for them to have there. He was also cooking more elaborate meals for them to have in the evening, giving the voice ever more requests for the finest ingredients while the going was good.

Time drew on, and Tony had worked out that their journey was now due to end in around one week's time. He had continued his studies in natural science, which had helped pass time, and in those last few days, each time he laid down at night, he couldn't help but anticipate how strange it was going to be on some alien planet, thousands of light years from Earth.

Chapter 5

One morning, Tony woke up to Zephyr prodding him with his nose; as he opened his eyes, he became aware of something he hadn't seen in months – it felt to him like natural daylight! Getting up from the sofa, he looked over at the window, where he could see a wide stream of light gushing through into the room. He walked cautiously over, squinting in the brightness. There, out of the window, he set his eyes on the landscape of a planet for the first time; they had landed.

Tony looked round at Zephyr. "My god, we're on another world, boy," he said. Looking back out of the window, he could see they had landed on a formation of rocks which surrounded them. In the distance he could see a river running through the landscape, which was made up of some kinds of trees, plants and grasses, as well as randomly scattered boulders. Beyond this, he could see what looked like a forest, and further still, planes of mist rising into the air. The sky was blue and the vegetation was green; what Tony couldn't see was any sign of civilisation – no buildings, no industry, just a natural and wild vista.

As he continued to curiously survey the outside terrain, the voice spoke. "Tony – as you can see, we have reached our destination. It is now time for you... to leave us."

"I see, I see," Tony replied. "So what happens now?"

There was a silence for a few moments before the voice spoke again. "You must follow me now, along the corridor to where you first entered the ship."

"What, like this?" he said (Tony was still naked).

"Yes, just as you are," the voice replied. "You will come to the ship's exit point with me, you will collect the items we have for you there, and then you will both be released."

"OK, so are you finally going to tell me why we're here, and what's going on?" he asked...

"Time to go," said the voice.

"Yeah, thought so," he ended by saying. They left their accommodation and followed the voice along the corridor to the point where it all began; the inner door opened automatically and they walked in. It felt strange to be back in the chamber, in what now seemed like an age since they'd left Earth. Tony looked to the left of him at what seemed like a bundle of furs on the floor which Zephyr was already checking out. He looked up. "This is mine?" he said to the voice.

"Yes," came the reply. Tony knelt down to take a closer look, first touching the item before lifting it as he stood back up. It was obviously some kind of animal skin in the form of a long, sleeveless one-piece garment. He pulled it over his head – after all it was better than being naked – then knelt back down to look at what was a large, long bag made out of the same substance as the garment. When he opened it, inside was what looked like some sort of butcher's knife; the blade was wide and about twelve inches in length. There were two stones, a large folded sheet which was also made from animal skin, and three wooden poles made from natural branch cuttings which were around five feet in length. As he stood back up, he noticed another wooden pole which was leant up against the wall and was around seven feet in length.

Tony leant down and picked up the bag, placing it under his left arm. Taking the pole in his right hand, he knew it would now be just a few moments until he and Zephyr would be setting foot outside. He felt apprehensive, but he wasn't going to show it, he never did that. He then looked up at the voice, saying: "Guess this is it then."

To Tony's surprise, the voice spoke to him for one last time. "We will remain here. You may come to us if it is necessary, but only absolutely necessary. Other than that, you are on your own, to make your own way."

"That suits me just fine," replied Tony… then, suddenly, the inner door closed and for a few brief moments they were encased in the chamber again. The outer doors then opened; there was a sudden breeze as the natural air rushed in. They stepped cautiously outside, walking down the ramp of the ship, before finally stepping out onto the rocks. They had now set foot… onto the planet.

Tony stood still for a moment to take a long, deep breath; the air was fresh and sweet, he could almost taste it. It felt good after all the months of being holed up in an artificial atmosphere. "Aaah," he sounded as he exhaled. Zephyr also appreciated being out in the open as he frolicked on the rocks. Tony turned to look back at the ship. It felt strange to see this massive structure from the outside again, and he thought about the thousands of light years it had brought them across the galaxy during the time they'd travelled in her.

As he continued looking, the ramp withdrew back into the ship, then the entrance closed seamlessly. He noticed the ship becoming more opaque, almost to the point of transparency, before becoming completely invisible. "My god," he said as he stepped back in shock. When he'd gathered himself he realised this was how they must have obscured themselves back on Earth to avoid being noticed. Tony turned back round and looked out onto the wide open spaces and terrain of the planet. He looked at Zephyr, who was looking back at him in excitement. "Well, Zeph, here we are. Let's see what's out there."

They made their way through the rocks in a downward direction towards the trees and vegetation in the distance that he'd seen from the window of the ship. He now had time to contemplate their new situation. He stopped in his tracks and sat on a rock to catch up on himself. It had now only been about an hour since he'd awoken, and events had not allowed him any time to even think about what had just happened. He thought about all the strange places and incredible situations he'd envisaged they would be in when they finally got to their destination, and here they were, on what seemed to be an Earth-like planet, free and making their own way to do… whatever! But for how long, and what the hell were they doing here anyway; why had these beings set them on this planet with nothing but a few bare essentials, and what *did* they want of them?

Tony's thoughts then turned to survival. One thing was for sure, if they were going to make it on this planet they needed to find food, water of some kind, and more than likely some form of shelter. His first goal was to reach the river as soon as they could, thinking that if there was a chance of finding some source of food, it was most likely to be near moisture. He stood up and picked up his pole and bag. "Come on, boy, let's get down there," he said. Zephyr was already ahead of him, sniffing along the ground as though to track for anything interesting as they made their way further into the unknown. Tony kept himself on high alert; his eyes were everywhere on their way down through the rocks. They were surrounded on both sides by large boulders, and with each step he meant to be ready for the possibility of some kind of attack as he started to think about whether any kind of life forms might be nearby, but the only thing to strike Tony was the total lack of any sign of complex life so far.

After around fifteen minutes, the thought occurred to him that it would be a good idea to ensure he could remember where the ship was. He decided to leave markers. Looking around, there was nothing else but rocks at this point; the most distinctive one he could find was almost black, with silver-like specks that reflected the light. He placed it in a gap between the boulders they were walking through, glanced around and took a photographic memory shot of the surrounding area. He continued to do this with the same rock of differing sizes each time he could find one, placing them down every hundred or so metres.

After around another twenty minutes, they were almost at the foot of the rocky area, and Tony made a mental note of the time it had taken them to walk down from the ship. They could now see and even smell the vegetation which sprawled before them. Zephyr lifted his head, his nose in the air sniffing with vigour as they both walked on to what appeared to be some form of grass and soil. Zephyr ran around with joy in the open grassy area,. The fact he was doing this told Tony the land must be good, not poisonous, to them, that is. He had to admit to himself how good it felt for him to be standing on natural ground again in a wide-open space. Since descending from the rocks though the air had become humid, the climate felt subtropical, and the grasses looked like nothing he'd seen before. The blades were wider and the colour a strange shade of almost blue-green, but still he did consider it to be some kind of grass.

He could now hear the sound of the gushing river in the distance; it was now only about five hundred metres ahead, he figured. "Come on, Zeph; let's get to it," he said. As they made their way, they came across differing forms of trees and bushes, some of which were bearing a variety of fruits. He was getting pretty hungry by now but didn't feel inclined to eat any of it, at least for now anyway. His main worry about food was Zephyr. Tony was no vegetarian, but he knew he could survive on fruits or any kind of vegetables he could find, as long as they weren't toxic that is, but Zephyr needed meat. This presented him with a dilemma: firstly, as an animal lover, the thought of killing one completely went against his nature and principles, and secondly, he still hadn't seen any sign of animal life in any case. But still he was prepared to do whatever it took for their survival, no matter how difficult.

He pressed on towards the river, thinking that if there were any answers to be found they'd lay there. Now almost at the bank of the river, the plant life was by now extremely dense, as well as huge. There were thick green stalks rising around six metres from the ground, with one massive kind of leaf sprouting from the top, creating a canopy at least ten metres in circumference. The air was damp from a wet spray. He knew they were close to coming through this thing by the noise of the river, but it was only when Tony brushed passed a large mass of vegetation that he got his first sight of complex life on the planet – flying insects, big and in their dozens. He stood back in shock as he watched them fly up to one of the canopies. The environment had become like a dense jungle by this time; they were now completely soaked from the ever-increasing moisture, but to his relief Tony began to see a few streams of light bursting through the huge leaves.

They finally stepped out into the clear and the bank of the river. Walking over to the edge, Tony could see the true and massive size of it, around two hundred metres across, stretching in a winding formation into the distance as far as the eye could see. Zephyr sat next to Tony as they looked out onto the forest at the other side. Tony looked down at the river. The water, if that's what it was, he thought, was a kind of crystal blue, with rocks sticking up from the surface creating a white wake of rapids. It was… beautiful, but it was flowing too fast and furiously for them to safely go down and take a closer look.

Tony looked at Zephyr. "OK, time to choose a direction," he said. He looked up to the sky; to the right of him was a huge mound of boulders on the bank, blocking the view and the route in that direction. To the left the bank was clear, and he could see they'd be able to walk through it. His eyes met with the glare of an extremely bright white sun. "This way," he said to himself. He was trying to get some bearing as to where they were going in relation to where they'd landed, so he made a mental note of where the sun was as they started out in that direction.

They walked for another hour along the unchanging bank, which was by now beginning to feel never-ending. Then, Tony noticed a break in the land about two hundred metres ahead. As they drew nearer, he could see there was a much smaller river flowing inwards from the main one, like a tributary. When they got there, Tony looked up at the sun again. He could see it was more or less in the same direction as before, except it was lower, so he figured if this planet revolved in the same direction as Earth then they should have headed west. He then looked to his left, down in the direction of the tributary – the land was lush, inviting and seemed much more hospitable. They were now both in real in need of water, and the river looked calm and accessible further down. "Come on, Zeph, that way," he said.

They hurried towards the bank of the secondary river, moving closer to the edge as they went. They finally reached the edge after about half a mile. Tony was seriously hoping the content of the river was some form of water-like substance they'd be able to ingest; it at least smelt like water, as far as he could tell. He intended to cautiously try it first, but before he could do anything, Zephyr bolted to the edge and started to lap it up. "Zephyr! Zephyr!" Tony called as he ran over to him, but it was too late. Already drinking, Tony pulled him away, but as he knelt down to watch him for a couple of minutes, he finally sighed with relief when he could see there were no ill effects. He then cupped his hands and dipped them into the river. Feeling pleasantly cool, he drew the liquid up to his face and took a first sip. It tasted like water, but so pure and clean, and better than he'd ever before experienced. He dipped his cupped hands back in and took another full scoop. Taking several gulps, it by now felt to him like the finest wine he had ever known. "Well, it's as good as water, Zeph, if not better!" he said as they both sat at the edge of the river. "Please god," he said to himself as he continued to sit there, looking around at all of nature, smelling the sweet clean air. "This planet must be teeming with life," he thought. He had by now more than realised that if this environment could support him and Zephyr then it had to make sense that something must have evolved here! He felt hot in the searing afternoon sun, and also noticed Zephyr panting in the heat. Now he knew the water was relatively safe, he thought it would be a good idea for them to cool off with a dip.

He stood up, slipped off the animal skin and took a walk into the river; Zephyr was no lover of water but Tony gently coaxed him in. They walked out a few metres until it was deep enough for Zephyr to swim. Tony then took a standing dive in. The temperature was ideal and he started to swim over to the other side, which was around twenty metres. As he did so he would duck under the water to cool his head; it was so crystal clear he could see the river bed. He decided to swim down to explore the bottom, which he found to be a mixture of silt, weeds and rocks, but as he swam back up to the surface, there, just above his head, giving him the shock of his life as he almost collided with it, he had his second encounter with another form of life.

It was some sort of fish-like creature but obviously like nothing else he'd ever seen. The sight of it caused him to expel the air from his lungs and he was choking as he reached the surface. He swam back to Zephyr and they made their way back to the edge. Walking back out of the river, Zephyr shook the excess water from his thick coat, causing a rainbow effect as he did so. Recovering from what he'd just seen, Tony's thoughts again turned to food. As he now realised in no uncertain terms that animal life did exist on this planet, then as far as Zephyr was concerned, he hoped there'd be small forms of land mammals, like rodents, that he'd be able to catch, kill and eat. He certainly knew Zephyr was well capable of this, and after all, it would only be the order of the natural food chain, but until anything else showed up, he decided to look for some kind of food in the form of vegetation that would keep them alive, for now at least.

They walked inland from the river to a group of strange looking trees and bushes around three hundred metres away. Some of the bushes had large, berry-like fruits on them, orange in colour with a kind of short fur-covered skin. Tony picked one; it felt fairly soft to the touch so he realised it could be ripe. "I don't know what I'm dealing with here, better handle this with caution," he thought to himself.

Reaching into his bag, he pulled out the large knife he'd been provided with and cut through the flesh inside until he reached what felt like a stone object in the middle, then cut round the circumference, separating it into two halves. Tony looked closely at the flesh of this strange-looking fruit. Lifting it closer to his face to sense whether it had any scent, it smelt fairly sweet. He knew from his studies of food science that in fruit this was usually a good sign, but who would know on this planet, he thought. As the juice ran out of it onto his hand, there was no adverse effect, so he could tell it wasn't corrosive, but was it poisonous?

"Well, it's this or starve, here goes," he said to Zephyr, taking the first bite. As his teeth sank into the soft flesh he could taste a mixture of sweetness and the slight bitterness of a citrus-like sensation. He chewed, swallowed and then waited to see what happened. After a few minutes, all Tony could feel was a slight sugar rush and the feeling of wellbeing from eating after having a hollow stomach. "Right, seems OK," he said. He then hoped Zephyr, who was looking at him intently, would be willing to eat the fruit. Taking the stone from the middle of the flesh on the other half, he knelt down and placed the fruit in front of Zephyr's nose. Sniffing at it before clasping it in his teeth, he finally gulped it down with a wag of his tail. "Phew, good boy! Right, we've got the means to at least keep us going, Zeph," he said as he reached back into the branches of the bush and picked all the fruit they would need for the rest of the day. "All right, time to think about setting up camp," he thought to himself.

They'd passed a large mound about a hundred meters back towards the river. "Best to occupy the high ground, Zeph. This way," he said. Reaching it, they walked up the slope and onto a plateau. The view was fantastic, and strategically very advantageous; they had a panoramic vision of the whole landscape. Looking around, Tony began to feel as though they were masters over everything they could survey.

He put his bag down. "This is home for now, boy," he said to Zephyr as he sat down beside him. Reaching into his bag, he pulled out some berries and his knife, cut a couple in half and they both savoured them as they devoured this veritable feast. Tony now started to consider the other items in his bag. He had realised the pole and knife were both useful as tools and weapons, but also realised the other contents must have been given to him for a reason. He got the items out of the bag and laid them on the ground. Looking at the two stones more closely, he could see they were flint from his native planet. "Of course, for starting fires," he thought. "Hey," he said with delight as he struck them together, causing sparks to fly.

Now looking at the posts and the large folded sheet of animal skin – although unable to know exactly why he'd been provided with these – he quickly worked out that the best thing he could do was to make some sort of tent out of them. "Good," he said to himself. Deciding he'd set this up before they would go back down to the river for the last time that day, he wanted to try and find some sort of natural vessel for carrying water back to what would now be their base.

Finding a decent-sized rock to drive the poles into the ground to form a triangle, he struck at the top of each one several times as they sank into the ground solidly. Then, draping the animal skin over them, he spread the edges out and over the ground. He was pleased to see that it was clearly going to be adequate in size for both of them, as well as leaving room for storing provisions. "Well, it ain't the Hilton, but it'll do for now," Tony said laughingly to Zephyr. He then found some good-sized heavy rocks to anchor it down. Finally, the one thing missing was an entrance, so Tony got his knife and cut a large slit down the middle part of the tent, which looked out onto the river. "There we are – luxury with a view, Zeph," he said as he laughed again.

As they made their way back towards the river, it was still hot and they were thirsty again. On the way, Tony looked for anything that might serve to carry water but couldn't see anything suitable; when they got to the river's edge though, he noticed more large vegetation growing on the bank, similar to the massive canopies they'd seen back at the main river, except smaller, and concave in shape. Looking at a large leaf growing out from the stalk, Tony thought he might be able to convert it into a carrying vessel. It wouldn't hold much, but it would do for the night through to the next morning.

After they'd had enough to drink, he cut one of the stalks down and took the large leaf into the water; the fabric of the leaf was thick and felt strong, with an oily feel to the surface. He immersed it into the water, clasped his hands around the top so as to seal in the water, before pulling it back up. "Perfect," he thought. Now he'd performed this operation, he realised he'd need something, or more than one thing for them to drink from when they got back to base. He looked around again and noticed there were several not yet fully grown versions of the same plant, which were much smaller. He walked back onto the bank, and with one hand still clasped around the water-filled large leaf, cut off four of the most concave small leaves and placed them in his bag. Picking up the bag with his other hand, they made their way back to the tent.

On their return, Tony knelt down and placed the small leaves just outside the tent. He cut a small slit into the side wall of the large leaf, filling the small leaves as the water spouted out. As he discarded the large one, it occurred to Tony the leaves could actually be poisonous, after all, everything at this point was a first, and it would all be trial and error. Looking at his hand, there was no allergic reaction at least. He decided to take a sip from the rest of the water in the large leaf and see what happened in an hour or so, but after less than an hour had passed, and he felt no ill effects, he thought it should be OK. He placed one of the leaves in front of Zephyr. "Yours, boy," he said as he looked around at the vast landscape, his thoughts once again turning to whether there were any life forms on land in the area. Although he had still seen nothing, it was difficult to imagine it not being so, on this seemingly lush and plentiful planet.

Evening was now starting to fall; Tony looked up at what was now a dusky and clear sky. It was already beginning to feel cooler and he thought he would try his hand at making a fire – besides anything else, it would provide light. He knew that if there were any dangerous predators which came out at night, Zephyr would sense them well in time for them to defend themselves, but the light of a fire would help them see what they were fighting. He looked at Zephyr, whose nose was in the air, reaching to pick up all manner of scents, and eyes were surveying everything that surrounded him. His natural instincts were really kicking in and he was displaying that wolflike stance of his. "What a magnificent creature," Tony said to himself.

Before it got dark, Tony grabbed his bag and they walked back down from their plateau towards the trees and bushes to get some dead, dry vegetation and branches for the fire. He knew they should easily be able to find some as he'd seen plenty just laying around on the ground earlier in the day. It didn't take long; they found the provisions and took them straight back to base as they were now rapidly losing daylight. Tony had managed to fill his bag with a good mixture of what could be described as a sort of tumbleweed type of material, dry twigs, and short branches that he'd found at the base of a clump of trees.

He placed a small amount of the dry weed into a natural dip in the ground just outside the tent, took the two stone flints in either hand and struck them together, aiming the sparks directly into the weed. Nothing happened to begin with, but he persevered until finally he got a flame. Quickly reaching back into the bag, he grabbed for more weed to throw on. It caught just as quickly and the flames flew into the air. Tony now threw on the twigs; he had to keep throwing more weed into the fire until the twigs finally caught. Finally adding some branches, he had a pretty significant blaze going. He turned to look at Zephyr, who was looking a bit apprehensive. "There we go, boy, our first fire." Tony was feeling pretty pleased with himself as he sat by the warmth. Zephyr finally came over to join him and he felt a sense that he'd really set up some kind of home. Not bad to say they'd only been on the planet for less than a day, he thought.

Night had now fully fallen during the time he'd been staring into the fire. He looked around into the velvet darkness of night, the flames of the fire casting strange shadows which flickered across the dim terrain. Then, looking up at the sky, the shock of what he saw caused him to rise to his feet and gasp. There, in the deep blue night sky, was the most incredible and spectacular display of stars. Tony had never seen the like of it back on Earth. He exhaled in sheer wonder at what he was witnessing; from his perspective there was no more than a six-inch gap between one star and another. "My god," he said to Zephyr as he smiled. "It looks like a pretty crowded galaxy from this planet."

As the flames of the fire died down, Tony began to feel tired; it had been a long, demanding day and he felt they'd managed to at least get a foothold in a land so strange to them. But he knew tomorrow would hold many more challenges; finding proper food, for one. They would need to be at their best to meet them. He looked back at Zephyr, who was now curled up in front of the smouldering fire. "Time to turn in soon, boy, I think." Zephyr got up, gave a long stretch, and they both went to get into the tent to bed down for their first night's sleep on this new world.

As they entered the tent, Tony kept the entrance open to allow some light in from the glow of the dying fire. He dragged his bag in and got some more fruit out. He had placed the makeshift bowls of water on the ground, Zephyr taking a few laps out of his. Tony cut a couple of berries in half. After they'd eaten these, he took a final sip from his bowl and closed the entrance. It was now extremely dark and he could hardly see; this improved after a couple of minutes, when his eyes adjusted, so he placed his bag up at one end of the tent to act as a pillow.

As they sat there in the darkness, the events of the day began to run through Tony's mind: of how only this morning when he had woken, he was still on the ship; of how incredible it was to think they'd gone from being in space on what was the most sophisticated travelling machine imaginable, to now being in the wild, in a makeshift tent and in the most basic of circumstances; and of how they were now in a situation where they would need to grapple with nature just to survive.

Tony smiled as he looked at Zephyr. "Just how we like it," he thought. He knew if anyone could come through this, they could. He knew they were the best of survivors. Maybe that's why they'd been put here, he thought. Well, never mind for now, it was time to get a good night's sleep. He took a deep breath, but then, suddenly and unexpectedly, the noises started, in the distance, seemingly from the forest on the other side of the river. First was a sound like a bird screeching, then the sound like a horn, but the like of which could only be made by an animal – a living being. This was followed by a distant sound of rustling of trees, made by what must have been a huge creature. Zephyr stood up and gave a deep growl; Tony looked outside the tent. There was nothing in their immediate vicinity, so no immediate threat for now, he thought to himself. He turned to Zephyr: 'Oh yeah. There *is* plenty of land life on this planet, boy," he said with a wry smile. They finally bedded down for the night, falling asleep to the haunting sounds of those life forms in the distance.

Chapter 6

The next day, as they woke with the break of dawn, Tony sat up and took a sip from his leaf bowl. Zephyr stood up, took a long stretch and shook himself. As he walked over to Tony, they greeted each other the same way as they would every morning. It made Tony think about their home back on Earth and that last morning he'd woken there, which now felt like a long time ago. Looking at Zephyr, his next immediate thoughts were of food. It was now nearly two days since they had eaten properly, and he knew they'd really need to find a proper source of nourishment to sustain them indefinitely.

As they stepped out of the tent, with the sweet smell of the fresh, pure air once again so apparent, looking out from their vantage point Tony could see a morning mist hovering over the river. "Fish! Of course," he thought. Now knowing there were fishlike creatures in there, he thought that if they bred anything like back on Earth, the river should be teeming with an almost inexhaustible amount for them. He also knew that if they were edible then fish meat would be the best and probably most healthy source of nutrition they could have – he would just need to find a way of catching them. Again, he still didn't like the thought of killing any creature, but this was a matter of survival for them. Besides, it was them who'd been put here against their will, and he'd make the death as quick and painless as possible.

Grabbing his bag, knife and pole from the tent, he got the remaining fruits from the bag and cut them in half for their breakfast. "OK, boy, let's go," he said as they made their way down from the plateau.

The sun had now fully risen and was already beginning to get hot; Tony could see the mist rapidly burning off the river. Zephyr did all his natural functions, toilet-wise; it then suddenly occurred to Tony that he now needed to 'go' himself. He had only needed to pee yesterday, largely due to having hardly eaten during that twenty-four-hour period, but now nature was taking its course from the fruits he'd had yesterday. Looking around, he realised it didn't really matter where he 'went', but going out in the open just didn't feel right. "I know, I'll go at the edge of the river and then clean off in the water," he thought. When they got there, he took off his top and did the necessary behind a nearby rock, then walked into the cool water to clean himself. "Luxury," he thought as he gave himself a good douse in the crystal-clear water. "You'd have to pay serious money for this back on Earth," he said to himself.

Tony walked back out of the river and put his top back on after drying off quickly in the now blisteringly hot sun. The first thing he decided to do was cut down another large canopy leaf to collect their water supply later, as well as some more small ones for their drinking bowls. He sat down on a rock and had a good think about how he would try to capture these fish. He realised he would need some form of bait, but what? What could he use? He decided to watch the water for a while to see whether any of these creatures would come to the surface to swallow something, thinking that if he could see what they were interested in, he could use it himself.

An hour or so had passed and Tony had seen nothing and felt he was now just wasting time. He was also getting hungry again and realised Zephyr must be as well; the fruit hardly even filled a hole. It was now searingly hot in the near-midday sun, so he coaxed Zephyr into the water to cool him off, dousing himself at the same time. He thought it would now be best if he collected their water for the day, and they went back to base empty-handed, aside from the water.

Later on, they went to collect more of the same fruits. Better than nothing, Tony thought. As they approached the trees and bushes, he spotted something which looked like a small brown mound sticking up from the grasses. At first he thought it was just a fairly large lump of earth, but as they got nearer, Zephyr stopped, pointed his nose into the air and started to sniff with purpose, before lowering his snout to the ground and walking forward to follow the scent he'd picked up. He was heading directly for the brown object; they were now only a few metres away when Tony suddenly stopped in his tracks. "My god," he said as Zephyr walked cautiously around it. "It's an animal. Zephyr, here!" he called. Zephyr walked back to Tony's side and they both stood still, just looking intensely at the creature; it was completely motionless and appeared not to be breathing.

Tony put his bag down and walked slowly towards it, gripping his pole in both hands. The animal was around the size of a large pig or boar, and covered in a kind of brown fur. It had fairly long legs and the head and snout were long and narrow with sharp features. Tony prodded it with his pole a couple of times, but he could already see it was dead. For the first time since being on the planet, he was witnessing some form of land mammal. There were what appeared to be at least three different types of insect crawling over the body. Tony felt a sadness for the lifeless creature, just lying dormant on the ground.

Two or three minutes passed as he looked more closely to try and see what had caused the death. There were no apparent injuries, so maybe it was just natural causes, but the thoughts he'd had since he first realised what they'd accidentally found were growing stronger in his mind. This was food, and Tony knew he now had the opportunity of getting what they were so desperately in need of. He considered the prospect, with the same possibility that it could be poisonous, just as he'd thought the water, fruit and plant life might have been, but again there was only one way to find out.

He walked over to his bag and drew his knife out, then stood back over the creature and thought about how he could best obtain meat from it. He was a pretty skilled chef, but not a butcher. As he surveyed the creature's body, just like most other mammals there seemed to be a good deal of flesh at the top half of the hind legs. Kneeling down, he began to cut into the skin of the hind leg. A small amount of blood, red in colour, poured out to begin with, but stopped after a few seconds, leaving the clear sight of a kind of reddy-pink flesh, and a lighter-coloured binding substance, which he figured must be the animal's sinew. "OK, meat," he thought.

Quickly and unskilfully, he cut two large slats of flesh from out of the leg. Zephyr circled around the animal in excitement, obviously smelling the strong scent of blood and flesh. "Right, that's it," Tony said, holding the meat in his hands. He moved away from the animal and grabbed his bag. As they walked away, Tony thought the safest thing to do would be to douse the meat in fresh water, and so he made his way back to the river.

Upon getting to the river's edge, he washed off all the blood still left on the meat. Although he didn't take what he'd had to do back there lightly, he had to smile when he saw Zephyr looking at him as if to say 'why aren't we eating this already?' Although he wanted to let him have a chunk right there, he thought it best to cook it over a fire and try a small sample himself first, just as he'd done with everything else.

Hurrying back to base, he collected more dead grass and twigs. Although it was only the second time he'd made a fire, Tony felt he was gaining more expertise, and this time it came more naturally to him. He saved the thickest twig he could find, and sharpened one end to skewer into the meat, placed it over the flames, and turned it constantly. Juices began to drip out into the base of the fire, causing the flames to rise higher. After a couple of minutes, the meat started to brown and slightly char as he kept turning it; after around another minute he was satisfied that it should now have cooked through.

Withdrawing the meat from the fire, Tony cut a small piece, tentatively placed it in his mouth and started to chew. It was tough, pretty tasteless, and didn't actually taste like anything he'd ever had. After swallowing, he waited a few minutes, all the time Zephyr staring at him as he shuffled impatiently. Although he had only ingested a relatively small piece, Tony was already starting to feel a flush to his face. Realising this was from the protein, that was good enough, he thought. "Right, Zeph, let's eat." Zephyr stood up eagerly. Tony cut two pieces from the slat of meat, throwing them immediately over to Zephyr, who ate them in less than thirty seconds. He cut the rest up and shared it equally between them and they ravaged it in double-quick time. Tony had now decided go back to the body of the animal to get more meat from the other leg, which would provide enough food through to the next day. Although he still felt hungry, and knew Zephyr could eat more, he decided to save the other slat of meat until that night. After all, he still didn't know when they'd next be able to source nourishment like this, at least not until he could work out how to catch fish, that is.

Later in the day, when they went back to the site where the animal still laid, Tony noticed that more flesh than he'd originally taken from the leg was missing, to the point that some of the bone was showing.

He could see by the way the flesh had been chewed and torn that this must have been done by a much smaller mammal. More proof of multiple species, he thought. Tony turned the creature over and performed the same procedure. Zephyr was a lot calmer this time, as though to treat the whole thing as normal, and in fact Tony found himself carrying out the task with far more ease this time. After washing the meat in the river, he cut down a canopy plant and wrapped the meat in it, thinking this would give it some protection from the outside elements, particularly insects.

Evening was now starting to fall by the time they got back to base. They sat there for a while in the calm of dusk before Tony started another fire and cooked off the second slat of meat, again cutting and sharing it out evenly. At the same time he was still trying to think of how he could bait and catch the fish, but at least they had food to last them for another day, he thought. "I'll think about all that tomorrow, boy," he said to Zephyr. For now though, they sat on the plateau like two silhouettes against the twilight sky, as they ate their dinner… under the stars.

After a good night's sleep on relatively full stomachs, they woke again at dawn. Tony laid on his back, looking around the tent for a moment. "Welcome to another day at the galactic Holiday Inn," he joked to himself as he got up and looked at Zephyr. "Well, we've survived another night to meet another day, boy." The first thing Tony did was to get a fire going again to do them a breakfast with the wood-skewered meat; after this, he was keen to get straight back down to the river for a bathe and to collect their water supply. They now had the luxury of already having enough food for the day, so he knew he'd be able to spend more time on baiting the river fish, or whatever they were.

When they got down to the bank, after bathing Tony cut down a canopy plant and went back into the river to collect the water, but after filling the leaf it split open due to a small natural tear in its wall. He tried again with different leaves, another three times in all but with the same result – each one would split. With the frustration of working against time to try to feed them, Tony's impatience got the better of him and he lost his temper. "Shit," he said as he tore up the leaf, throwing pieces of it out into the middle of the river before stomping back out onto the bank. "Bloody thing!" he shouted in a rage as he turned back towards the river.

Stomping back to the canopies to cut another one down, and still swearing under his breath, he suddenly heard several splashes in the water. As he turned to look at what was causing this, a big smile suddenly came to his face. To begin with he could hardly believe it, but the splashing sound was being made by the fish, thrashing around on the surface of the water; at least a dozen of them, all going crazy for the pieces of leaf... He'd inadvertently found his bait. "OK, first step to a permanent food supply!" he said as he looked at Zephyr.

Sitting down on the bank, he thought about how he was actually going to handle catching the fish; he didn't exactly have a fishing rod and hooks! But after a while he realised he was going to have to make some kind of enclosure to entice them into, a kind of well within the river's waters. Looking around, there were plenty of rocks about, which he thought would do the job well, and knowing time was a factor, he got straight to work, rounding up all the rocks of the right size he could find – each was around the size of a football.

Having to eventually go further afield for the right size of rock, it was hard, hot work in the searing glare of the sun, and his hands were starting to blister in places. Tony thought how glad he now was for all those hours he'd spent in the gym on the ship; the rocks were now piled six feet high by around three feet wide and he figured this should be enough for now.

After going back into the water to cool off and have a good drink, he cut another canopy down to fill with water, this time making sure there were no splits in the wall! They then made their way back to the tent, but when they were about a hundred metres from base, Tony noticed something moving. As they got closer, he could see two mammals, about the same size as Zephyr. Shocked to begin with, he then stopped to try and get a good look; this was the first time he'd seen a 'live' land creature since they'd been here. "Of course! The food!" he said. "They're after the meat." Quickly picking up the scent of the animals, Zephyr bolted in their direction, running at them with incredible speed, a deep growl coming from the depths of his chest. As the two creatures caught sight of him, after briefly freezing where they stood, they darted into the distance. Tony had his bag and pole under one arm and was carrying the canopy of water in his other, so he couldn't move too quickly but ran behind as fast as he could, until he could just see the mammals disappearing into the distance as Zephyr got to the tent. He was continuing to chase them but Tony called him off.

When he eventually got to the tent, Tony threw everything on the ground and knelt down to Zephyr, praising him. "Good work, boy, we've seen our first alien invaders off," he said with a smile. Realising they'd now caught the attention of all and any wildlife that lived in the area by storing food in the tent, Tony knew they'd be back again to try their luck. He and Zephyr would now need to guard it, as well as themselves. Zephyr walked around the tent and surrounding area, marking their territory with a cock of his leg every few metres. "That should at least serve as a warning, for now, anyway," Tony thought.

They rested for a while before going back to the river, this time taking the meat with them in the bag. Tony had given more thought to how he would build the well; when they got back, he set to work with a sense of urgency. Firstly walking back into the water to submerge himself to waist height, he placed the first rock on the riverbed. His plan was to build a wall in a semi-circle from that spot back to the bank, and then repeat the process on the other side. The structure would stand about two rocks high above the surface, and the circular shape would stand strong against the moderate current of the river. He'd place the leaves within the structure, then, by taking away a few rocks from one or either side of the walls, would allow the fish in to take the bait, before replacing the rocks.

He worked through until the light level began to drop. The task was lengthy and difficult and the biggest problem was to make the rocks balance steadily under the water so the wall was solid. Tony got pretty frustrated a few times, but once he'd got the foundations right, it all started coming together. He finally managed to complete the first wall before finishing for the day. On their way back to base, he collected the usual fire material to cook the meat for dinner. It had been another long day and they were both ready to eat; when they got back, Tony started up the fire and they fast devoured the meat.

Sitting by the fire to warm themselves in the cool of the night, Tony started to think about how this was now only their third day on the planet, and of how far they'd come in just that short amount of time. It had been a good day's work and he felt a sense of satisfaction and progress, but how he wished he had some of his libation to sit and relax with after a hard day. He was beginning to miss that; at the same time, he realised that it was probably a good sign that other thoughts were now starting to come to mind other than just food, water and shelter; it meant they were gaining more means of survival with every passing day. He was only too conscious though that tonight they would need to be well alert to the wild animal life which was now aware of their presence in the area, and judging by the deep, loud sounds they'd heard in the distance throughout the last two nights, they could be having to fight off some pretty large predators. As they laid down to sleep that night, Tony kept his knife and pole closely by his side.

Late into the night, he woke with a jolt to hear Zephyr ferociously barking. Quickly grabbing the knife and pole, he opened the entrance of the tent. Zephyr shot out into the night like a bullet, and Tony straight after him. In the dark of night, he could just about make out that it was the same creatures from that afternoon, about six or seven of them this time, standing together in a pack. Zephyr charged straight at them, scattering the pack, but they circled back round and regrouped. Tony ran towards them, wielding his pole before bringing it down to a thud on the ground in front of them. As they spread out again, Zephyr leapt on one of them, bowling it over onto the ground and pinning it down, biting it in the neck several times. Tony carried on swinging the pole, running at one creature, then another, and another. This time the pack completely dispersed, each creature disappearing in a different direction into the night, all except the one Zephyr now had at his mercy. Tony called him off; the creature was lucky; there were only a few superficial marks to the throat, as far as he could see, and the animal scurried away, limping on one hind leg.

After the dust had settled, all Tony could hear were the distant and diminishing sounds of the creatures getting further away into the night. He turned and smiled at Zephyr. "Well that gave um something to chew on, boy." They settled back in the tent for what was left of the night. Zephyr lay alert, just inside the entrance, and Tony had no qualms about getting back to sleep – Zephyr was doing his job brilliantly...

The next morning, Tony woke up later than usual. It was already fully light and starting to get hot; he felt like he had a hangover from a broken night's sleep as the events of last night came quickly flooding back to him. He ached all over from lifting all those rocks yesterday, and wasn't exactly feeling like doing any more today, but it had to get done. They were now out of food, and he would first have to collect some fruits again, just to keep them going for the day.

They walked down to the trees and Tony picked about twenty of them. Zephyr looked unenthusiastic, and in truth Tony didn't have much of a stomach for them either. The thought of being on these things all day didn't exactly whet his appetite, especially since they'd had meat for the last two days. When they got back to the river, Tony cut up a couple of the fruits for them. There was one good thing –
having to eat these things again gave him even more incentive to complete the well today. "OK, time to get to work," he said to himself.

Setting about the task, he grabbed the first rock. Putting aside the pain he felt in his hands, still sore from yesterday, he walked back into the river and began laying the foundations for the second half of the wall. After a short time Tony was shocked to see some of the mammals appear at the river. They must have followed his and Zephyr's scent, realising there might always be a chance of food wherever they both were, but Zephyr soon chased them away, leaving Tony able to carry on uninterrupted.

The hours went by as he worked through the fierce heat of the day, his hands now bleeding and most of his body in pain from the back-breaking work of constantly carrying the rocks through the water, then running out of the nearby ones and having to go further afield to collect around half as many again. Eventually though, by the late afternoon, as the heat gradually began to subside, he started to see his work come together, and the end was nearly in his sight. Finally placing the last of the rocks at the top of the wall, Tony walked out of the river and sat down to admire his work; he'd managed to build what was effectively an arch-shaped isolated pool within the river, around twenty feet in circumference.

Ignoring his cuts and aches, he smiled with satisfaction as he looked at the structure, and then laid on his back in near exhaustion. Zephyr walked over to where he was laying, looking down at him to check he was all right. Tony sat back up and put his hand on him. "It's OK, boy," he said. Zephyr quickly picked up on the wounds on his hands and started to lick at them, in the healing way that dogs do. "OK, boy, let's get some bait." Tony went over to the canopies, cut another one down and ripped it up, took two rocks away from the right-hand side of the wall to create an opening in the middle, and then threw several pieces of the leaf out into the river to create a trail, before tossing a few within the pool itself. And then... he waited.

The fish quickly started taking the bait, but only the pieces of leaf that were further out in the water. Tony then threw a few more pieces nearer to the entrance. Slowly but surely, they began to come in, getting ever closer to the entrance. He threw a few more pieces into the pool area,, then suddenly, a large one swam straight within the boundaries of the pool. Tony quickly grabbed the two rocks to place them back onto the wall, but before he could manage to get there, the creature swam back out just as fast as it had entered. He exhaled in frustration, but he knew he was close. The method he was using was working, which only gave him more encouragement to keep trying.

Repeating the process several times, eventually another large creature swam into the pool. Tony was nearer and more ready this time and swiftly replaced the rocks before it had a chance to swim out again. The first fish had been caught; he leapt into the air with excitement. "Yes, Zephyr, yes," he shouted, but his joy soon turned to dread when he thought about what he was going to have to do. "Let's get this over with," he said to himself as he stepped off the bank and walked into the pool. He knew it wouldn't be easy to get the fish out of there but he meant to do it as quick as he could, and he'd left his knife on the bank where he could see it and most easily get to it.

To begin with, the fish was too fast and slippery for him, but eventually he managed to get a grip of the creature as it lunged toward him. Throwing his arms up, he tossed it onto the bank, then ran straight out of the water; Zephyr ran over to the fish as it wriggled and thrashed around on the ground. Tony reached straight for his knife, and with one swift, strong swipe, lopped off the head… A small stream of blood gushed out and the creature's wriggle began to subside. He grabbed what was left of the canopy leaf and placed it over the fish… it was done. Tony felt sick inside, but at the same time a great sense of relief that it was over, and that he had been able to make the act as quick and hopefully painless for the creature as possible.

After sitting back down to gather himself, he stood back up and grabbed the fish, wrapping the leaf around it. "OK, Zeph, back to base." He placed the fish in his bag, and they made their way up; evening was now again beginning to fall on a *very* long, hard day, and they both needed to eat.

Tony's appetite was starting to return as he continued to put behind him what he'd had to do back there. He unwrapped the creature from the leaf. Looking at it, he knew that if it had the same anatomy as most fish back on Earth, it would need gutting. He'd done this many times and expertly slit the creature's underside. Unusually, there was not much to scrape out, but thought it best done anyway. The flesh was dark in colour; again, he thought if the same was true as back home, this meant the meat would be rich in oils, making it even more nutritious. "Who knows though, this thing still might even be poisonous," he said to himself.

He got the fire started, cut the tail from the fish and skewered it onto a slim stick of wood. It didn't take long to cook through as he turned it over the fire. He was going to try it himself as usual; Zephyr came nearer, licking his lips in anticipation. "Well, whether this is edible or not, it sure smells good," he thought. Drawing the fish away from the fire, he could see the cooking process had revealed an inner skeleton, but he was able to pull this out with relative ease. Tony cut a small piece from it. The skin had gone crispy, which added to its appeal. His mouth was now watering as he took a small bite; the taste made him salivate even more. It had a slightly dark, earthy flavour to it; he thought it tasted somewhere between trout and salmon, with even a bit of sea fish thrown in, but had its own unique taste all at the same time. Maybe it was because he was so hungry, but he could hardly remember having anything better. He'd now waited five minutes or so, and again nothing sinister had happened and he felt fine. Swiftly chopping the whole fish up and sharing it out with Zephyr, they ate the delicacy ravenously.

It was almost dark now, and as Tony sat on the ground eating and drinking the cool, pure water, he felt as though it couldn't be better; as if he was in a five-star restaurant with an open-top roof, eating the best food and drinking the finest wine money could buy... He realised today had been a very significant turning point for them. No longer would he have to worry about when they would next be able to eat properly again; they now had an almost inexhaustible supply of good food. Knowing this was going to make a massive difference to their chances of survival on this planet; he felt that, for now at least, they had conquered the elements and the world was theirs. He was now able to think about making more progress, and give more thought to why they were actually on this far distant world, and what they were supposed to achieve!

For the first time since being there, his thoughts turned back to the ship, and the beings who had brought them here – what *did* they really want from him? They had treated us well on the vessel, for sure, and it was now clear they'd intended us to survive. By the normal laws of nature, this planet's probably got some pretty inhospitable areas – deserts, ice sheets and barren, rocky terrain. They could have put us in any of those places, but no, they put us here. OK, it's too hot at times, but it's lush, food-bearing and habitable. They didn't give us any technology to use for our advantage in this situation, any food, or any other provisions, but they gave us the tools to get a foothold in the environment: the knife, the means of making shelter, and the stones for fire. These didn't exactly come with any instructions, I had to use my initiative and intelligence to put them to good use, but they've come in pretty handy! Well, we'll explore the area further down the river soon. There have to be answers out there, he thought, and he was determined to find them...

Over the next few days, Tony got more adept at catching the fish, and they began to settle into a daily routine, feeding themselves up after their initial lean period. But, as dawn broke one day, Tony could hear a sound he hadn't experienced since he'd been on the planet – rain. He went straight over to the opening of the tent and cautiously looked out, eventually holding his hand out…

"Yes, it's pure, simple rain!" he said to himself. It felt fresh and was a relief from the constant heat. Tony slipped his jacket off and got out of the tent, standing out in the rain completely naked, with his arms stretched out and face upwards to the sky. "Aaah, that's good," he said. Zephyr eventually ventured out and stood beside him, not looking too impressed and looking as if to wonder what the big deal was. The rain stopped suddenly and Tony could see and feel the fierce glare of the sun breaking through the diminishing clouds. He rubbed his face and body with his hands as Zephyr shook the water off himself. Going back into the tent to prepare for the rest of the day, Tony felt refreshed and exhilarated after his first shower on this new world.

He decided that morning that this would be the day they'd start exploring further afield, just as he'd promised himself that night. As they started out towards the river, the sun was already turning the fallen rain into a steamy mist, and visibility was down to around ten metres. This had also brought out the large flying insects he'd seen when they first landed. When they got to the river's edge, Tony decided to go left, into the direction the sun. After they'd walked for about two miles, he was noticing the river narrowing and becoming shallower, until it was eventually possible to walk across. They were still directly opposite the huge forest, which extended far beyond. "Come on, Zeph, let's go look over there," he said.

They walked across the river and up onto the bank on the other side; the edge of the forest was now only around fifty metres ahead of them. As they slowly approached this mass of vegetation, Tony could hear the sound of rustling through the trees. From what he could make out, these noises were being made by both very large and smaller life forms. He could also hear and sense the presence of large, birdlike creatures in the treetops, some of which were at least two hundred feet high. The mist was still pretty thick at this point; the forest had an almost mystical look and feel to it as they got ever nearer to its border. They passed a large, strange-looking bush, with reddish-coloured fruits which Tony hadn't seen before, and they were now less than ten metres from the trees.

Suddenly and without warning, the ground shook to the sound of what seemed like thunder. There was a deep, growling-like sound, then the clump of trees they were stood in front of parted as a huge creature lunged out from behind them. It was larger than an elephant, with a thick, muscular body mass, and its hind legs were nearly as wide as some of the huge tree trunks. It had an extended neck and a head similar to a rhino, but with a long snout. Tony and Zephyr almost froze at the sight of the terrifying beast as it hurtled towards them. Tony looked at Zephyr. "Run!" he said, as he put his hand down to push him, but before they had time to take even two paces, the creature had reached them.

Zephyr let out a ferocious growl and deep bark, baring his teeth at the same time. Tony raised his pole and struck one of the creature's front legs. Zephyr then struck out with his teeth at the other leg, sinking a vicious bite into it. But their actions were to no effect on the beast, and they were both struck in turn with its massive legs, knocking them about six feet into the air.

As they fell back down to the ground with a hard thud, they found themselves underneath the beast. In truth, Tony thought they might have breathed their last, but he took hold of Zephyr and tried to get up to look for the best way for them to escape from under it. Then, to his surprise, the creature just kept walking, paying them no attention at all. They stood back up as soon as they were clear of it. Tony looked on with amazement as it went over to the bush and started to bite off whole branches from it with clumps of fruit attached... "It's a vegetarian!" he shouted. "It's a bloody harmless vegetarian." He stood there smiling as he watched the magnificent creature half-demolish the bush; he thought the size and general look of it was similar to one of Earth's dinosaurs. He knelt down to Zephyr to check him over. When he could see he was fine, they walked cautiously over to the creature. Zephyr started to growl but it still took no notice of them. "Come on, Zeph, let's move on while the going's good," Tony said. Glad they were both still actually alive, he decided to go back over to their side of the river and carry on walking along the bank to see where it would take them.

Chapter 7

They had walked on another few miles and the river was by now just a diminishing stream; as they went still further, the stream had completely dried up, and Tony could see a large white landmass in the distance. When they drew nearer, he could see a series of cracks running all the way through it; he could also now see the reflection of the sun bouncing off this brilliant, totally white landscape. Tony was intrigued with this discovery and increased his pace to reach it.

When they got there he could see it was round, about two hundred metres across. Stepping cautiously onto it, he looked down at Zephyr, who was curiously sniffing the ground. He then bent down to touch the substance. It felt strangely cool, which was surprising in the midday heat. Zephyr then started to lick the ground. Tony quickly stopped him, but he knew there must be a reason he'd done this; looking more closely he could see the substance of the ground was made up of crystals, white crystals. Scraping up a few of these to hold in the palm of his hand, he could see that Zephyr was fine after licking them, so he eventually placed a couple on his tongue. "Salt, it's salt," he said. "My god, it's a salt lake!"

Tony knew from his natural science studies that this could have formed by the river at one time having consisted of saltwater. The rains had now replenished the river with pure water, but at one time it must have flowed into this lake, then, due to some geological changes, time had eventually dried out this whole area. This was a really important discovery; back home he'd used salt water to treat wounds and infections on himself and others with a great deal of success, and had always believed there was nothing better for that purpose; another use that immediately occurred to him was that he would actually be able to season the food! But, even more importantly, he knew he'd be able to preserve their food for a time by wrapping it in the salt; this would also deter any wildlife and insects from scavenging, and allow him to build up a few days' supply. Tony was almost celebrating. In the circumstances they were in, having to rely on the natural resources this planet had to offer, finding salt to him was like striking oil back on Earth, and he now had a virtually limitless supply of it.

When he'd calmed down, he took hold of his pole and struck the ground in a downward motion, breaking chunks of the stuff away until he thought he had enough to last for a few days. After putting them into his bag, he decided they'd need to start making their way back to base. They must have walked about five miles,it was now getting towards mid-afternoon and he needed to catch fish for dinner before nightfall, so they started back. They were glad when they'd reached water again, and stopped for a drink and a dunk to cool off in the sweltering heat. As they finally got back to their part of the river, they rested for a while. Tony caught more fish than usual this time, intending to stash a few for the next couple of days in his new found salt. He also gathered an extra couple of the large water leaves to wrap them in.

When they got back to base, he lit the fire and cooked off a couple of the fish, and chopped Zephyr's up, but instead of putting the chunks on the ground, this time he decided to cut a piece of leaf off to put them in, as though to make a bowl for him to eat from. He then sprinkled some salt crystals over his own share – it tasted fantastic. Savouring every bite, he decided to afford them the luxury, and cooked another off. Looking to see if Zephyr had finished, he noticed he'd eaten the leaf bowl as well. Tony didn't really take much notice to begin with, but then he started to think: if Zephyr had eaten this, it must mean he'd instinctively sensed there's some goodness in it. He didn't really fancy eating a raw leaf, so after cutting a piece off for himself, he decided to let some juice from the fish he was cooking drizzle onto it, then lightly toast it over the fire. Taking a bite, he could taste a sweetness, and thought it strangely enough tasted a bit like spinach. "Sure has been a day of fortunate discoveries," he thought. This was another form of nutrition for them, and hopefully some form of vitamin, the like of which are provided by vegetables back home, so he cut another piece off for Zephyr to have with his half of the fish.

After they'd eaten, Tony gutted the rest of the raw fish and placed them into two separate whole leaves, smothered them with salt, and wrapped the leaves around them, before placing them in the tent. He then threw the fish guts onto the fire, as they'd only attract unwanted visitors, before sitting back down at the fire with Zephyr. "Well, that's been an adventure today, boy," he said. "First we encountered a monster and got away with it, then we found ourselves a salt lake! And finally we've found something new to eat, thanks to you!"

Night had now fallen again, and Tony returned to his thoughts of the night, thoughts of how he wanted to try to find those answers to why they'd been brought here. "OK, it had been a good and productive day," he thought, but he was still no nearer to finding any of the answers. At that moment, an old record he knew came into his head: 'There Are More Questions Than Answers'! He sat back, looked up at the star-spangled sky and laughed out loud, so loud it echoed into the darkness of the night. Zephyr turned his head and looked at him inquisitively, which made him laugh even more. "OK, boy," he said as he placed his hand on his head. "Don't worry, I'm not going crazy – not yet anyway!"

After his laughter had died down, he still couldn't help but think again about the beings who'd brought him here, and the fact they couldn't have done it just for him to live out his existence like this. Still, they'd only been here for just under two weeks now; maybe he should just wait and the answers would come to him in time, but that wasn't in his nature, to just wait around; he couldn't stand that.

After giving more thought to everything he decided they'd go even further afield, to really see what's out there. This appealed much more to him, and, after all, he now had the means to stockpile food to take with them. He'd seen the same dried out materials he was using to build a fire laying around everywhere on their hike today, so he'd be able to make a fire anywhere, and they could take the tent with them. Yes, it was definitely time to move on, he thought.

At the break of dawn the next day, they went straight down to the river. Tony wanted to catch more fish for the day's food, intending to save those he'd wrapped in salt for their expedition the next day; he also wanted to take some of the water leaves with them for their newly found food supplement. He'd thought of taking some of the fruits from the surrounding trees as well, so they'd be able to eat on the move.

After completing all the preparations for the next day, he planned for them to get some rest before starting out. They'd probably need it... for whatever might lay ahead of them.

As the sun rose that next morning, Tony started to get everything ready. Although he'd only been there for a couple of weeks now, he felt a strange sadness at leaving the spot where they'd begun their struggle for survival, but he knew he needed to do this. Besides, he was looking forward now, forward to what they'd eventually find out there. Planning for them to walk beyond the salt lake on this first day and set up base there somewhere, he knew he would need to stay within walking distance of their part of the river for catching fish, so in this respect they were limited to how far they could go. But he thought that if they could get set up on the other side of the lake, then they could explore the wider area in different directions each day, providing he could catch enough fish and store them for long enough that is, and, as the river still ran up to a relatively short distance from the lake, they'd be OK for water.

The sun had almost fully risen by the time they set out. With the fish and everything else in his bag, Tony was now carrying a fair bit of weight and knew they'd need to stop periodically, but as it was very early, he figured they should make it to where he wanted to and be able to set up base before nightfall. Their first stop was near to the place where they'd encountered the huge creature; they could still hear the deep, dull thuds of the beast as it trudged through that area of the forest. This made Zephyr uneasy and he let out the odd growl. "It's OK, boy, it won't bother coming over this way," Tony assured him.

After drinking from the river, they moved on. Tony knew he would need to fill a water leaf further on before they hit the end of the river. As they walked on, he could see this time round that the surrounding terrain was sloping upwards, which would explain the river having eventually dried up. Looking at what used to be the riverbed, he could see what looked like a collection of brownish, rust-coloured rocks scattered everywhere. Looking more closely at them, "Metal, there's a kind of metal in the rock," he thought. Again thinking back to his science studies back on the ship, he knew metals such as iron could be formed in rocks by a chemical reaction with the oxygen in fresh waters.

"Interesting," he said to himself. "But this isn't Earth, so who knows!" he concluded as he tossed the rock back to the ground.

The day was getting long by the time they reached the salt lake. Again, the sun was fiercely reflecting off the lake's white, crystalline surface, which made it impossible to walk on, so they had to go around it, making the journey even longer, but they finally reached the other side by late afternoon. Tony took a good look around. The whole area was flat, rocky and barren; no vegetation would grow around here. He realised this was due to the salt and complete lack of water, but, in the distance, through the heat haze, he could see an area of relatively small cliffs rising up from the rocky plain, surrounded by green vegetation. Being such a contrast to the rest of the landscape, he thought it might even be a mirage, but if they were going to stay this side of the lake, they seriously needed to get out of the heat which now bore down on them. "This way, Zeph," he said. The fact that they were already hot and tired, made crossing the rocky stretch of land extremely tuff going. "Please god for that, at least it's real," Tony said as they finally approached this new-found area.

They headed straight for a clump of trees for immediate shelter; both almost completely exhausted, and close to heatstroke by now, it was a huge relief to get under the cool of the trees. "OK, let's rest here," Tony said, as he was very worried about the effect of the heat on Zephyr by now. Throwing his bag down and dropping to his knees, he opened the water leaf he'd brought with them. Placing his hand into the water, he drizzled it over Zephyr's head and back as he lay there panting. He quickly took a leaf bowl from his bag and filled it for him, before taking a few good gulps for himself.

They both laid there for a while and Tony was relieved to see Zephyr was looking all right. He could also feel himself cooling down and his strength returning. Not quite knowing whether it was the effect of the heat on his mind, but as he sat up he thought he could hear what sounded like running water in the near distance, coming from the other side of the clump of trees they were in. Keen to see what lay beyond the trees anyway, this only increased his curiosity.

Getting back on his feet, he gave Zephyr the signal to follow him in the direction of the sound; it was getting more pronounced the nearer they got. Tony smiled to himself at the now unmistakable noise of gushing water. Stepping through the border of trees and back into the clear daylight, "Wow" he said to himself as the smile on his face gradually got wider. The more he took in of what was now revealed to him, the more he realised the importance of what they'd found. "Like an oasis in a desert," he thought to himself.

To his left were the series of the small cliffs he'd seen from the distance, which were sloping backwards, making them accessible to walk up. The running water was in the form of a moderate waterfall flowing from the top of one of the cliffs, which ran into a lake about fifty metres across. The whole area was lush with grasses and vegetation, some of which he hadn't seen before; bushes and trees, but even better, his now familiar water leaves, were all growing around the side of the lake. Tony realised the water must be from another offshoot of the main river. "Incredible what a bit of water can do," he said to himself as he looked around the area again. Observing the series of cliffs more closely, he could see that each one of them had a series of fairly wide holes at the rock face. "Come on, let's go and check this out," he said excitedly to Zephyr.

They made their way up the face of the first cliff wall. Tony laughed as he watched Zephyr with his four legs breeze up, down and around the rocky, slanted surface with the ease of a mountain goat! He wondered what he might find within the holes of these cliffs, but each one he looked in turned out to be just a small empty cavern. "Come on, boy, let's try the next one," he said as he made his way back down.

The next cliff had four openings on its face, the first being the same as on the other cliff. Tony then moved along to the second and largest opening. "Now that's more like it!" he thought. The entrance was wide enough to let a good amount of light in, and the cavern went fairly deep into the rock. As he took his first step in, he could also see it was a lot wider inside than the actual opening, and had a ceiling of around five metres in height. The atmosphere inside was pleasantly cool and dry, and the ground relatively smooth. He could see a shaft of light streaming through from the ceiling near the back of the cavern, around ten metres away. "Come on, Zeph, in here."

Once Zephyr had entered, they walked towards the source of light, which was coming in through a narrow slit about twenty centimetres wide and a metre in length, which ran up through to the roof of the cliff. Tony looked at Zephyr. "Well, it's light, airy, spacious and dry – we'll take it!" he joked. "Our new home!" They walked back to the entrance, and Tony put his hand out to lean on the rock wall. "This is perfect," he said to himself as he looked down at the lake and vegetation below. "It's solid, secure, and with a good vantage point. And we've got fresh running water on our doorstep. It's what an estate agent back on Earth would call a high-end property." He turned to Zephyr with a smile on his face: "Come on, boy. Let's go down, get our stuff, we're moving in!."

Evening was now starting to fall, so once at the bottom of the cliffs, Tony decided to cook their dinner. There were plenty of dried dead branches, twigs and grasses in the area, and he quickly gathered enough material to get the fire started. Before doing so, he took two of the fish wrapped in salt over to the lake to wash them off. It was whilst he was doing this that a thought suddenly occurred to him. "Of course! I can start the fire in the cave." Realising it would draw air in through the entrance, the crack in the ceiling would act as a kind of chimney. Excited at the prospect, he hurried back to the base of the cliff to gather everything together.

They quickly made their way back up and into their new-found accommodation. Tony set up his materials immediately below the vent and started the fire – the theory worked perfectly. To him, what they'd found today was like moving out of a small room in a guest house and into the penthouse suite of a five-star hotel. "Perfect," he said again as he turned to Zephyr, who was anxiously waiting for his dinner. The fish had preserved well in the salt, Tony thought, and needed no extra seasoning.

After eating, they just sat there for a while, watching the blanket of night fall through the entrance of the cave, the flames of the fire casting strange shadows across the walls. Tony started to think about the logistics of where they were now; he wondered whether there'd be any fish in the lake. He would check at some time, but he didn't relish the thought of building *another* well to catch them in, and besides, he hadn't seen many loose rocks laying around the immediate area to do it with, so he worked out they would have to go back to their part of the river to fish every three days or so, and would need to start out early in the morning and come back in the evening to avoid the heat… "Yep, life's just getting more complicated," he said to himself as he laughed. But for now they had enough food, so he intended to do as planned and get out and explore the wider area at daybreak.

Chapter 8

They woke the next morning to the sun rising low in the sky, the light penetrating through the cave, blurring Tony's eyes as he opened them. He had that thing where he had to think where he was for a moment, like waking up in a strange hotel room after the first night; he still felt tired as he rubbed his face. Zephyr stood up and stretched. They were both a bit bombed out from the day before but they'd had a good night's sleep, and Tony was keen to get started as early as possible "OK, boy, let's hit the road." Tony felt it was now safe to leave the food and his bag behind in this virtual fortress, he wanted to travel as lightly as possible, and just take items of defence with them.

He grabbed his pole and knife and they started out, only stopping briefly at the foot of the waterfall to wash and fill a water leaf. The area around the lake was surrounded on all sides by trees, so the obvious choice of direction was to go through the opposite way to which they'd entered. Tony had a feeling of anticipation and hope at the thought of what they might find out there, but knew he had to keep a cool head, and be totally on his guard for whatever dangers might lay ahead of them. Even so, this was exciting, and the fact they now had a strong permanent base gave him, in a strange kind of way, a sense of greater security. He felt ready to take on anything this planet had to throw at him, just as he did in life back on Earth.

What lay beyond the trees was at first much the same as the landscape they'd crossed beyond the salt lake: flat, barren and rocky. The land however seemed to disappear about four to five hundred metres in the direction they were walking, so Tony was interested to see what was, or wasn't, there. As they got nearer to where the land ended, they approached slowly and cautiously; they were now only about thirty metres away and the view started to reveal itself.

"My god," Tony said as they got to the edge and he could see what was before them. He initially had a spell of dizziness, before quickly reaching down to put his hand on Zephyr's chest to make sure he didn't get too close to the edge. Standing there in silence and wonderment, he looked out onto a massive canyon, the like and size of which he'd never experienced. He'd not visited the Grand Canyon back on Earth, but thought this must be at least equal in size, except this one had masses of vegetation growing around all of its interior.

A virtual rainforest lay at the base, stretching the full length of the canyon and fed by a huge waterfall running down the right-hand side of the face at the far side, which was giving off a massive cloud of spray and causing a rainbow to run through it. "Jesus, Zephyr, this planet's certainly full of surprises, if nothing else. Even if there's no intelligent life here I've got to admit it's a pretty spectacular place."

After an hour or so, Tony decided to move on in another direction. He'd looked all around the edge of the canyon, but it was clear there was no safe way down. He could see another row of cliffs in the distance, although these appeared larger; apart from that there was nothing else to this flat, barren landscape. "That way, Zeph." As they got closer to the cliffs it became obvious this was a huge cluster of rocky mounds rising up to a high elevation. Upon reaching the base of the front face, Tony could see inlets into the cliffs and walked over to the entrance of one of them. In front of him was a ravine, stretching over a hundred metres through a virtual labyrinth of huge boulders, cliffs and caves. There was an eerie silence and feel about this place. Zephyr gave a deep, low growl and could obviously sense something. They both looked at each other as though to acknowledge each other's thoughts, but Tony knew he just had to go in. "Come on, boy, let's see what's here."

They cautiously took their first few steps into the pathway and Tony was, as always, more than glad to have Zephyr by his side. After fifty metres or so, the silence began to break with the sounds of something in the distance. Unable to discern what these sounds were, they walked on. The sounds got louder and Tony now started to notice plant life growing out of some of the rocks. Further on, the path began to widen; they passed by fruit-bearing bushes like the ones around their cave. Tony now felt a strange air of expectancy, as though he could almost sense he was about to encounter something. Gripping his knife and pole tightly in his hands, he got ready to defend himself.

Now near the centre of the mass of cliffs, they could hear a sound like rock banging on rock, and odd, sort of grunting noises. Tony could see an opening between two boulders coming up on the left of them, and was just thinking about turning into it when he came to a startled stop... from out of the entrance walked two figures –fairly small, upright and on two legs; hairy and ugly. They were both carrying tree branches which had been trimmed and fashioned for a purpose. They were obviously primitive, but Tony realised in an instant that this was an intelligent life form!

The few seconds that passed as they all stood, just staring at each other in a still silence, felt like an hour. The moment was then shattered suddenly and quickly by the sound of Zephyr barking as he ferociously lunged at them. Tony called him off, but the two figures swiftly disappeared back through the opening from which they'd first appeared. He ran straight to the entrance to catch sight of where they were going, with the intention of following them, but when he got there he stopped again at what he could now see.

As he watched the two figures running away as fast as they could, Tony saw a whole community of these creatures against the backdrop of a large waterfall running into a series of lakes, each being around the same size as the one at their cave. There must have been about thirty of these beings, all scattered around this massive area nestled within the huge cluster of cliffs, but there wasn't much time to observe: the two figures were by now back within their community, grunting loudly and pointing in Tony and Zephyr's direction. Tony could see some of them looking their way. "Come on, boy, let's make ourselves scarce, for now, anyway," he said.

In double-quick time they made their way out of the cliffs and back into the open landscape; as far as he could tell, they weren't being followed. Tony decided to get them back to their cave, regroup and have a good think about this unexpected discovery. En route back to their territory, Tony carefully took a detour to the edge of the canyon. That way, if they were being watched, the creatures would think they'd come from that direction. He didn't think they'd come out into the open to follow him; for one thing he was a lot bigger than they were, and it was certain they hadn't encountered anything like Zephyr before! He stayed at the canyon's edge for a good hour again before doubling back to base.

On their return, Tony stopped just inside the clump of trees and stood watch for a while, just to make doubly sure they'd not been followed. When he was sure the coast was clear, they finally went back into their cave and Tony prepared the food, with the discovery of the creatures still so fresh in his mind, and not yet really sunk in properly yet. "Well, Zeph, we wanted to see what was out there and we sure found it!" he said as they ravaged their dinner.

As dusk began to fall, Tony started to think for the first time since they'd landed here just how much he was missing things in his old life; his home, his old chair, a glass or two of whisky in the evening, even the TV, and especially a choice of what he would have for dinner; even the ship where he had those same things. "The ship, my god I never thought I'd come to miss that!" he thought as he continued to ponder the situation they were now in. "I wonder what those beings on there are doing now? Are they watching us, I wonder, are they able to, I wonder? Have I just ended up doing everything they wanted me to so far, just playing into their hands? "Well, one thing's for sure: I've done what *I* needed to do so far," he said as he looked over at Zephyr. "We'll show 'em, boy, we'll show 'em!"

His thoughts then returned to their encounter with the creatures that day, of who and what they really were, but whatever their origins, he couldn't deny they were definitely humanoid; that was a pretty big leap from the life forms he'd seen so far on this planet. He just knew he'd be compelled to go back and observe them again; he didn't really know why, but it was like a magnet to him. Tomorrow though they'd need to go back to their river for more fish; they'd go back to the community the day after, he thought. As he continued to contemplate the days ahead, the nagging feeling hung over him that of all the beings he could have imagined he might have found here, he now knew the most dangerous animal of all existed on this planet, a form... of man!

Setting out before the sun had fully risen to avoid the heat that day, they made the trip back to their part of the river; getting there early meant Tony had plenty of time to spend catching as many fish as he could carry back in his bag. Spending the whole day there felt like a break from everything they'd done in the past few days, like a day out, in a strange kind of way, but still Tony knew they'd found a proper place to live now, and they needed to think of it as their main base.

They made their way back in the cooler temperature of early evening as planned and got back just before nightfall. After they'd eaten, Tony started to formulate a plan for the next day; he knew where the beings would be this time, which he hoped would give him an advantage, and they should be able to stealthily observe the community without being detected this time. He didn't know what he would gain by this, but he'd found the only sign of truly intelligent life so far and felt compelled to investigate.

Again, they started out at daybreak; they knew where they were going now so it only took them about thirty minutes to reach the series of cliffs. They trod through the path leading through the ravine once more, until Tony could hear those same sounds emanating from the rocks and boulders which hid the settlement so well. Approaching the spot where he'd encountered the two beings the day before, he noticed a pile of boulders which reached up to a ridge. Working out that this should overlook the community, he gave Zephyr the signal and they scaled up, being careful to keep their heads down when they were close to the top. Tony slowly and carefully peered over the rocks; he could now see the beings clearly, and was in a perfect position so as not to be spotted.

He looked on with fascination as he scrutinised the actions and interactions of these life forms; almost equally fascinating was the thought that they were being observed by *him* – for all intents and purposes an alien being from another planet way across the galaxy. It wasn't difficult for Tony to see from their general form, look and features, and everything else about them – the way they communicated through use of gesture and vocal sound, the wearing of animal skins, and the formation of a basic but cohesive society – that they were not dissimilar to an early form of human. Even the genders were clearly distinguishable: some of the females were nurturing infants, whilst the men were picking fruits from the bushes which grew randomly around the series of lakes, and carrying the food back to the mother and child in the respective plots which they occupied. OK, they were hairy and relatively small, but they were a higher sentient life form.

He'd had plenty of time to think as he sat there in his vantage point, and again the questions as to what and why he'd been brought here crossed his mind. Now that they'd discovered these beings, the questions at the forefront of his mind were: "Are they the reason I'm here? Am I supposed to make contact with them? Am I supposed to do something for them?" He thought to himself, but then, the ominous thought of… "Am I supposed to... breed with them!" finally dawned on him. "My god, *my* genes into theirs, no way!"

With that thought, he grabbed his pole and prepared to make a swift departure, but just at that moment, out of the corner of his eye, he spotted something going on – there was some kind of disruption happening over on the far side of one of the lakes. He couldn't really see this properly, because the group it was coming from were being partly obscured behind one of the bushes. Then, suddenly a single female came running out from behind the bush, closely followed by a group of six to seven others, both male and female, all picking up rocks and throwing them at her in close pursuit. Tony watched the female for a few seconds as she ran frantically away from them. There was something different about her; she was cleaner, taller, and from what he could see at that distance, lacked the hair on her arms and legs. She was heading for the exit of the community and the males in the group were gaining ground on her; Tony knew he had to help her. "OK, Zeph, let's get back down, boy".

As they landed back on the ground, the female came darting through the exit and was heading straight towards them. Her head was in a downward position as she looked at the ground, still running as fast as she could. She was now about ten metres away from them when she suddenly lifted her head; the shock of seeing Tony and Zephyr standing there brought her to a skidding stop. She stood motionless before them, breathing heavily, just staring, her eyes wide and mouth open. Tony put his hand out. "Come with me," he said.

At that moment, the group started to appear, running through the exit still in frantic pursuit. She turned her head to look at them before looking back to Tony, then moved quickly to position herself by him and Zephyr. The group also hadn't noticed them yet, but Tony stood there as they drew nearer, clutching his pole in one hand and knife in the other. Zephyr started to growl, and let out a deep, loud bark, causing the group to look straight at them. They all came to a gradual stop, standing their ground and looking at him with a curious expression on their faces. Tony stared into their eyes one by one with a penetrating glare; he knew him and Zephyr could take them; if they didn't back off in the next few seconds, he was going to make the first move.

As they continued to hold their ground, he and Zephyr looked at each other. Tony cocked his head towards the group: "Come on, boy, let's go for it!" he shouted, breaking the silence. They shot towards the group. Tony gave out a battle cry, wielding his knife and raising his pole above his head; Zephyr was snarling viciously, baring and flashing his impressive teeth. It was all over before they could reach the group; they scattered and fled back through the entrance to the community faster than they'd come from it, Zephyr continuing to chase them before Tony called him off. "Good boy," he said to Zephyr as he leant down to speak to him.

A few moments later, Tony looked up to see the female standing over them, still looking worried and shaken up and staring at the entrance, obviously concerned the group might appear again. Tony stood back up and spoke to her. "Don't worry, they're gone… gone," he said as he waved his arms from side to side in gesture. "Anyway," he said as he put his hand on her shoulder, "I'm Tony, and this is Zephyr." "This way," Tony said as he pointed down the pathway leading to the way out. "Come on, let's go." She cautiously started to follow them, her eyes fixed on Zephyr, gazing curiously at the like of which she'd never seen before.

As they continued to walk back through the ravine, Tony began to look more closely at the female. She looked like a cleaned-up version of the other creatures, more human even, in a strange kind of way, he thought. But what exactly was she? … And why was she being persecuted by the rest of her kind? … Was it because she looked different? Whatever the reason, and whatever she was, he instinctively knew he'd had to help her, but what now? And what… was he going to do with her?

They were now about halfway back across the barren, rocky area and headed towards home. Tony kept looking over his shoulder to check whether they were being followed, but so far he'd seen nothing. The female was by now starting to look exhausted in the midday heat and Tony guided her to a large rock that she could sit and rest on for a while, but the sun's heat was blazing down and bouncing off the rocks and he knew they needed to get back to base. Before moving on, Tony took another look back at the cliffs in the distance; this time he could just see three humanoid figures standing there. They were too far away for him to tell for sure, but they seemed to be looking and pointing in his direction. "Come on, rest time over," Tony said as he grabbed the female's arm.

When they finally got back to base, he pointed to the lake and looked at her. "Cool off?" he said, but she just looked back at him, still seemingly unsure about what was happening. "Well I'm gonna cool off myself, that's for sure!" He was about to strip off and plunge into the lake when he suddenly realised: "No, I can't strip in front of her, it just wouldn't be right!" Tony gave this a bit more thought but came to the same conclusion. "This being might be a different breed, but it's still humanoid, and it's female. Better wait till later", he decided.

Meanwhile, Zephyr had already walked over to the lake; Tony looked round just in time to see him submerge himself in the water by laying on his front, with just his head protruding above the surface. He laughed out loud. "It's all right for some, Zeph," he said enviously. As he looked back at the female, he could see her also looking at Zephyr, and to his surprise, she was smiling. "Now that's better," he said as he began to walk over to her, but before he had the chance to reach her, she walked straight past him and over to Zephyr and sat down in the water beside him. Tony looked on with fascination as she started to touch his head affectionately. Zephyr began to sniff at the female, eventually licking a cut on her arm. "Well, good to see *you two* have made friends," Tony said with a hint of sarcasm. "Dinner time," he said as he looked at Zephyr. Zephyr stood up quickly and shook himself, soaking the female with an intense spray of water. Tony laughed as the female gasped in shock. "That'll teach ya. Well come on, if you wanna eat," Tony said as he gestured to the female to follow them. She tentatively stood up out of the water and began to walk behind him and Zephyr.

She followed them up the face of the cliff, stopping warily at the entrance to the cave. Tony looked around at her again, this time putting his arm out, his hand flat and pointing in the direction of the inside, as though to welcome a guest into a hotel. "Welcome to my apartment," he joked. She slowly stepped in, her eyes cautiously looking everywhere. Tony guided her to the back of the cave, sitting her on a smooth and relatively comfortable rock which he normally sat on. "There we are, make yourself at home." He grabbed a few handfuls of dead grass and sticks that he'd now been storing in the cave for the fire, then grabbed his stones from the bag. Striking the stones against one another in the usual way, the sparks were as always quick to start a flame in the kindling, which took hold in seconds. Suddenly startled by a piercing screech from the female, Tony turned to see her bolt out of the cave, disappearing back through the entrance a hundred times faster than she'd entered. "Of course," Tony thought as he realised she must never have experienced fire before. After he'd gathered himself, he saw the funny side of this and smiled. "Come on, Zeph, let's go find her," he said as he walked from the cave laughing.

As he started to make his way back down the cliff, it wasn't long before he spotted her, crouched, hiding behind one of the rocks. He walked round to the other side of the rock and knelt down to her. "It's alright," he tried to say calmingly as he reached out to gently hold her hand. Zephyr sat reassuringly by them before Tony slowly pulled her up. Still holding her hand, they all walked back into the cave; the fire was now burning slowly as the flames licked against the back wall. He sat her back on the rock. "OK, let's eat," he gestured by pretending to put food in his mouth.

Grabbing one of the leaves, he unwrapped a fish and brushed off the excess salt, skewered it in the normal way, and began to cook. The female's eyes were fixed on the whole process as she moved her head from side to side in curiosity. After he'd finished cooking, he boned it in the usual way, then cut it into three equal portions and gave Zephyr his share. Breaking a piece off from one of the other portions, Tony placed it into one of her hands, once again making the gesture to eat.

She held it up to her face and sniffed, then slowly took a first bite, closing her eyes as she began to chew. He could see she was obviously enjoying it. "They don't call me the best chef on this planet for nothing, ya know," he said jokingly as he gave her the rest of her share. It was a fair bet she hadn't eaten for a while, Tony thought, which was made even more obvious by how fast she ate the rest of it.

After eating his share, he quickly cooked three more fish off and they each sat enjoying what felt like a virtual feast. As night began to fall, there was a soft glow in the cave from the smouldering remains of the fire. The female's eyes were now growing heavy and she moved herself over to a near corner. As she laid down on her side, Tony watched as she gradually drifted into sleep, observing how closely this resembled human behaviour. "How do you communicate, I wonder? Can you talk? I haven't heard a sound from you since we first met back there," he said to himself. He looked at Zephyr, who was now laying on his front in contentment after his dinner. "Well, Zeph, what are we gonna do about this one then? Whoever she is, we'll need to go back up the river for more food tomorrow. Shall we take her with us? Uh, whatever, we'll decide in the morning."

Thinking back to the events of the day, Tony now realised he had another problem: he was sure the other humanoids had seen them coming back to base, and would need to be on the lookout for a curious visit from them. Whatever they were, and however primitive their culture, as they were complex, intelligent life forms he knew this made them dangerous.

It was now feeling like it had been a long, eventful day, and Tony decided they'd better sleep nearer to the entrance of the cave, just in case the creatures tried to pay them a night visit! He took his bag up to the closest point of the opening, then, clutching his knife, he and Zephyr laid at the entrance to sleep for the night.

Chapter 9

As Tony woke the next morning with the events of yesterday flowing back to him, he got up and immediately walked to the back of the cave to check on the female; she'd gone without a trace. As he turned back round toward the entrance, he saw Zephyr standing at the opening, looking outwards. Quickly walking back to where Zephyr stood, he looked in the same direction – there she was, bathing in the lake, looking completely oblivious to everything around her. Tony smiled to himself: "Not a care in the world, huh."

He decided it *would* be a good idea to take her with them to the river that day after all, mainly because of the possibility of her fellow beings coming to find her, only to finish what they'd started yesterday! But there was something else. Beside the fact she couldn't communicate verbally with him, he still thought she'd become good company for them in time, and the fact she seemed to like Zephyr so much had made him warm to her.

Walking down to the lake to greet her, Tony handed her the animal skin she'd left at the edge, turning his back whilst she got out. As he took her back up to the cave, he made the 'eating' gesture to her and she followed eagerly; he cooked off the last two fish he'd stored away and shared them out. After they'd eaten, Tony grabbed his bag, pole and knife; looking at the female, he pointed towards the exit. "Come on," he said, gesturing that it was time to go. She got up and followed reluctantly, as though wary about what was happening. "It's OK," he said, continually looking round at her.

By the time they'd reached the bottom of the cliff she seemed more at ease, and Tony was easily able to coax her from out of the confines of the lake area. He'd started out early again to avoid the heat and they crossed the barren, rocky area in good time; as they got to the salt lake, the female stopped and gazed in wonder at the totally flat, brilliantly white phenomenon, eventually holding her hands up to her eyes to avoid the glare. Tony smiled to himself. "OK, let's move on," he said, grabbing her arm to guide her around the edge of the lake.

Finally getting to the lush land of the flowing river, Zephyr began to frolic and run through the grasses in excitement; the female smiled at the sight and ran over to him. Tony was both surprised and pleased to see her kneel down to stroke him before joining in the run around. He watched in amusement as Zephyr ran rings around her. Finally jumping up, he pushed the female backwards, sending her reeling for several feet before she fell to the ground. His amusement soon turned to amazement as there came a sound of something he'd not expected to hear –

laughter. The female let out a loud sound of laughter; apart from this being the first time he'd heard any sound from her at all, Tony realised that to make the sound of laughter she must have a voice box, meaning she could have the ability to talk.

Walking on until they got to their part of the river, they sat down to rest before Tony got started on catching the fish. The female began to look at him as though to wonder why they'd stopped there. "Fishing," he said as he pointed to the well, but as Tony watched her stroking Zephyr again, the thought occurred to him that to actually see him catch the fish, and do what he had to do in the process, might completely freak her out.

With this in mind, he decided to create a distraction for her, with Zephyr's help. He took the female up to the grass mound where they'd first set up base and took a couple of rocks with him. He knew how Zephyr loved to chase after and retrieve rocks or large stones that he threw for him on the beaches back on Earth, so, when they reached the top of the mound, he looked at Zephyr as he threw one of the rocks. The female watched and smiled as Zephyr ran excitedly after the object before bringing it straight back to him. Tony then placed the rock in the female's hand and gestured her to throw; with a straight arm she chucked it as far as she could. When Zephyr retrieved it, dropped it at her feet and looked at her to throw it again, her face filled with delight. "Job done," Tony thought as he gestured for the female to continue. Then, looking at Zephyr, "Stay, guard," he said before he left to go back to the well; Zephyr knew what this meant as Tony had said this to him many times in their travels back on Earth.

Tony started to make his way back to the river, looking back a couple of times and smiling to himself at sight of the two of them having a fun time. Back at the well, he went about the business of catching the fish in the normal way; in just over an hour he'd caught a good clutch and it was now time to bring Zephyr and the female back down. On his return they were both laying on the grass. "It's OK for some," Tony said as he put down his fish-laden bag.

Drawing breath he looked around at the stunning panoramic view; it brought back memories of those first few days on the planet, which now seemed like months ago rather than just nearly three weeks or so; in fact it seemed like weeks since they'd been back here. "Come on, time to go, Zeph," he said while gently grabbing the female's arm to let her know they should start out. As they walked back down to the river, the female turned to look at Tony and smiled as though to tell him how much she'd enjoyed the day. This took him by surprise, but after they'd gone a few more steps he looked round and nodded to her. "You're welcome," he said.

Upon getting back to the river's edge, the female sat on one of the large rocks whilst Tony and Zephyr walked into the river to cool off. It was now mid-afternoon, so they had some time to spare as they needed to wait until the heat of the day subsided, and with the main task of the day done, Tony felt he had time to relax for a while. He looked curiously at the female as she sat there so upright, as though an ornament set on a plinth, her legs crossed with her head turned in a gaze at everything which surrounded her. "My god, she could almost be striking a pose," he thought. At that moment, the record 'Vogue' by Madonna came into his mind and he started laughing before nearly choking as an intake of breath caused him to take in water.

When he'd stopped laughing, and choking, he looked back at her again. He was beginning to notice just how different she really seemed from the rest of her race: so more refined, in looks and more than likely in ways, from what he'd seen of them so far. In fact, she was starting to seem almost comparatively human to him.

Walking out of the river to sit at the edge and dry off in the intense heat, Tony started to think about how the living arrangements were going to work with this 'being'. Again, he thought about the fact that it was female, and if her breed felt the same way about gender differences she'd need her own privacy, and so would he. "I mean, I feel responsible for her in a way now," he thought to himself. It then occurred to him that he could let her have one of the other caves back at base. Like having her own room, he thought, laughing to himself. "OK, we'll give it a couple of days and just see how things go," he told himself.

When it got to early evening, they began to make their way back to base, only stopping at the lake for Tony to collect more salt to coat the fish. By the time they got back to base it was beginning to get dark, and as they walked back through the surrounding woods, Tony could hear sounds, sounds he was now only too familiar with – the basic grunts of the other humanoid creatures. Zephyr started to growl deeply. "OK, boy," Tony said in a half-whisper. He looked back at the female; she seemed to be eagerly listening, as though trying to decide whether the sounds were coming from beings she recognised. Tony signalled to the female to stay where she stood. He laid his bag on the ground, reached into it for his knife, and he and Zephyr made their way slowly through the woods until they reached the edge.

Looking down at Zephyr, he gave the signal 'go'. As they burst through the trees, he could see two figures turning to look in shock at the sight of Zephyr running towards them, closely followed by Tony, knife in hand and letting out a yell. They stood frozen for a second or two, then turned and fled into the waters of the lake. Tony called Zephyr back as the beings stood half-submerged in the water; if he had been back on Earth he'd swear they had an expression of fear on their faces.

He and Zephyr walked to the water's edge; Tony now had a chance to take a really good look at them. "My god, they're ugly bastards," he said to himself, but as he continued to stare at them, he saw their eyes suddenly move to look beyond him. He was taken aback to see them begin to smile and point, which eventually caused him to look round; it was the female, standing behind him and smiling back at them. She moved towards the water's edge. Tony was profoundly shocked when the female began gesturing to him, pointing at the beings then pointing at herself; he could see she was trying to tell him something, tell him they belonged with each other maybe. "Wow," he thought. "She's picked that up just from being with me for a day." "OK," he said, standing back to let them out of the water. As they walked to the edge the female rushed toward them, and they held their arms open as though to welcome her, before they all eventually held each other in an embrace.

Tony stood in silent fascination as the beings began to converse with each other in a relatively complex way. They were using some kind of language, or at least that's what he assumed the seemingly basic vocal sounds were. The sounds were also being aided by the use of hand gestures and facial expressions, Tony thought as he tried to understand what they were saying. From what he could make out, they appeared to be recounting the events of yesterday when the female was chased out of the community. The males seemed to be telling her what had happened to them after she'd gone, and by the looks of it, it wasn't good; he could see fresh wounds and bruises on their upper bodies and faces.

The female turned to look at and point to Tony, then continued to converse with the males; he figured she was telling them about how he'd rescued her, brought her to this place and fed her. "Maybe, who knows," he thought. The conversation continued for around another two minutes, then, after a brief silence, the female slowly walked over to Tony. To begin with, he thought this was 'goodbye, thanks for everything but I'll be going with my own kind now'. "Fair enough," he said as he nodded in acknowledgement, but to his astonishment she pointed to them and then to one of the caves in the cliff; she was asking for them to stay! Tony put his hand up to her, gesturing to let him think about this; he walked away from the group and sat down on a rock with Zephyr by his side.

The thought had already occurred to him that these other two beings were now outcasts, but where they went, what they did, wasn't his concern, or responsibility. "I don't need two more mouths to feed either," he thought. "But, on the other hand, this place has got potential – the potential to be cultivated. That's going to need a lot of work, and they must know what grows and where to get it round here, hopefully.

They could also come on the fishing trips with me; if we can find a way of making another bag or two we can bring much more food back, enough to last for a week or so – the salt will preserve it for that long. Yes, yes, my god, this could work!" he concluded as he decided to give it a try.

Tony walked over to collect his bag, then back over to the humanoids. "OK, follow me," he said as he beckoned them towards him. The female smiled as they scurried behind him. Leading them up to the cliff face, trying to decide which cavern to put them in, Tony stopped for a moment to think. This caused the two humanoids to stop immediately behind him; as he looked round, a strong scent hit him full on. "The cave furthest from mine. Apart from being ugly, you smell bad," Tony said to them with a wry smile on his face.

As they reached the opening to the cave, the two beings became excited, rushing into it before Tony had a chance to even point them in. "Hey! Your new home, boys," he said as they smiled and flung their arms in the air with excitement. "Christ, it's only a cave," Tony thought, but as he walked away he realised that to them it was much more – it was a place to be, a place… with their own breed.

Tony also thought this was now a good time to give the female her own cave, the next one along, so that she could be near to her fellow beings. When they got there, he turned to look at her and gestured. "Yours," he said. She looked back at him with a troubled expression on her face, moving her arms from side to side to gesture 'no', then pointed to his cave. Tony didn't know why, but she obviously wanted to remain in his place. Maybe because it was big, maybe because of her friendship with Zephyr: either way he accepted her choice.

When they got back to the cave, Tony unpacked a few fish and got the fire started. He gestured to the female to bring her friends in for dinner as he started to cook off; he'd also decided to do a couple of extra fish for them all to have for breakfast. When the female returned with them, they approached the fire cautiously; they were just as wary of it as she'd been the first time; the time which had passed since then seemed like days ago now. As the two humanoids drew nearer, he could smell them again, so he quickly got up and sat them on a rock at a reasonable distance.

Tony shared the food out and served it on pieces of the leaves which he'd wrapped the fish in. He watched as they devoured the meal, each one looking at the other as though to agree they'd never eaten anything as good in their lives before. When they finished the fish, Tony looked on with even more interest as they started to eat the leaves; it looked as though this was totally normal for them. "My god, they know these things are good for eating, just as I've discovered." He knew there was really no reason to be amazed by this – he already knew they must know what vegetation to eat – but it was just that initial realisation of a mutual discovery which made him feel a kind of link with them. They each looked at Tony, holding their arms out to him; he could see this was some kind of gesture of appreciation. He looked back at them. "That's OK, boys. You'll work for it in payment," he thought with a smile on his face, before returning the gesture.

After they'd all eaten, Tony took the two of them back down the cliff to the waterfall and showed them how to shower under it. They didn't like it but Tony directed them in, firmly. When they'd finished he smiled and gave them a thumbs up. He couldn't think how to tell them to do this every day, so he would just bring them here again tomorrow evening, and the next, and the next, until they realised this was part of the daily routine.

In a similar vein, although it had been the last thing on his mind over these last few weeks, he'd become increasingly aware of the growth of his own hair and facial hair. Never having liked beards or long hair, and deciding this was the time to do something about it, he went back up to the cave for his knife. Aware of the need to keep it sharp anyway, he walked back down and found the smoothest, hardest rock surface to scrape the edges of the blade against. Going back over to the lake, he knelt over the glasslike surface to catch his reflection. Tentatively raising the blade to his face, he pinched a tuft of beard and sliced it off close to his skin; repeating this process many times before starting on his hair, the whole thing took close to thirty minutes. "Well, it ain't exactly the Turkish barber's, but it'll do," he said, laughing to himself and deciding he'd do this every couple of weeks from now on.

Before it got dark, Tony decided to have a fresh look around the lake and surrounding area to have a good think; a think about how he could start to cultivate this land. He could see it had everything; everything necessary for growing whatever kind of plant life or vegetation he could find which would produce food. The earth looked good, and there was plenty of water, but the problem was mainly the sheer strength of the sun; there were large patches of parched ground on the outer rim, which were furthest from the lake, and some of the bushes had gone dry and brittle, which had caused them to stop producing leaves, or maybe even fruit. The land closer to the lake was more moist, which was why a wide variety of wild vegetation was already growing there, like the water leaves, as he'd come to call them. But the earth there was stony, uneven and littered with boulders too large to move, whereas on the far side the dry earth looked more pure, and was flat and even. "Irrigation! That's the key."

He thought about how channels could be made to run from the lake and flow water over onto the more fertile ground. He knew this wasn't exactly his field of expertise, but "nor was building a well in a river to catch fish", he thought to himself. "It's going to take a bit more thought, but God knows I've got time! And with my two new-found helpers on board we should be able to make good progress, once I work out how we're gonna do it, that is."

As night began to draw in, Tony felt a sense of excitement at the prospect of creating another source of food. Apart from fruits on bushes, which he already knew about only too well, the thought occurred to him that surely there were forms of vegetables that must exist on this planet. A job for tomorrow, he thought. "Tomorrow I'll try to communicate to the humanoids what I'm planning; try to find out from them what, and where, any food grows. OK, time to call it for the day." As he made his way back to the cave, he felt that all that surrounded him was his for the keeping, and was beginning to feel a strange sense of responsibility for it. Upon getting back to the cave he found the female asleep next to Zephyr, who got up to greet him. They both sat down and Tony put his arm around him. "Well, Zeph, tomorrow we work the land, boy, we work the land!"

Early the next morning, Tony was keen to get started. He chopped up the two fish from the previous night and shared out a couple of pieces each with Zephyr, leaving some aside for the female to eat later.

Taking two pieces each for the males, he grabbed his pole and knife then called to Zephyr that it was time to get going. They went straight down to see the two humanoids, who were already awake and looking out onto the horizon as the sun rose. "Morning, boys. Sleep well?" Tony said as they looked at him blankly. He gave them their share of the fish, which they keenly ate. "OK, come with me." Tony waved them on towards him and took them down to the outer rim of the area. "This is going to be difficult," he thought as he tried to work out how to communicate the object of the exercise to them.

His plan was firstly to find out whether they knew of one single place where a variety of edible vegetation grew. By the look of it, although their kind were pretty small, they all looked fairly well-fed, and the community he'd discovered back there was quite well-populated, so he figured they must have a reasonable source of food. The fact they were small could be down to a lack of protein through not eating any kind of meat, in which case vegetation would have been their main source of nutrition.

After severable unsuccessful attempts at trying to convey his thoughts through actions and gestures, while watched on by Zephyr, Tony was getting pretty frustrated, sometimes turning his back on them both, throwing his hands in the air and swearing to himself. Suddenly, Zephyr let out a deep bark; the two males froze, it was obvious they were still very wary of him. Then there was a silence as Zephyr walked over to one of the bushes, pointed towards it with his snout, and then looked back at the two males.

He continued to walk past the bush and on towards the border of trees leading to the outside, pointed again with his snout and let out an incredible howl, the like of which even Tony hadn't heard before. He then finally turned back to give the males a very, very meaningful stare. The humanoids looked at each other, made a kind of grunting noise coupled with some hand movements in the direction of the bush, then looked back at Tony.

A brief moment passed before he noticed a look of relief and enlightenment emerge in their eyes, closely followed by smiles of acknowledgement, along with the sound of excited vocal noises. They began to throw their arms in the air, pointing to the bush and then in an outward direction beyond the trees. For a moment, Tony stood motionless, his mouth open. "My god, they've understood! Zephyr, incredible! Clever, clever boy," he said, walking towards him with his arms stretched out in amazement. The sun had fully risen, and Tony now knew the ground was laid for the expedition. "Lead on, gentlemen," he said, gesturing them in the direction of the trees.

When they emerged on the other side, the two males started to walk in the same direction Tony had done when he'd first set out to explore the area those few days ago. As they began to cross the rocky, barren area, Tony was aware that there were two good reasons for them to be starting out at daybreak: one being that it was cooler; and two, they could easily be spotted by the other humanoids from the community. There was less chance of this happening so early in the day; after all, he didn't really want to attract any more attention until he'd found what he was looking for.

They were now fast approaching the edge of the canyon and Tony was starting to wonder why the two males were continuing in that direction. He was well aware that the inner area was a virtual mass of vegetation, but although he'd already looked around the immediate rim when he was last there, he saw no safe passages to descend from, at least not on this side of it, and the rest of the vast edge which surrounded it looked pretty inaccessible anyway, so this was going to be interesting to say the least, he thought.

The sound of gushing water could now be heard from the massive waterfall on the far side, so he knew they were nearly there. The humanoids then turned to look at him. Tony stopped as they pointed in the direction to the left of him, bringing his attention to a fairly small mound of boulders pretty close to the edge of canyon. He nodded to them in acknowledgement, but didn't really understand what this had to do with finding vegetation – the mound was as barren as the rest of the landscape! Tony turned back and shouted at them: "OK, we've come all the way over here and that's it! Just a pile of rocks!" Turning his back on them and looking up to the sky, he took a deep breath, before swearing to himself in frustration again.

By the time Tony turned back round, the two males were already walking over to the mound. "Oh, come on, Zeph," he said as he began to follow them. "I've gotta see this!" he said sarcastically. The humanoids walked around to the back of the boulders, disappearing from view, and Tony was really starting to wonder what the hell was going on.

As he and Zephyr reached the mound and also began walking round to the back, Tony could hear them both grunting to each other. "So, what's this all about?" he said as he got to them. The two males started to point again, this time to a dark, fairly large opening at the foot of the mound. "So what!" Tony said as he looked back at them. The males then walked through the opening, beckoning for him to follow. "OK, Zeph, let's see what's in there," he said reluctantly as they ventured in.

Once inside, they were just able to follow the outline of the humanoids by a pale light of day which still shone through. The rocky passageway sloped downwards to below ground surface, and as daylight faded completely, the atmosphere became cool and damp. Tony was now having to feel his way past the rocky walls until his eyes adjusted to the dark, whilst Zephyr relied on his sense of smell to guide him.

The route became more difficult as the wall began to bend round to the right, and they were now turning back on themselves; for a while they were moving through complete darkness. Tony put his hand down to Zephyr to make sure he was following OK. After another dozen or so paces, he felt a sense of relief as he saw a thin shaft of light hit the wall a few metres ahead of them. The two males, who obviously knew their way through only too well, had now disappeared into the winding corridor which lay ahead, but Tony could now see his way forward as the light grew stronger. "Thanks for waiting for me, boys," he called to them.

They were still moving in a downwards direction and yet the daylight was now increasing with almost every step. Tony smiled to himself as he began to realise what was happening. "Of course, well whaddayaknow – those boys really do know their stuff!" It was now almost fully light and he could tell they were only a couple of twists and turns away from coming out into the open; now hearing the sound of the mighty waterfall more clearly, he could smell the lush vegetation.

They cleared the last bend and the first thing Tony saw was the two humanoids, who were stood waiting for him.

As he approached the opening to the outside, the sheer scale of this explosion of nature hit him full on and he had to stop for a moment to take it all in. "Wow, boys, wow! Well done," he said as he walked up to the two males. Standing before them he patted each one on the shoulder and gave them a thumbs up. "OK, let's see what's here then." As Tony looked around to get his bearings, he could see they were standing on some sort of huge ledge, about a hundred feet below the rim of the canyon.

The atmosphere, although hot, also had a damp feel to it, which took the edge off the glaring heat of the sun. It was obviously a perfect environment for plant life of any kind to form and grow, and what surrounded him certainly didn't disappoint; the sheer size, variation and scale of vegetation was staggering. The abundance of new smells in the area had sent Zephyr into a sniffing frenzy as he shot from one new bush, plant or tree to another.

Then, Tony noticed him suddenly stand still and intensely sniff the air, before bolting into the thick greenery. Tony quickly ran after him, closely followed by the two males as they weaved in and out of the massive trees. By the time they'd caught sight of Zephyr again, he was standing, looking over the edge and barking constantly. Tony got there as fast as he could, worried that he might eventually fall over it.

Grabbing hold of Zephyr, Tony took a good look over; what lay below was the sight of a spectacular second ledge, about another fifty feet down. He soon noticed a rocky pathway jutting out from the main cliff face, connecting the two ledges. Walking over to it, he was thinking about venturing down there when he heard the two males grunting. Tony could instantly tell there was a sense of urgency to the sounds they were making; he quickly turned his head to see them waving their arms in a virtual state of panic. He almost laughed at the sight of this, but on a serious note, he realised there was obviously some kind of danger down there, knowing that they must have been there many times before. But what could it be? What *was* down there?

It wasn't long before Tony's thoughts were answered. He'd already called Zephyr away from the edge and they'd all began to walk back to the trees they'd come through when Zephyr suddenly stopped, turned and started to growl deeply, raising his fur and arching his back. Tony immediately knew Zephyr had sensed something; he could also see the two males knew what was happening as they darted back through the trees. Zephyr by now had stopped growling and Tony felt as though a blanket of silence had formed around them. This was short-lived as a curious sound of what seemed like the movement of pebbles started to emanate from the rocky pathway. Whatever it was that was lurking beneath that ledge didn't sound too ominous, but he trusted Zephyr's senses absolutely, and stood on full alert for any eventuality.

The next few seconds felt like an eternity, until something finally showed itself. Tony was shocked and relieved all at the same time when the head of some kind of harmless birdlike creature appeared over the edge, closely followed by another, eventually jumping up to the surface to fully reveal themselves. They stood about four feet in height, their legs disproportionately long in comparison to their body size, and were similar in shape to an ostrich. They had no feathers, just a thin covering of fur, and had a dry, tough, almost elephant-like skin.

Tony and Zephyr stood motionless as they watched these creatures hop around and peck at the ground. Tony observed from their general look and movements that they seemed to be only very young. "They're babies, just babies," he thought. "Hold on though, where's the parent? Come on, Zeph, let's get out of here," he said in a raised voice, but it was too late. Before they could move, there came a sound of heavy rumbling. Simultaneous ear-piercing screeches could be heard from the pathway below, then, a split-second later, a giant of a creature leapt up from below the edge.

Two massive taloned feet landed on the ground with a huge thud, causing the earth beneath to tremor. It stood well over ten feet in height, had a neck extension like a python, and the top of its legs were at least a metre in circumference. The ferocious appearance of this 'thing' was daunting; it was not only big, but fast and agile in its swift approach towards them, and Tony exhaled in relief when it came to a sudden stop.

As it stood there, glaring and screeching at them, Zephyr began to snarl at the creature defensively. Tony noticed it also had a fine set of sharp-pointed teeth in its armoury. Gripping his pole and knife tightly in either hand, he knew he was going to have to think fast here. If they ran, the thing could easily catch them, he thought, and apart from that, it would probably send the wrong signal, so, against all his natural instincts, he stood firm. "OK, Zeph. Stand easy, boy. It's all right, it's all right," he said, trying to calm Zephyr down.

Just at that moment, Tony noticed the creature's attention switch to its young. "OK, it's just protecting the offspring. That has to be the natural instinct of any animal, whatever planet you're on!" he was telling himself. "So, if we just move back slowly, keeping eye contact, that could be the way out of this." The creature swiftly flicked it's huge, beaked head back in their direction, its eyes piercing them with an icy stare. "Let's keep moving, Zeph... nice and easy." Tony kept slowly walking backwards, keeping a fix on the creature as they stared into each other's eyes. Being very careful not to make any sudden moves, he got closer and closer to the trees, until he and Zephyr finally slipped from the creature's main view.

Once fully out of sight, they turned around and continued to walk away at a steady pace. Tony let out a big gasp of air. "Wow, that was close, boy, that was close," he said to Zephyr, who was looking pretty calm about the whole thing. As he started to laugh, another screech could be heard coming from the creature in the distance. "Looks like the kids are in trouble, Zeph," he said jokingly as they made their way out of there.

Upon getting back to the entrance of the ledge, Tony was amused to see a look of surprise mixed with relief on the faces of the two males. He'd already realised that some of their breed might well have come to a sticky end at the hands of that creature, and appreciated the fact they'd actually stuck around and waited to see if he and Zephyr made it back, even if they were about two hundred metres away!

The first thing Tony did was gesture to them by pointing to the bushes and the ground, and then putting his hand to his mouth as though to eat something to get them started on showing him where the food grew around there. Gesturing back at him to follow, they led him to a shaded area under the canopy of one of the many trees. One of the males pointed to a leafy bunch of stalks. As Tony looked around, he could see the whole area around the tree trunk was littered with the same things. The male leant down, placed his hands around the base of the plant from where the stalks grew, and with one quick and fairly expert tug, pulled the plant up by its roots to reveal the fruits of its yield. Tony looked inquisitively at what he could now see; what dangled from the roots were similar in shape to small potatoes, but the striking thing about them was the colour, which ranged from shades of pink through to purple.

The male stood up and handed the plant to him; Tony picked off and held a couple of these things in his hands; they were hard and the skin had a rough feel to it. He took his knife and cut one in half to reveal a similar but more faded colour running through it. Crispy but moist, the male took one half from his hand and took a bite to demonstrate that it could be eaten. Tony then tentatively took a bite from the other half; apart from being slightly bitter due to the rawness, it had a strange combination of tastes – a mixture of potato, onion, garlic, and some other flavour he'd never tasted before. "Well, it's not haute cuisine, but it's not bad," he said tongue-in-cheek to the male. On a more serious note, he could tell it would be quite tasty if it were cooked properly, and, if it's genetic make up *was* anything like a potato, it would be rich in carbohydrate, the great energy provider. "But again who knows," he thought, once more having to remind himself this wasn't Earth. "Apart from anything else though, it'll be good to have something on the menu other than just fish!" he thought to himself.

Looking up, he noticed the other male pulling up more of the plants; although similar, some of these things were orange and yellow in colour. Pleased to have found another food source, the next priority was to get these plants back to base, and quickly. The earlier he could plant them in the earth, the more chance there'd be of them taking root. The next thing that came to mind was the problem of digging the irrigation channels; he wasn't going to do it today, but he knew it was going to be vitally important in the grand scheme of things. "Well, boys, time to get back," he said, turning to the two males. As they gathered the plants together, he realised he'd better bring his bag next time. They could carry about ten of these things between them for now, but some of the actual vegetables, or whatever they were, would probably start to fall off on the way.

Before starting back, Tony wanted to take a good look at the breathtaking scene which lay below them. As he and Zephyr walked over to the outer edge, he started to hear noises he'd not yet heard on the planet. He couldn't really make them out, but a strange mix of haunting hoots and high-pitched whistles increasingly filled the air. Reaching the edge, he looked down onto the canopy of the forest below, and the origin of the sounds became immediately evident... "Birds, my god, dozens of them."

Just like the first time he'd looked over the edge of the canyon a few days ago, he began to feel slightly disorientated by the fact he was actually looking down onto these things soaring high above the trees. He could see whole groups of exotic and brightly coloured birdlike creatures, all perched sporadically throughout the treetops. As far as he could tell, these were making the piercing whistles; the far deeper, almost horn-like sounds were coming from the large raptors; darker and more plain in colour, they gracefully hovered over all they surveyed.

As he stood there, he was reminded again of just what an Earth-like planet this was, and how much it only stood to reason that Earth-like creatures would have evolved and developed here in the same way, including his new humanoid friends back there. He thought about how much life there must be right here, thriving in the huge, lush forest below. "Gotta go take a look down there sometime, Zeph. Anyway, no more time to think about it now, boy. Let's get moving."

When they got back to the two humanoids, Tony noticed one of them tugging at the cliff face near the entrance to the ledge, while the other one seemed to be striking at the earth with something. As he got closer, he could see the one at the wall was trying to prise off a disk-shaped piece of rock; it was sharp and jagged around the edges and the humanoid's hands were cut and bleeding. Finally pulling it free, he turned to hand it to Tony, then pointed to the ground. Tony looked around at the other humanoid, and could now see he was striking the ground with the same kind of disc-like rock, cutting a hole in the earth as though to test it out, he thought, and pretty efficiently at that. "Of course! Spades! They use them as digging tools." With this revelation, Tony quickly went over to the cliff face to help the humanoid pull more of these out from the rock face. "OK, OK," he said as he gestured the other to stop and come over to him. Standing there all together, Tony looked straight at them. "You're not as stupid as you look, boys, not by a damn sight!" he said with a massive grin on his face. "Now let's get back and dig these in then."

Going back through the dark, upwardly sloping passageway, they carried an equal share of their harvest and one digging tool each; Tony was excited about all the new discoveries of the day and was thinking about how he'd get more of everything in his bag next time.

Upon reaching the surface, they made their way in the best possible time; as they returned back to base, the female came down from the cliff to welcome them. Tony realised she'd probably been worried about them from the time she woke to find them not there; finding this strangely endearing, he smiled as he watched her hug the two humanoids in affection.

Keen to get the new bushes planted, Tony began to look around for the most suitable spot to place them, but before he'd even had the chance to fully consider the matter, he looked back to find the two males already expertly digging holes at the edge of the lake. "OK, boys, you know what you're doing – carry on then!" he said in retrospect with an air of slight embarrassment. At the same time, although he appreciated that they *did* obviously know what worked, this would only do for now. To make a real difference, he knew he'd need to carry out his plan to cultivate the potentially fertile land on the far side, and with the newly acquired tools, they now had the means to do it.

In the heat of what was now mid-afternoon, Tony decided they would get started on the project at dawn tomorrow. For now, he thought, the boys had earned the rest of the day off, but first he took them over to the waterfall to shower. After this, he communicated as best he could that it was now free time for them; he did this by pointing to their cave and then stretching his arms towards the rest of the land. Whether they really understood was another matter, but they did nod and walk back to their cavern. As far he was concerned, he planned to take the new-found vegetables up to his cave to do some experimental cooking with them. As he walked back over, he saw something which made him realise they were definitely good to eat – the sight of Zephyr standing over the pile, having a good chomp on one of them. He let out a loud laugh as he got closer. "Well I'm glad I got back here just in time! Come on, mate, let's fetch the bag and get this lot inside. Then you can try 'em when they're cooked!"

Back in the cavern, Tony now had more time to properly study these 'alien potatoes' as he'd come to think of them. He cut another in half to reveal its flesh to his full range of culinary senses: touch, smell, sight and taste, as he knew from his chef's training. Everything about these things told him they'd be best baked or roasted, but as he didn't exactly have an oven, that wasn't going to happen, he thought. But, as the flesh was so moist as well as crispy and firm then slicing and griddle would be an option.

He sat back, had a good think and looked at what was around him. "That's it!' he said to himself excitedly. He'd remembered seeing a long, thin piece of rock laying around near to the entrance of the cave, about one metre in length and another half metre in width, with a relatively smooth surface. Quickly getting up to bring it in and over to the site of the fire, he estimated that if he could place it about thirty centimetres high above, then it would serve as a kind of hot plate. He could easily build a wall of rocks on either side of the fire, and "Hey presto, a homemade griddle," he thought.

He gathered a few rocks together and the thing was built; he now just had to try it out. As he didn't really know how long it would take for the rock to heat up sufficiently, he put extra materials in to burn under it; after one minute or so from lighting the fire, he discovered he needn't have worried. Tentatively touching the surface, he nearly burnt his fingers, so, time to cook off, he thought. Slicing one of the 'potatoes' up and placing the pieces on the rock, it felt strange for him to hear the sound of frying for the first time since they'd left the ship. Watching with a sense of accomplishment as the slices sizzled, discharging an oily type substance onto the surface of the self-designed hot plate, he quickly grabbed a thin, small, flat piece of handheld rock to turn them over with.

They seemed to be fully cooked on both sides within around three minutes. As he picked the slices off from the now extremely hot surface, it occurred to him that he could also cook the fish in this way; that would mean he could do two, three, or maybe even more at one time. Carefully taking a first bite from one of the slices, he was full of apprehension. They actually smelled good, but how they would taste was foremost on his mind, or even whether cooking had somehow made them poisonous. "Maybe they should be eaten raw? Who knows, but here goes," he thought.

His doubts about the taste were soon put to rest as he began to chew the still crispy flesh and skin, before turning to Zephyr. "Wow, it's like a sauteed potato cooked in garlic with a hint of onion." He then, as always, waited for a few minutes in case of any adverse effects; when none came he shared it out with him.

Late in the afternoon, Tony went down to see the two males and the female to let them know he was about to do dinner, giving them the usual gesture. They all followed him eagerly back up; as they sat down, he keenly presented his new invention to them. They all looked curiously at it, then back at him. He laughed in amusement, both at the look of confusion on their faces, and even more so at the fact that he felt as though he was, to all intents and purposes, hosting some kind of primitive dinner party. But as his laughter subsided, he began to realise that somehow this felt good, and a feeling of communal belonging came over him, something he hadn't felt since leaving Earth, all those months ago.

Chapter 10

The next morning, Tony directed the two males to begin digging the channel. He started one of them off at about two metres from the edge of the lake, then took the other in a straight line up to about a third of the way towards the outer area. Walking himself another third of the way, again in a straight line, he began digging himself. The logic in doing the dig in this way was that by the time he'd reached the land to be irrigated, the other two would have dug their thirds and it would be complete, hopefully!

The work was gruelling and over the next few days Tony got them into a routine: start early, break at midday, start back late afternoon, and finish at dusk. By day four, their hands were so cut and sore that they had to stop for a few days. Tony needed to go back to the river to get more fish anyway, so the day after they'd stopped he decided to take one of the males with him, mainly because it would mean more fish, as he could carry a few himself; he'd leave the other behind with the female.

That day, Tony, Zephyr and the male started out at the break of dawn. As they passed a certain point en route to the salt lake, he noticed the male looking around, curious about where they were going; he looked lost as he followed them and Tony could tell he or his kind had probably never been this way before. "What a boring life they've had up to now," he joked to himself.

As they reached the lake, Tony looked on as the male stood still, gazing with an expression of amazement on his face, just as the female had done, and just as he had when he'd first seen it. He turned to look at him with a smile: "Yeah, always a big tourist attraction, huh. Come on, this way," he said as he guided him around it in silence. The silence though was suddenly broken with what sounded like the ominous roar of the massive creature in the woods beyond, causing the male to stop in his tracks again. Tony looked round and beckoned to him to keep walking.

When they finally reached the spot where the creature lived on the opposite side of the river, a mild tremor could be felt through the ground, and there was the sound of loud cracks as thick branches were being snapped like twigs. Zephyr began to instinctively growl and Tony smiled to himself as he knew just what was happening. He could see the male was getting really spooked, but the best he could do was to calmly reassure him with a strong and steady signal to just carry on. But just as they'd all gone a few more paces, there was a sudden and frantic rustling in the trees as the huge head of the creature burst through into full sight. That was it – the male shot into the distance as fast as his legs could take him. Zephyr let out a deep bark, and Tony laughed so much he fell to his knees, only stopping to shout out: "At least you're going in the right direction, mate!"

They walked on another couple of hundred metres to catch up with the male, who was now sitting on the ground, overcome with fear. "God, man, I've not laughed as much as that in a long time. Come on, let's get some fish," he said, helping him up to his feet.

They were now almost at their part of the river when Zephyr stopped, put his nose up to sniff the air, and began to quickly walk over to a small grassy mound to the right of them; Tony knew there must be a good reason for this and so followed him. Zephyr went straight over the top of the mound, disappeared around the other side, and started to bark. Tony ran to the top of the mound and looked down – it was one of the wild mammals, laying motionless. The male had followed and now stood next to Tony at the top; spotting the animal, he appeared strangely excited and quickly ran down to look at it.

As Tony got there, he could see the creature was dead. The male started to prod it but Tony stopped him. He gestured for them to move on again, but as he did this the male pointed to the creature, and then to himself, as though to claim it was his. Tony didn't really know why the male wanted it, but obviously knowing he could utilise the mammal as a good source of food, he nodded to him in agreement, then gestured that they should go now and come back for it later.

Finally reaching his well at the river's edge, Tony got straight to work on the whole fishing process. The male watched keenly, but his interest turned to a kind of shock when Tony did what he had to do with his knife when he'd caught the fish. He filled his bag with as many fish as he could carry. As usual, it was mid-afternoon by now, so he routinely gave it a couple hours before starting back; he took a bathe in the river before getting the male to do the same, and then put some cooling water over Zephyr's coat.

Resting in the heat of the afternoon, he started to think about the culture of his new-found humanoid allies. It was now even more clear to him that they had no idea of how to catch or cook food, or to cultivate a reliable food supply; apart from being able to plant and grow the odd vegetable bush, they were, to all intents and purposes, scavengers. He began to wonder if he was doing the right thing by changing this, or even showing them how to do things which were, at least at this time, beyond their capabilities. He'd always been a leader, leading many of his own kind back on Earth, but was it right to influence these people? And if he did, would he be interfering with the whole course of their future, the consequences of which could be untold?

It was time to start back; Tony grabbed his bag and they walked to where the creature still lay. He figured he owed it to the male for the help he and the other had been so far, so he hadn't caught as many fish as planned as they'd have to carry the creature back to base between them. As they stood over it, the male took one end by the front legs and Tony grabbed the hind legs. Smaller than the first one he'd found, it was relatively light to carry between them. He could see they'd done this before; it seemed as natural to the male as the harvesting of the vegetables. He still wondered why and for what purpose he wanted the dead animal, but he knew there had to be a reason, and he was keen to learn. When they got to the lake, Tony stopped briefly to pick up extra salt, as he would need more for the meat he intended to get from the carcass of the creature.

Evening had begun to fall, and as they walked on, Tony started to notice a strange, faint, disc-like object appear in the sky. He was struck by how high it was, as it seemed to hover directly above them, but he couldn't see it clearly enough to make it out, and besides, it was starting to get dark and they needed to keep get moving. When they got back to base, the male went straight to his cave, carrying the animal with him. Tony was prepared to let them have it for the night; it was dark by now, but he knew in this heat that he would need to get any meat from the creature by the next morning and get it salted.

Later that night, after he'd done feeding them all and the two males had gone back to their own cave, Tony decided that he and Zephyr should pay them a visit to see what, if anything, they were doing with their seemingly treasured possession. On their way down he couldn't help but notice the night seemed just slightly brighter than usual, then as he looked down at the lake he saw what looked like a saucer of light reflecting from its surface. "The disc, the disc I saw in the sky earlier!" he thought as he simultaneously raised his head to look above. "There it is, there it is! … A moon!" Small but bright, and higher in the sky than the one on Earth, but there it was, a moon, the strange sight of the bottom half partially bathed in light. Tony looked back down to Zephyr. "Makes you feel at home eh, boy."

Still excited at the discovery of the celestial body, and looking to the sky every few seconds, he got to the males' cave to see they'd just left the animal outside the entrance. He could see they were getting ready to sleep. "OK, good night then, boys!" he said with a tone of confusion to his voice. None of this made sense to him, but whatever they wanted with it they had just until morning to do it, then he'd take over. "Come on, boy, time to sleep for us too, I think," he said as they walked back up to their home, guided by the glow of the planet's moon. The female had long since turned in by the time they returned. "God, is that all anyone does around here at night?" he said jokingly to Zephyr.

Sitting there watching the female sleep, he again started to contemplate the possible effects of his interactions with these beings. Although he still felt troubled by this, as he thought on an idea began to occur to him. From the time he'd first made contact with this breed, so much had happened he'd hardly had time to continue thinking about the reasons as to why he was here, the reasons he'd so determinedly set out to find. Maybe now he'd 'found' the answer, maybe this was it, the reason already so clearly staring him in the face. Maybe the beings on the ship who'd brought him here had done so for this very purpose, maybe… maybe. But the more he thought about it, the more sense it made that this was it! He decided there and then: "If they've dropped me here on this planet to help develop and advance these aliens, then I'll show 'em what a bloody good job I can do of it! Then, then they might take me home, let me go, God knows, somehow give me my old life back, just as they'd promised they would when first we met... on that fateful evening back on Earth."

Tony woke the next morning fuelled by his thoughts from the night before; he felt a new sense of enthusiasm and enlightenment. "OK, let's *really* get this started, Zeph," he said, grabbing his digging tool and knife. Making their way down to the males' cave, he was getting himself ready to cut the meat from the dead animal. As he got closer, he saw the humanoids were already awake and standing outside as they did every morning. They seemed to be standing over the creature, looking down at it, and he wondered why, but as he walked on he didn't need to wonder for long – the males parted as he got close to them to reveal a gruesome sight; they'd skinned the animal!

Tony looked down in horror at the sight of it, whilst Zephyr hovered around the creature, sniffing at the raw flesh and sinew that was now fully exposed. His eyes moved back to the males, a look of shock on his face; they, on the other hand, looked back at him with a smile, then pointed to the skin of the animal as it hung on the rocks, still dripping with blood. Although repulsed by it, Tony knew he needed to accept this is as part of what they did. He hadn't even considered it before, but the animal skins they were wearing obviously had to come from somewhere, just as the skin he wore himself!

As he looked back at them again, he saw they were holding the digging tools in their hands, still also dripping with blood. They must have fashioned them last night to have sharp enough edges, he thought. In truth he had to admit to himself they'd done a pretty good job, and taking a deep breath he nodded to them with a subtle smile of acknowledgement.

Notwithstanding his respect for the animal, Tony gripped his knife and knelt over the carcass. The two males watched on as he crudely carved out slats of meat from its hind legs and loin; although still pretty unskilled at doing this, he was finding the whole process much easier than the first couple of times as he hadn't had to cut the skin away first, so he was also able to get the full amount of meat from the creature. Stopping briefly for a moment, he glanced up at the males, who were looking down and smiling. He realised they now probably knew the reason he was doing this – food. When he finally finished, he stood up and started handing the cuts of meat out evenly to the two males and himself for them to take back up to his cave.

After salting the meat and wrapping it in leaves, before they did anything else Tony took them all back down to bury the animal. The males looked confused and reluctant about this, but apart from the exposed carcass being likely to attract all kinds of unwelcome wildlife and insects, he wanted to teach them to have a respect for other life forms, whether they were living or not. He tried to do this by gesturing to them in the best way he could, by trying to convey to them by making a comparison, an example that it would be no different if one of them had died.

Hoping they'd understood, they all went back up to their cave and brought the animal skin back down to the lake to wash it before it dried in the sun. Tony remembered something about salting the skin being beneficial; he thought this was probably right anyway, as it would stop the growth of bacteria, and again keep the insects away, so he took the skin back up to his cave to treat it, then got them geared up to get back to digging the channel. Just as they were about to start, the female, who had just woken as they'd taken the meat into the cave, came walking down to join them. She looked at Tony and clearly gestured that she wanted to help in some way. "OK, sex equality and all that then!" he said to himself.

Remembering that they'd brought a few spare digging tools back with them, he went back to the cave to get one, then took her to the edge of the far side of the land to be irrigated to show her what to do. He'd set her on course to dig backwards towards his part of the channel in a straight line, so they'd join up at some point; this way he'd hoped to finish his part earlier than the other two, giving him time to oversee the final completion.

Again, they dug through until midday and broke until late afternoon. They hadn't eaten before taking their break, so Tony took them all up to the cave and cooked off some fish. Starting back, he was aiming to get the channel fully completed by the next day. They'd all have worked pretty hard by the end of the day, so he was planning to cook some of the meat off that night. Although he'd wrapped it well, given the scent it was letting off it was likely to attract scavengers, so he'd left Zephyr up in the cave to guard it. They finally finished for the day as dusk fell. Tony had realised the female had worked well; walking over to show his appreciation, he put his hand on her shoulder and gestured by pointing to what she'd done, then gave her a nod in recognition.

They'd all eaten and slept well that night and Tony had woken just before dawn; he felt an air of excitement at being able to finish the project that day, but hoped the whole thing was actually going to work! He laughed to himself at the thought that if it didn't, the others would wonder what the bloody hell they'd done all this for anyway! Standing there in the peace of an early hour, he and Zephyr watched the moon so high above them fade into the sky as the sun rose. "Yeah, another day, another dollar, Zeph," he said, kneeling down to him. "But where in the galaxy are we, boy, huh? Guess we'll find out one day. Well, in the meantime, let's get this job finished." He went back to wake the female, and then down to raise the males.

Once they got started, knowing they'd nearly finished seemed to drive them all on to work even faster, so by midday, with the help of the female, Tony's channel was joined and complete. The two males didn't have far to go either; instead of breaking he gestured for them to carry on, making sure they kept on track in the crucial last few metres. When they finally finished, he looked on with a sense of achievement at what they'd accomplished; between them they had managed to dig a trench around a hundred metres in length, down to about four feet below the edge of the lake; the only thing left to do now was dig out the final six feet or so leading up to the water.

Tony walked swiftly over to the lake, then turned to look at the humanoids. "This is it then," he said as he struck at the ground to begin making the job complete. A few moments later, he looked up to find they'd all come to join him in the task; for a moment he felt a sense of camaraderie at this, a fleeting thought that they now all shared a common goal. This part of the ground was particularly hard and stony, but in less than an hour they'd got right up to the border where the ground met the water.

It had all gone to plan so far, and all that remained was a wall of earth, laden with rocks and standing like a dam between the water and the channel. Tony walked into the lake, first digging out the rocks and then pulling the rest of the earth towards him. One of the males then started to help from the other side and they were almost there; only inches now remained as they continued to strike at the earth, their hands now sore and bleeding again. Then, a small trickle began to flow over the edge; as they carried on digging the trickle turned into a steady flow until they cleared the last remaining rock. A huge surge of water then gushed into the mouth of the channel and the force of the water nearly took Tony with it. All that was needed now was to watch the water flow like a river as it tumbled through to the land on the far side; they'd done it!

Tony breathed a sigh of relief – it was working fine. He looked round at the others, who were all clutching each other in an excited embrace. Feeling pretty happy about everything himself, he actually joined in with them, letting out a shout of "Yes, yes!" several times... When they'd all calmed down after a few minutes had passed, Tony realised there was still just one more thing left for them to do – they would need to dig out a series of narrow gullies to run from the main channel evenly over the fertile land to allow the water to spread properly. But for now, with an inexhaustible source water, he decided that tomorrow would do.

The flow of the water had now slowed to the rate of a stream. Tony knew this would eventually end up being more of a steady trickle, except when it rained heavily, but this would be more than adequate over time. With much of the waterfall feeding into the lake, the excess water would now always overflow into the channel, instead of just seeping through into the stony ground, giving the desired effect.

The next day, as they all walked back over to the channel Tony was pleased to see the project performing as he'd hoped; the water had continued to flow all the way up to the other end. Following the channel up to the other side of the land, he smiled to himself as he began to virtually smell the water, which was already starting to infuse into the ground. He beckoned the others to join him.

They got to work on digging the gullies out, splaying out across the land from the main channel; he'd positioned them equally apart down one side, and then the other. In the soft ground they'd completed the job by midday, and Tony thought it was now best to just leave things alone for a few days, and let the land develop naturally. In time they'd go back to the shelf of the canyon to bring back more of the same vegetable plants for planting, along with anything else they could find. Knowing they'd need to make several trips, Tony would need to plan out the logistics for this. To begin with, apart from taking his own bag, he wanted to try to get the animal skin in shape for carrying as well. They could do two trips a day, one starting in the early morning as usual, and maybe one again late afternoon; that way it would give them time for planting throughout the middle of the day. "Yeah, really looking good," he said to himself as he thought of the benefits and the satisfaction it would bring to cultivate a pretty large piece of land for them all.

That evening, after Tony had done dinner, he took Zephyr down to the lake, thinking to himself it had felt like a long time since they'd just gone for one of their walks; that simple pleasure of the two of them just making their way out amongst all the best that nature had to offer. Just then it occurred to him how settled they were now becoming in their new environment, in their new life, as it had now come to be.

He picked up a hand-sized rock and began to throw it. As he watched Zephyr keenly retrieve and bring it back to be thrown again, he started to think about the walks they'd had every day in that artificial outside environment back on the ship. Such a surreal experience that now seemed. His thoughts then turned again to the aliens – those alien beings who'd taken them to the stars and dropped them here – and again to whether they were still there as they said they'd be. But with the sun setting on a beautiful evening, and the two of them enjoying their walk on the land, a land he'd now come to think of as being theirs... he didn't really care.

Over the next few days, they all did as planned, managing the two trips a day. Taking Tony's bag and the new animal skin, they were able to bring back around ten plants on each trip, which they would plant as soon as they'd get back. The males had also introduced him to a strange fruit-bearing bush; the skin of the fruit itself was orange and had an eggshell-like quality, but the inner flesh was white, gelatinous, had a hint of sweet and sour to it, and tasted fantastic. The actual bushes were quite big so they took just five of them back in total.

The whole operation went pretty well, with only the ferocious sounds of the predator in the distance disrupting their work from time to time. This would really freak the two males out; they'd run for cover and it would take nearly half an hour before they were ready to come out. Although Tony understood, going on their last encounter with it he figured that if they didn't bother it, then it wouldn't bother them. One thing did trouble him though; he'd noticed they'd been spotted by some of the other humanoids from the community; this had happened more than once on their way to and from as they crossed the rocky, barren land. He'd seen at least two, but sometimes up to four of them as they stood in a group outside of their entrance. He was pretty sure now that it would only be a matter of time before they'd be paying them a visit, as curiosity would eventually run high.

By the end of the fifth day, they'd completed planting; the earth was now moist, and all that needed to happen was for nature to take its course. They all stood back to look at the newly created plantation, which had around forty vegetable plants, including the fruit bushes. Tony thought they might have gone a bit over the top! But given that he didn't really know how many would take root and survive, he wanted to make sure they were left with enough, whatever happened.

Turning to the two males, he shook their hands for a good job done; they looked a bit confused by this, but Tony thought he saw a look of understanding in their eyes. The female was sitting on a rock in the shade of a small tree with Zephyr a few feet away; although she hadn't been on the trips with them, she'd again worked hard and well on the planting process. Tony walked over and offered her his hand; as she took it he bent down and kissed her lightly on the cheek. Putting her hand to where his lips had been, she raised her eyes and gave him the slightest smile. "Huh, nothing much impresses you then, I can see," he said with a snigger in his voice.

The days went by and Tony was amazed at how quickly the plants were taking root and growing, even though about a quarter of them were beginning to die off. As he walked around though he had to admit it all looked pretty promising. He couldn't really tell yet how the bushes were doing, but realised this would take more time, although they looked OK for now. "All looks good, Zeph," he said with a smile.

Just then, a loud crack from the surrounding tree border broke the silence, followed by what sounded like something running through leaves on the ground. Zephyr let out a flurry of barks as they both shot straight through the plantation and over to the woods. When they reached the trees, Tony put his hand out, signalling for them to stop. Whatever was in there, he wanted to draw it out, rather than them go in blindly. Using his pole, he held it at one end and started to rustle some branches with the other; then came the sounds of a series of almighty shrieks from behind the trees. Tony nearly jumped out of his skin as the sounds echoed through the air. "What the hell is going on in there?" he shouted. When the shrieking died down, the one thing he was sure of was that this was no animal; he was pretty sure the sounds were being made by the humanoids.

Moments later, Zephyr began to growl – he'd sensed something coming up behind them. Both swiftly turning round, Tony held his pole up in readiness to strike at what or whoever was there; he quickly lowered it when he saw it was the two males, looking knowingly at the woods as they continued walking towards them. Tony could see by their expressions and posture that they obviously knew what was happening. They stopped and looked at him, and both pointed inwardly at themselves and then to the woods, as though to gesture that they wanted to go in. Tony gestured back, extending his arm towards the trees to usher them on.

After they'd entered, he could hear the general grunting they usually made to each other. A few minutes passed and Tony's usual impatience was starting to get the better of him; for one thing he was getting bored, but mainly he wanted to know what this was all about. Nearly fifteen minutes had passed before the two males emerged from the trees, closely followed by three other humanoids! Two were male, one female; the original males beckoned them to come closer, raised and held their arms open to Tony, and then did the same to the three 'visitors' in a gesture of introduction.

Tony nodded. "Christ, you do all look the bloody same, don't you?" he said, looking them up and down. Aside from the female, he could hardly tell them apart. "Of course," he thought. "Given the size of their tribe, they're probably all related in some way." The female though was nothing like the one who was already there. Slightly smaller, and with characteristically no facial hair, and only a light covering of bodily hair – these were about the only features which clearly distinguished her from the males, Tony thought. "OK, so what do they want?" he said as he turned to the original males, gesturing with the flat of his hands. One of them stepped forward and pointed to the visitors, and then to the ground! Tony knew exactly what his humanoid friend meant; they'd come over wanting to stay, maybe even to take refuge, like the two of *them*, he thought.

Then, in a gesture of conformation, one of the visiting males walked over holding an animal skin; it was in the shape of a bag of sorts. Standing toe to toe with him, the male opened it to reveal a mix of the vegetables Tony was now growing himself; fruits, some of which he'd not seen before; the digging tools that he was now so familiar with; a whole collection of what looked like other stone tools; and pelts of animal skins.

The male took a couple of steps back and placed the bag on the ground, looked at Tony, pointed to him, and then to the bag. Realising this was meant as a gift, Tony had a slight laugh to himself, but knew he needed to think hard and fast about what was happening here. Unlike the reservations he'd had with the first two males, he felt positive about this from the start. Things had moved on now, and to all intents and purposes he realised he was building a community of his own. The first thing that came to mind was 'strength in numbers'; the new arrivals could make a valuable contribution, he thought, and apart from anything else, this would fit well with his plans to develop these beings, which he was now convinced was the reason for him being there.

He'd made his decision; holding his arms out wide in a welcoming gesture to them all, "Come with me!" he said. They all stood still for a moment. "Well come on then," he said again. As they now began to follow on keenly, Tony looked behind him to see one of the males and the female walking with their arms round each other – they were obviously a couple. "How sweet," Tony said to himself sarcastically. He'd planned to put the two males together and give the female a cave of her own, but this would now obviously need to change. Remembering that the second largest cavern was close to the top of the cliff, near to his, he'd give that to the couple, and there was a small cave near to the one with the two males, so the single male could have that one.

There *was* just one other thing though: Tony had picked up on the fact they smelt as bad as the others first had when they'd got here, so before he took them to their new accommodations, he gestured to the two males to take them to shower. He smiled to himself as he stood there watching the five humanoids all walking towards the waterfall together. "Yeah, they're learning, they're learning, boy," he said to Zephyr as they all disappeared behind the rocks. In the meantime, he began to think about what to do with these new additions to the fold..

Later that evening, Tony brought them all up to his cave, before cooking the food as usual. The female welcomed the three new humanoids with an embrace of instant recognition, but there was something about the reactions and expressions on the faces of the recent arrivals that caught Tony's attention. After their initial greetings, the three of them stepped back, began to look her up and down, then all looked at each other as though there was something they didn't really understand. As he looked back at the female himself, the reason struck him as to why they might have acted in this way. Tony realised that it must now have been nearly three weeks since they'd seen her, and although he'd looked at her every day over that time, even he couldn't help but notice certain changes. No one specific thing was obvious, but as he stood observing her in that moment, it seemed to him that some kind of general enhancement had taken place in her appearance.

The differences between her and the other humanoids had become even more pronounced; not only had she now lost what little bodily hair she did have, but her skin was looking smoother and more refined, her female form had in some way become accentuated. It looked to him as though she'd even become more... human. Tony put this down to the better lifestyle she now had – good food and plenty of it, and a good place to live – and he thought he could sense that, in a way, she was content. It was either all of these things, or his eyes were just playing tricks on him, he thought laughing to himself.

One thing was for sure, he now had a growing community to feed, and they would need to go for food again tomorrow. He'd decided to take his first two males as well as the single new male with him; they now had two animal skins as well as his bag and so the four of them could carry even more fish back.

As they set out in the morning, with the help of the first two males Tony tried to gesture to the new male who they were leaving behind, that he should stay there to look after things. Taking him to the border of trees, Tony also gestured to the two males to explain the direction they were going in, so if there *was* a problem he could try to come and get them. He watched as they grunted and gestured to the new male. Whether he'd understood or not, Tony didn't know, but he was now well aware that if the nature of these beings in any way resembled that of humans, then many of the humanoids in the original community could now be potential enemies. There could be resentful leaders, he'd thought, seeking revenge for the losses of their followers; there could be jealousy in the ranks, from those also wanting a new start in a new community; or it could just be curiosity, fuelled by envy. Whatever the reason, he knew he now had much to protect, and protect it he would.

On their return that evening, Tony could see the day had passed without event; everything was in order and he began to salt and wrap the large amount of fish they'd brought back with them. After he'd finished, he began to think about the increasing amount of communication he was now having to carry out with these beings. He and the first two males were now managing to understand each other pretty well, in fact the speed and level of competence at which they'd picked up on his conveyances had surprised him, but it was still difficult in some ways, still not great.

He'd now witnessed the beings verbally communicate with each other many times and was thinking there should be no reason why they couldn't learn a far more complex language. He couldn't be sure about this by any means, but it would definitely be worth a try; he decided to start with the first female, and he'd begin tomorrow.

That morning, as Tony woke he realised that for the first time since they'd been on the planet, they actually had nothing they had to do that day – they had a large stash of fish and vegetables, there was no urgent work to do on the land, and he had plenty of fuel for the cooking fires. He walked over to where the female was still sleeping and put his hand on one shoulder, causing her to wake with a start. "Sorry, sleeping beauty," he said with a smirk. Walking over to the back wall to bring her some water, he started to think about the task ahead. "This is gonna be interesting," he said to himself as he tried to work out how he was going to even begin to teach this alien being how to speak English!

Once the female had fully woken, he took a deep breath and got started. Knowing he obviously needed to begin at the most basic and simple level, he made his first move. "YOU," he pronounced in an exaggerated tone of voice as he pointed to her; "ME," he said in the same way, pointing to himself. The female looked confused to begin with, and he couldn't blame her. He thought of himself being in her situation in an effort to understand what this might be like for her, but he continued to repeat these words and actions; over an hour had passed and he didn't seem to be getting anywhere.

He was about give it up as a bad job, but he suddenly detected a spark of understanding in her eyes. "Yes... yes," he said loudly. Inspired to carry on, he was uncharacteristically patient, and began to try to show her how to shape her lips to form the words properly. But for all this, the female showed no sign or intention to even try to mimic these simple words. "Time for a break, Zeph," he said as he stood up to go outside for a while.

Standing on the ledge of his cavern, he looked round as he heard his new neighbours stirring in their cave. "They better not be noisy," he said to himself. "Still, don't suppose they'll exactly be having any late-night parties, not on this planet, anyway," he thought, laughing to himself. "Well, if they're a pain in the arse I can always just move them anyway."

Just at that moment, a strange sound from within the cave caught his attention. Tony ran straight back in, thinking Zephyr might be warning him of something. "What's... going...on?" he said, staggering his words and stopping abruptly in his tracks.

The sound was coming from the female. "Woo... woo," she was saying with a strange pitch in her voice as she pointed to Zephyr.

"My god... she's doing it," he said, looking at Zephyr excitedly. Walking over to the female, he began to speak to her... "OK, OK, but you're not saying it right," he said, smiling at her, but he could see she was trying to repeat one of the words, and the right one as she pointed to Zephyr. "Clever girl... clever girl!" he said, giving her a nod. Now he knew she'd actually understood the meaning of what he'd been trying to teach her, he planned to perfect her on a few simple words, then try her on stringing them together!

After continuing through the morning, Tony decided to go and see what the others were doing with their day. As he and Zephyr headed down the cliff towards the lake, the humanoids were nowhere to be seen. Walking past the lake, Tony thought he could hear a sound like the chopping of wood; he ran over towards the sound to see what was going on.

As they got nearer, Zephyr ran ahead, growling deeply, and disappeared into a small clump of bushes; Tony thought there must be intruders on the land and stepped his pace up. Following Zephyr, he leapt through the bushes. Standing on the other side in a clearing, there was almost a complete silence, broken only by the low murmur of a growl from Zephyr. The resident humanoids, all of them, stood there looking shocked, their mouths open and their eyes in a fixed gaze on him.

A few moments passed and Tony's adrenaline turned to laughter. "What the hell are you all doing?" he said, looking around at some chopped off branches. One of them knelt down and picked up something they'd already fashioned and held it out to Tony, gesturing for him to take it. They'd made a straight, solid pole; it had a smooth feel to the surface and a good balance to it. This was pretty skilful work, Tony thought; they were using the same sharpened version of the tool they'd used for digging, and he was now beginning to realise just how multi-purpose these things were. As he handed the pole back, Tony nodded in recognition.

Over the next couple of hours, he watched with fascination as they continued to make more of them; and observed as they impressively worked together as a team. He watched as the males took turns, two of them holding a large branch at either end, while a third would trim the bark and cut away excess wood in order to make the pole even in circumference. The female would then finish it by smoothing the surface using the flat of the stone tool. Seeing how they did this made him realise that these beings must have these skills taught to them from an early age; each generation handing down to the next and so on, he guessed.

Thinking back to when he'd first encountered this race at their community, Tony remembered them carrying these poles. The advantages in terms of their use as crude weapons or instruments of self-defense was obvious, he'd used his in the same way, but for these purposes he realised there was one thing missing. While he'd always had his knife, he had not thought it necessary to modify his pole, but to make these things into a fully efficient weapon, they could easily make it to have a sharpened point on the end.

Realising they'd not even thought of this, he wondered why; their level of intelligence suggested they were well capable of the innovation, but maybe they just didn't have the homicidal tendencies of his own race, he thought. At that moment he did think about showing them how to do this and why, but stopped himself with the single thought that this might be an intervention too far in their development. For now, he was just pleased they'd done what they had this day, realising they would probably need them in times to come.

Over the next few days, he continued to try to teach the female more words; although it was difficult and even frustrating at times, he persevered and was eventually surprised at the speed with which she was progressing; she could now pronounce 'me', 'you', and other words clearly. He'd now started her on various inanimate objects, like the fire, his bag, the fish. She was picking these words up with ease, including his and Zephyr's names, but still there was no way for him to tell just how much she really understood what these words meant, if at all. He *was* close to taking the leap of trying her on stringing things together with the use of connective words though; at this point one very important and significant thing occurred to him – she didn't have a name! Not one that was tangible to him, anyway.

One day when Tony was listening to the female recite the words she'd learnt, a small scar on her upper arm, obviously caused by a previous injury, caught his attention. He couldn't help but notice how it resembled the letter 'J'. As he sat there thinking of her past and what might have caused this mark; of what kind of life she'd had so far; a thought flashed through his mind like a wave of inspiration. "That's it!" he said as he rose to his feet. "Julie, I call you... Julie!" he said to the female as he pointed at her.

It wasn't clear to begin with whether she'd understood what he'd said to her as she smiled at him, but as the day went on, and he began to introduce a series of nouns and pronouns to place in front of the words she already knew, such as 'the fish', 'my bag', 'him, Zephyr', and so on, she suddenly did something that incorporated everything he'd been trying to teach her. Looking directly into his eyes and pointing inwardly to herself, she uttered the words: "Me, Julie." Tony leant back onto the wall where he sat, half in shock and half in excitement. That one action, those two simple words, displayed to him that she had every level of understanding, every level of self-awareness equivalent to any human back on his native Earth; it was... a revelation.

Chapter 11

Over the next few weeks, the community went from strength to strength. The land they'd cultivated was doing well; with around half the vegetable plants and fruit bushes having survived and taken root, they were now reaping the benefits. On the fishing trips they were bringing back enough to last them all for a week to ten days, and Tony had begun to teach the first two males how to actually bait and catch the fish themselves.

The female, 'Julie', was progressing with her linguistics at an incredible rate, and was now relatively fluent, even conversational by the use of certain sentences she'd learned. It was also becoming increasingly apparent to Tony that she was quite artistic. She'd got hold of some of the stone items which were in his animal skin bag – the one the group of three humanoids had given him when they'd first come over – and by using the stone pieces she'd started to draw pictures on the cave walls. He had always been interested and impressed by drawings, since this was something he'd never been able to do, and although these were fairly crude and basic, he could still see there was a definite flair which came through on the imagery she'd etched into the rocks.

Tony found that these drawings were having a homely effect on the cave in an odd kind of way. She'd drawn plants and bushes, which reminded him of what they'd all collectively achieved so far, and a picture of Zephyr (his favourite, of course). Although still basic, he could pick out that Julie had actually managed to portray that almost indefinable look on his face he'd often have; she'd even etched this above the place where he usually slept.

During the next couple of weeks, Tony started to hold group sessions to start to teach the other humanoids to speak. This time, with the help of Julie being able to mediate between him and them, it was going relatively smoothly, even though they were slower and not picking things up anywhere near as well as she had, their level of understanding was sufficient enough to have already improved the quality of communication between them. All of this had given Tony a sense of satisfaction; he felt he was achieving everything he'd set out to do with these beings a few weeks ago.

There was one nagging thought though, and it was starting to play on him; he'd begun to realise that he was starting to feel like he was now becoming a part of this world, and it a part of him. He was increasingly finding that by developing these 'people', as he had now come to think of them, he was actually building a life for himself – a new life – and he now started to wonder how willing he'd be to let this go, how willing he'd be to go back to his old life back on his native Earth, when or if that time ever came.

As the days came and went, things were running ever more like a well-oiled machine. Tony had given every individual an equal part to play in the community, and everyone knew what duties they needed to perform on a daily basis. He'd allocated different jobs according to the abilities he reckoned each one of them to have, whether it was harvesting the fruit and vegetables for the day, going out to gather dead wood and grass for the cooking fire, or disposing of the subsequent ash and any waste pieces of food material, which they'd scatter over the cultivated land to nourish the earth. Everything was now carried out as a matter of routine; he'd even let the first two males do a couple of fishing trips on their own, which they'd completed successfully.

In time, even more humanoids came over to this new community; two couples and two more single males. Tony gladly accepted and integrated them into the fold in same way; there were now twelve humanoids in total, and nearly every cave was in use. A strange and slightly ironic thought came to mind one day as he stood by the lake and looked around him at them all – some in their caverns, some carrying out their duties, some just standing, communicating with each other. "Yes," he thought. "My god, it's like I'm running a hotel again!"

That wasn't all. The humanoids as a group were now beginning to display some of the traits of his own race, arguing between themselves about who should have what, what belonged to who, and who'd done something to someone they shouldn't have – even theft was an issue in some cases. Tony was therefore now also finding himself using his legal training, sorting out these problems they were having between themselves.

To try and administer justice fairly, he would use the same principles of civil or criminal law which a court would back on Earth to determine what should or shouldn't happen. He was fast becoming aware of the need to lay down firm rules, rules which he would make clear to them and would be considered as law in their community. But, for all of this, it wasn't long before his prediction of a hostile visit from some of the members of the original community came to be.

One day, a few of them were working the cultivated land, digging up unwanted weeds which would spring up constantly on the now lush and fertile land, and trimming the bushes and plants of dead branches and other foliage to keep them in the best of productive health. Tony always brought Zephyr with him when they did this; he liked to chew the sticks and this was good for his teeth.

It was around midday, and Zephyr suddenly stood up and started to growl toward the border of trees; from that moment Tony knew there was a problem. Zephyr was now used to people coming into and going out of the community area, so he wasn't doing this for nothing. Tony quickly grabbed hold of him, not wanting him to go rushing into the trees on his own, then told everyone else to stop what they were doing and stand in silence. He listened carefully; a rustle here and a snapping twig there, as well as a general sense of presence behind those trees told him they were no longer alone as a group.

The humanoids had made around twenty poles in all; Tony had stored them all in one of the few small empty caverns. He directed two of them to run back to bring some down so that they could arm themselves; when they got there they alerted the rest of the males to join them. Tony ran straight back up to his cave. Quickly grabbing his pole and knife, he told Julie to stay in there. He, Zephyr and six males fast made their way back toward the trees, but as they reached the lake, Tony's suspicions… were confirmed.

There they were, ten males he counted in total, all armed with poles and standing side by side in the area between the lake and the cultivated land. He was now close enough to see their eyes roving as they surveyed everything which surrounded them, but it wasn't this that really caught his attention. There, in the middle of their line, stood the one he realised must be the leader. The other males were all roughly the same size as these beings normally were, but this one was something else: much taller with a thickset body mass, he stood out massively from the rest, his eyes fixed on Tony as the group now looked on at him, as though to wait for his instructions.

There was a feeling of tension in the air, which cut through the uncomfortable silence that now existed between them. All Tony's males had now stopped and he found himself and Zephyr walking towards the group on their own. He stopped to look round at his group. "Stand firm," he told them and gestured as he continued to move forward. Then, suddenly, the leader himself began to walk towards Tony. Zephyr was growling deeply. "All right, it's all right, Zeph, steady," he said as he and the leader stopped; they now stood eyeball to eyeball and the tensions were now at a pinnacle.

Then, the atmosphere was suddenly shattered when one of the visiting group, who must have got jittery, made a sudden movement and started quickly making his way in their direction. This caused Zephyr to bolt towards him like a bullet, snarling ferociously. It was all over in no more than two seconds. Almost before Tony had time to look, the humanoid was on his back, pinned to the ground with Zephyr staring down at him with that menacing deep growl coming from within his chest, and two of the visitors had actually ran back into the trees. Tony moved past the leader to call Zephyr off: "OK, Zeph, stand clear, stand clear." Zephyr stepped off the humanoid, leaving the stunned male wondering what had just happened!

As they walked back to the leader, Tony could see a look of intelligence mixed with hatred in his eyes. "What can I do for you then?" Tony said in a cocky tone he sometimes used in situations like this, but in truth he knew they'd now won the day with the display Zephyr had just put on. The leader looked Tony up and down in curiosity, took another look around the community, then nodded to him with a look as though to say "it doesn't end here."

He took a step back, and with one wave of his hand his party all began to make their exit towards the trees. Tony knelt down. "Great work, mate," he said to Zephyr, knowing he'd given the intruders something to think about before coming back. But come back he knew they would; the leader was someone to be reckoned with, and today would only be a start to the problems which now lay before them.

That evening, Tony called a meeting with all members of the community. He knew they had by now almost learnt enough basic language to understand the main points he needed to make, and Julie – now so advanced linguistically that she would be able to interpret – could relay to them anything which he might have trouble getting across.

He began by explaining to them that because their group had now grown in number, and were becoming strong, successful and productive, the members of the original community probably now saw them as a threat. He explained how this would mean danger for them, and how they would now need to defend themselves, and the land, for the good of their community. He didn't even try to explain the material and psychological reasons for this, which he knew only too well; it was enough for now that *they* just knew it was so. Besides, they'd shown already to have many of the traits of his own human kind, so maybe deep down they had their own inherent and instinctive way of knowing what he'd said to be true.

At the same time, as he spoke to them Tony couldn't help but think of Earth's history; of how it all must have started deep in his own world's past; and of how wars between communities just like these had begun, only to be replicated through time on an ever-increasing larger scale, all in the same way, and all for the same reasons. Was the sheer fact of him being here now driving this world towards the same fate as his, he wondered. Could he have done anything differently over the last few months? Done anything to prevent this situation? He knew deep down within himself that to have done so would not have been in his nature, so these were questions he could never really have the answer for, in any case. In reality, things were the way they were now, and it was here and now, not in the past, and not in the future; what needed to be done, must now *be* done.

From the next day, he arranged for two humanoids to be on guard duty every night on a rota basis. Everyone would take a turn over a seven-day period, including the females; this would start from tonight by him and another one of the males taking the first shift. During the day, Tony also got the males together to put a battle plan in place; he knew the other community was bigger and they would probably come back in greater numbers, so he'd need the elements of stealth and surprise on their side.

He devised a strategy for two of them to take guard duty in the daytime as well; they would take position in the border of trees, one at each end, looking outwardly towards the other community. "This will provide for an early warning to alert us if or when we see them coming," he said as he had Julie continue to help interpret some of his words.

During the few next days, they prepared themselves to fight. Tony picked out mounds of rock and thick wild bushes and trees for them to conceal the poles so they'd have them to hand at these strategic positions at any given time. His plan was that as soon as the alarm was raised, they would also conceal themselves in these places to lay in wait for their adversaries. Tony also planned for them to fight in pairs, back-to-back; that way, if each pair got outnumbered it would be harder to overwhelm them, each one watching the other's back. He would of course have Zephyr with him, watching *his* back, and he'd told them he would take the leader.

Although Tony realised they'd more than likely be outnumbered, his people did have one other advantage: it was more than noticeable that due to the nourishment of the good, cooked food over time, they'd got bigger in body mass and grown stronger than their counterparts. Nevertheless, day after day Tony had them rehearse the event, from the early warning, for which he'd taught them to shout two simple words 'in-come!' to each pair running to their respective point of concealment; then from lying in wait and silence, to finally jumping out to attack at the sound of a high-pitched whistle, which would come from him. As well as this, he'd also taught them to let out a loud battle cry.

Time after time they practised this, until they were able to execute everything perfectly. In the end, when Tony told them this was good enough and they could go back to normal duties, the look of relief on their faces made him smile to himself. The next night, he took his cooking facilities down to the lake, cooked off extra food for everyone, and arranged for them all to eat socially together, thinking that this would boost morale and camaraderie.

Later that night, after they'd all eaten and gone back to their caves, Tony looked on as Julie sat with Zephyr in their cavern. They'd become closer over the last couple of months, and she'd devote any spare time she had to taking him for walks around the lake, throwing rocks for him to retrieve, and playing chase games. Tony watched as she looked so affectionately on him. It was obvious she was now becoming so much more advanced in many ways; with the passing of each day he could see an ever-increasing look of self-awareness and intellect growing in her eyes; this went hand in hand with the simultaneous development of a more advanced personality.

He didn't really find this troubling in any way, in fact it all seemed to be happening totally naturally over time, but it was beyond his understanding, and he could no longer just put it down to good food and a better way of living. There was something else that *did* truly bother him though. He'd almost not wanted to admit it to himself, but she was starting to become attractive to him. He saw not only the beauty which she now possessed in physical form, but that which she possessed within; he didn't know what to do about this, but it was a fact he could now no longer deny.

Over the next few days, life in the community carried on as normal. Tony had been getting up extra early for the past few mornings; this was mainly to oversee the changeover from night guard to day watch, even just to make sure it actually happened. One morning, just before sunrise, he and Zephyr walked into the trees to see the two males who were just finishing their night shift. Everything was quiet so he let them both go before the daytime lookouts arrived. Just as he was watching the huge red sun begin to come up over the horizon, the slight image of something moving in the distance caught his eye.

To begin with, it was just one dark flicker against the background of the sun, then there were two, then three, then four or more; he could eventually see up to around ten of these objects before he knew what they were. As they drew nearer and got larger, he finally realised. "The humanoids," he said to himself. "The time's arrived. Come on, Zeph," he said, grabbing his pole. They ran back out from the trees towards the lake, Tony shouting "incoming... incoming" repeatedly until they reached the caves.

Once he could see everyone had awoken, he mobilised them as fast as possible, knowing that if his plan of attack was going to work, they'd need to be in situ *before* the intruders came through the border. Like clockwork each of them knew exactly what to do, and all quickly took their respective positions.

As they lay there in silence, Tony began to hear the rustling of branches he'd come to know so well, as the enemies made their way... through the trees. He watched from his vantage point as they began to appear. As expected, first came the leader, flanked by two other humanoids walking either side of him, before most of the others appeared – again they were all armed with poles. Tony counted nineteen to begin with, but could see some of them were barely more than children.

When a final three more appeared, he realised they were outnumbered by nearly three to one, or at least over two to one if he discounted some of the very young males, but his side had a plan, and if they stuck to it this would give them a chance. They remained in silence as the other side drew nearer; eventually the leader brought them to a halt.

It was now half-light and Tony watched him as he looked around and listened to see what situation they were faced with. He could tell this male was obviously intelligent, and that he sensed something was around him. "OK, it's time to go for it," Tony thought. On the sound of his high-pitched whistle, they all jumped out into the open, letting out the battle cry he'd taught them. Tony looked around him for one split-second as they rushed towards the enemy with all guns blazing. "Ha, proud of you already, boys," he thought as he went to single out the leader.

As soon as Tony came into his view, the leader raised his pole fast above his head, bringing it down with great force. Tony blocked this with equal speed and their hand-to-hand battle began. On and on they slugged it out, constantly wielding their poles at each other, both blocking the other's blows, all except for the odd one hitting its target.

Built like a tank, the leader was an immovable object; Tony was throwing everything he'd got at him but he just kept coming. He looked round at Zephyr, who was keeping one of the humanoids who'd been at the leader's side from getting to Tony. He could see blood running down his arm from a vicious bite. He then suddenly felt a jarring thud from the leader's pole as it struck his face.

Just managing to stay on his feet, Tony lunged at him and they locked poles, each one of them trying to push the other to the ground. The leader's strength was almost insurmountable, and Tony was starting to get real problems just trying to contain him. Then, he got lucky; the leader slipped and pitched forward. Taking full advantage of this, Tony rounded on him, bringing down a powerful blow to the head from his pole. The leader fell face down to the ground, before rolling over onto his back in a semi-conscious state.

At this point, Tony could so easily have killed him. Holding his pole vertically with both hands, the butt of it hovering above the leader's face, he was about to strike a last few fatal blows when the sound of someone crying out in pain distracted him. As he looked around he could see that most of the young males had fled; his males, although still outnumbered, were holding their own.

Tony ran over to where a group of three of the enemies were beginning to overwhelm two of his own. As he struck out to disperse them, he suddenly noticed the members of the other side begin to back off, all of them moving to one side. Tony realised what was happening; they'd spotted the leader was down. As they rushed toward him, two of them helped him to his feet and they began to walk towards the trees, the leader unsteady on his feet, his thick arms around the shoulders of the helpers as though they were crutches.

The rest of them followed as they all began a silent retreat. Three of Tony's males followed them and started to raise their poles; he called them off. Apart from not being completely ruthless, he thought it best to let them go back to their own community with the wounded leader and tell the tale, the tale of how they'd been defeated that day.

Tony quickly walked over to Zephyr, making sure he was all right; he'd also seen blood coming from puncture marks on the leg of another one of the enemies, again caused by a vicious bite. "Well done, boy, well done," he said as he knelt down beside him.

Tony stood back up to see all of his people standing in a group around one of them, who was lying motionless on the ground, with another kneeling by his side. Walking over, he could see the male had sustained severe head injuries. He quickly bent down to see what he could do. The fact he didn't know anything about their anatomy made this difficult, but they seemed so similar to humans that the first thing he did was to check for a pulse in his wrist. Feeling nothing, he decided to go straight to CPR. Tony grabbed one of the males to show him how to do chest compressions while he himself started to breathe into his mouth.

They carried out the procedure for a good three to four minutes before he told the male to stop. Clenching his fist, he struck six hard blows to the injured male's chest, then continued CPR for around another three minutes. Finally stopping to take another good look at him, checking for a pulse in his neck this time, he could still detect nothing – the male lay motionless and not breathing, his eyes open in a blank stare, and Tony now knew… he was dead.

Getting back up to his feet, he looked towards the rest of the group, waved his hands from side to side and shook his head. He could see they'd all understood as they lowered their heads and a look of sadness appeared in their eyes. One of them, possibly a relative, he thought, sat down next to the body and began to cry. As the humanoid held the hand of the dead male, Tony saw for the first time that these beings could feel sorrow and grieve. He singled out the original two males who he'd buried the carcass of the creature with a few months ago. Looking directly at them, Tony pointed to the body, and then to the ground; they immediately knew what this meant.

Running back to the caves to fetch the stones for digging, they returned with Julie and two other females, all clutching one of the multi-purpose tools in their hands. Julie and the two males handed a stone out to Tony and the other males; as he started to dig, Tony listened as the three of them explained to the others what was happening, and why. As everyone then began digging with him he not only felt humbled, but a sense of respect and admiration came over him towards this race. He began to realise that not only had they understood what he'd try to say that day they buried the creature, but had held those values close enough to carry them forward, and pass them on to their own kind.

They completed the burial and only the usual mound of earth marked the place where a body now lay. As they all stood silently around the plot, most of them still bloodied and bruised from the battle, the motionless gathering was suddenly broken when one of the females walked over to the plantation.

They all watched as she bent down and pulled a young and recently planted fruit plant from the ground, walked back and knelt over the grave. She parted a small area in the soft earth at the head of the mound and planted the young bush. Tony looked at the female and smiled. Knowing and understanding why she had done this, and the meaning of her actions, he felt it now fell on him to put this into words. Looking around at them, and with the aid of some hand gestures, he uttered a few simple words: "As this plant grows bigger and stronger, let this man grow stronger in our hearts."

After he'd finished, he found his eyes drifting over to where Julie was standing. She was already looking at him, and as their eyes met he detected a very slight, almost indefinable smile appear on her face. At that moment, he knew she'd understood his words and shared them with him. "Well, I think we all need a good shower now, and we'll eat together again tonight. Well done everyone!" Tony said as he tried to lift the moment. Julie took Zephyr off for their usual walk around the lake and Tony went back to his cavern to get salt to treat the injuries they'd sustained, which he'd administer after they'd all washed their wounds of battle.

Later in the day, he took the original two males back to the wooded border to check and make sure the other community weren't planning any reprisals yet. They stayed there on lookout for at least a couple of hours before Tony put one of them on guard duty for the night, arranging for the other to relieve him to eat later on. It felt strange to him in a way, but he'd become aware that he had come to trust these two males now, more than he'd ever done with most of his past friends and associates back on Earth. He also felt a pretty strong bond with them in some strange way; at that point it struck him that he'd not thought of a name to call each of them either.

Deciding to remedy this, he went through all the letters of the alphabet, coming up with all sorts of the usual names, but unlike when he named Julie, he had no point of reference for them. He began to think about a more unusual handle for these beings of a different planet.

Being pretty familiar with the use of Latin through law, Tony started thinking along the lines of that same language. He was just going through the ancient alphabet when it came to him. "That's it!" he said as he joked to himself about a 'Eureka moment'. "Alpha and Omega – the beginning and the end," he said, pointing to one and then the other. "You Alpha, you Omega," he repeated. He laughed out loud as they each in turn started to repeat their own names to each other. "Great names for you both, boys. Two great names," Tony said as he left them in the woods.

On his way back to the cave, he began to think about how he would see Julie back there, and how he'd grown to look forward to this; to look forward to the talks in a broken form of English they'd now have every evening, and just having her general company at the end of a day. When he returned, after a greeting from Zephyr and a 'hi' to Julie, he grabbed a few wraps of fish to take down the cliff with him to start preparing for a communal dinner.

When he turned to call Zephyr to go with him, something on the wall behind Julie caught his eye. As he continued to stare at this, the realisation of what it actually was gradually revealed itself to him. Filled with almost disbelief, he dropped the wraps of fish to the ground and walked slowly over to the wall, finally kneeling down close to where Julie sat.

"Oh my god," he said and turned his head to look at her – etched into the rock was a picture of the alien spaceship. Having drawn this while Tony had been out for most of the afternoon through to the evening, she looked into his eyes, then at the picture, and finally back to him.

"Me, you?" she said, pointing to herself and then at him.

"You were there?" he said, putting his hand on her shoulder. "You *were* there! How? What happened?"

She began to tell him what she remembered as best she could.

"Was walking by self one day. Thought I hear noise, then felt tired, sat, and sleep. Then, woke there. When left I was… different. Me same, but somehow… different."

Tony listened as she tried to explain what had happened to her when she was on the ship, but she didn't have the vocabulary for this yet, so it was unclear. But two things *were* clear to him: the aliens had taken her there, and altered her in some way, for some reason, but why? That was the big question on his mind. He realised immediately that as he himself must appear very different to her kind, she'd obviously assumed that he must somehow be associated with the ship.

Thinking back to when they'd first met, it all made sense now – the humanoids he'd rescued the female from had turned against her because she'd become different, different to them; her community had rejected her because of this. "Huh, typical of my world, really. Reject and attack that which you don't understand, through fear of the unknown," he said to her as he took her hand. "OK, don't worry now. It's all right. It's all right, Julie."

Tony did dinner that night for everyone just as he said he would, but he couldn't help being pre-occupied the whole time by what he'd learnt that day. It had been a very long one and he decided to put it all aside for now and have a good think about the whole thing tomorrow. In the meantime, Julie helped him clear up and take the cooking slab and stands back up the cliff.

When they got back to the cave, Tony lit a fire to provide some light before they bedded down for the night. He looked over to Julie smiling at Zephyr as he lay beside her, the flames of the fire casting flecks of light over them all, and he thought to himself about where they go from here. Maybe it was now time to go back to the ship that he was now pretty sure would still be there, to finally try and find out what was really going on… maybe, maybe. But again he decided to think on this tomorrow; it was time to bed down.

As the flames of the fire died out that night, they began to take up their usual sleeping positions. Tony was almost asleep when he heard Julie start to move and eventually stand up. Still in a state of semi-sleep, he wondered what was wrong, but before he had a chance to look round his thoughts were answered when she laid down beside him, wrapping one arm around his upper body.

He opened his eyes and half turned his head in surprise. He felt awkward to begin with and didn't know how to react, but it had felt like a long time since he'd felt the warmth of a female body next to him, that tender feeling of soft skin on his. A minute or so passed before he reached for her hand. Caressing it gently, they both fell into a deep sleep.

When they woke in the morning, their bodies entangled, Tony looked at Julie as she opened her eyes. "This doesn't mean we're married, ya know," he said with a smile. From that moment, a blanket of silence prevailed as they got up to start the morning. That day and the next passed without incident, and the community settled back in to its normal routine, but there remained an uneasy, even edgy atmosphere between Julie and Tony. Feeling some regret about this, he hoped their relationship as it stood had not been spoiled.

On the third day, Tony and Zephyr went straight down to check in on the newly named Alpha, who'd stayed on guard duty that night; he had nothing to report and there'd been no sign of movement from the other side; all was quiet. They spoke for a while before Tony finally relieved him. It was later that morning than he'd usually get up and the sun had already fully risen.

He and Zephyr walked through the woods to the outer side; as it was completely light there'd be a clear sight over to the other community. They walked a couple of hundred metres out onto the barren rocks so he could get an even better view. As they got nearer, he could just about see what looked like no more than a dot in the distance, just outside the huge rock cliff. Curiosity finally got the better of him when he thought he could see the object moving, then seemingly disappear. He now suspected it was one of the humanoids, but had to find out for sure as they walked still further.

Only slowing when his suspicions were confirmed, he could now see a whole group of the humanoids as they appeared from behind the rocks, pointing at him and Zephyr. Realising they'd been spotted, Tony brought them to a halt. He smiled wryly. "So you're now doing the same as we are, huh?" he said to himself. "OK, come on Zeph. Time to get home."

Walking back to the wooded border, Tony realised this wasn't over. The fact that the other community were now posting guards and lookouts, just as he was, meant they were fearing an attack from his side now, but the reality was that if he did nothing, the other side would only be encouraged to mount another attack on them. "That's how it works," he thought to himself.

Getting back to base, he began to weigh up the possibilities, and cast aside any thoughts he'd had the other night about seeking out the alien ship. He needed to prioritise matters closer to home right now, and he found himself giving the community precedence over anything else. As he thought on, though, he realised that to mount an attack on the neighbouring humanoids would be a pointless exercise – they certainly had nothing he, or any member of the community, for that matter, wanted. Besides, he had nothing to fear from *them*; they were a primitive species with all the limitations which came with that. This was all about the defence of *his* territory now, and if others did attack, it was going to be important for his community to show they were more superior, to the point where the other side would realise the futility of ever trying it again.

He thought on about how he would he achieve this; apart from the element of surprise they'd used – which would be unlikely to work again – they were pretty evenly matched. He didn't like to admit it to himself, but the only option he could think of was the one thing he'd already dismissed. In this basic culture, he could see no other way... no other way than to 'spike the poles'. Thinking back to why he'd not done this before, he reminded himself how he hadn't wanted to introduce this race to an instrument of killing, particularly when they'd clearly not thought of it themselves, yet!

As the matter continued to play on his mind, before the day was out he began to philosophise either way on the subject. Yes, this might take their ability to carry out acts of violence to another level, that would be the philosophy of any court of law back on Earth, but he could direct them to only use these weapons in defence, just to wound the enemy, not to kill. Another side of the argument would be that the other side could respond by making the superior weapon themselves, once they'd seen what it could do, but at the same time it would also teach them the consequences of battle, causing the beings on either side to be more wary of conflict, much like nuclear weapons back on Earth did.

At that point, he stopped this train of thought, smiled and said: "Or are you just convincing yourself here, Tony?" By this time though he'd already made up his mind. These weapons could save another battle like the last, and another death, so using a legal analogy, on the balance of probabilities, rightly or wrongly, he'd decided on this course of action.

Late in the day, Tony found himself gathering everyone together again. With his knife in one hand, a pole in the other, and an ominous sense of being caught between right and wrong, he began to hack away at one end of the pole. By the time he finished, he'd fashioned a crude, long and very sharp point at the tip of the pole. As he looked back up at all members of the community, their eyes fixed in bemusement at what they were looking at, he began to explain it in the usual broken English.

He began by telling them that they had to realise there would be another attack from the other community, and as before they would be outnumbered, so this time they needed a better weapon, and this… was it. "But, this can kill," he said as he pointed to the grave of the fallen one. Tony went on to explain that the weapon should only be used in defence, and never as something to end a life, just because it can. "Only in the most extreme case of self-defense must it be used in that way. Defend, only hurt, not kill," he finished by saying.

Chopping the upper part of the pole off with a few blows of his knife, gritting his teeth, then holding the tip towards his body, he demonstrated. In a split-second they saw what it was capable of as he thrust the point into his upper arm; with a yell of pain he dropped the weapon. The blood running down his arm was all it took; from that moment on they knew the power they would now come to wield. Tony exchanged a knowing glance with them all. "I go for short time," he said as he walked off to bathe and salt his wound.

On his return, they all carried the stored arsenal of poles out into the open, and Tony began hacking to form the pointed tips. Again, the first two tips were crude and uneven and he wasn't really happy with them, this was until Alpha walked over and knelt down to look at them, picked one up and took it to Omega. Tony stopped as he looked on at them consulting with each other. After examining the weapon, they both ran back in the direction of their cave, eventually returning with the stone tools.

Tony watched as they began to ply their considerable skills which he'd now become familiar with; he again looked on with admiration as they honed the tips to fine, smooth points. "Nice one, boys," he said, walking back to the poles. They continued on with this process: Tony doing the initial cutting, whilst Alpha and Omega fashioned the points to a perfect finish. When they'd completed them all, they placed the poles back into store.

As he stood back to take a good look at the newly created arsenal, Tony was taken aback by how the sharply pointed poles looked as though they'd almost been produced on a lathe, all solid and almost perfectly even! He turned to look at his two friends with a wry smile on his face. "We're ready, boys. We're ready," he said as he pumped a clenched fist.

As they walked back to their caves, Tony noticed Julie sitting by the lake on her own. He and Zephyr went over and sat beside her to find she was looking at her own reflection in the water. Touching her face as it stared back at her from the surface, she wore a curious frown on her forehead. "See, doesn't matter what we do, it still looks the same," Tony couldn't resist saying. "Come on, let's go." Putting one hand on her arm, he quickly put his other hand in the lake, swished the water and flicked some in her face. "What's done is done. Can do nothing for this now," he said as they began to walk back to the cave.

Julie turned to look at him. "Feel better, me feel better," she said with a slight grin.

Tony put a hand on her shoulder. "Well, that's what I'm here for," he said with a laugh in his voice. Later on, the three of them went for a walk around the grounds of the community, in the cooler calm of the evening. Tony threw a rock for Zephyr; Julie had a faraway look in her eyes as she watched him bound after it. "What bothers you now?' he said as he noticed her gaze.

At that point she stood still and turned to him... "Where you two come from?" she asked.

"Well that's a question!" he said in a hesitant tone. "Place like this, long way from here," he finally replied. "If only she knew!" he thought to himself.

"You from place they took me?" Julie said.

"No, no, they... took me there too," he finished by saying. She had that curious look on her face again as she stared at him with innocent eyes. Tony then felt a compulsion, the compulsion which only comes when that almost indefinable chemistry occurs between two people; he instinctively knew she felt the same, that knowing when it feels almost as though a psychic bridge had formed between them at that synchronised moment in time. Tony gently placed his hand on her face, she moved ever closer, then in a second, which felt like an hour, their lips met in a tender... lasting kiss.

There ensued a few silent moments between them that spoke a hundred words... this was suddenly and abruptly broken by the sound of Alpha and Omega running towards them and shouting Tony's name. Zephyr dropped his rock, let out a bark and made his way towards them. The two males were there to tell Tony that the night watch had spotted a gathering of the enemy outside of the other community. "See you later," he indicated with a smile to Julie as he put his hand on her arm. "Come on, Zeph," he said as he and the two males made their way to the wooded border.

They arrived to see eight figures in the distance, in what was now the twilight of evening, one of them being the far bigger, taller frame of the leader. They seemed to be looking up at the thinly-lit silver new moon which was just beginning to appear, the leader pointing to it, then across the rocky, barren area, towards their community. Tony looked up at the celestial body so pale and high in the sky. "That's it," he thought. "They're planning to attack at night this time."

He'd thought they could be waiting for a full moon to light their way across the rocks, then straight into the heart of his community as they all slept. If his guess was right, this could be the best early warning he could have hoped for. Not knowing how long the moon on this planet took to change from new to full, he'd have to monitor it each night, but first gauge the difference between now and tomorrow – that would give him a rough idea of the length of the cycle. From this he could pinpoint when they'd need to be ready to within a day or two. They stayed until dark, when the figures of the enemy disappeared behind the walls of their community. "OK, boys. Me, you and all males meet in morning," he said as they walked from out of the woods.

His feelings were mixed as he walked back to the cave. "Shit, that was bad timing," he said to himself. "Just in the middle of a 'moment' with Julie there, and now this!" When he and Zephyr got back, he told her of the situation and explained what he thought would happen.

"I worry for this," Julie said as he lit the fire to do the food.

"Forget for now. We eat tonight, worry for tomorrow," he joked, but he himself couldn't forget, and as he built the fire up, he began to think out his battle plan. Later on, when they bedded down, he and Julie slept in each other's arms again that night. Although the thought of what was to come weighed heavily on his mind, he knew he would need to sleep well this night; he'd need an early start the next morning to prepare himself, and everyone else, for what he now believed would be an inevitable chain of events.

In the rising sun of the next day, Tony gathered Alpha, Omega and the rest of the males together at the site of the concealed weapons. He explained to them everything he expected would soon happen, and of how he thought the enemy were planning a night raid, and how he would, by using the moon's cycle, work out when this would happen so that they'd be ready for them when that night came. He asked them all to go in and each take a weapon, then, using Alpha as the subject, he demonstrated how they should use it, and most importantly, where on the body they should concentrate on; arms, legs and upper chest plate; but to particularly avoid anywhere around the torso from under the ribcage to above the upper leg. Afterwards he made each one of them practice this to make sure they'd understood.

They'd all followed his strategy pretty much well in the last battle, so Tony was sure they'd understand the one he was planning this time. He stood them in a concave semi-circle in relation to the wooded border, then placed them each around twenty feet apart. Using a mix of signs and broken language, he told them there would still need to be an element of surprise, so when the time came one of the females would be on lookout in the woods. They would need to be in this position but lying flat, covering themselves with freshly cut branches from the bushes; that way, as it would be dark they'd not be seen as the other side approached. They'd let them enter in as they'd done before, but this time they would be walking into a position where they'd be surrounded.

"At that point, we stand up," he said, "and move in with our weapons pointed in on them." Tony went on to explain that once they got close up, they would already have the advantage of keeping the enemy a pole's length away from them. "We wait for them to strike out with their poles. This will leave one side of their body open, then we lunge, stabbing at them until they back off, or run, but... we not kill," he finished by saying again.

After this, they continued to rehearse long into the day, even down to cutting the bushes to camouflage themselves. As they practised the operation time and time again, Tony's thoughts turned to the leader of the other community; he knew he'd need to be the one to deal with him, as he had before.

Although he was obviously the same breed as all the others, Tony realised how far more mentally and physically superior he was to the others, and he wondered why. Was he a throwback, or more likely a leap forward in the species? "Well, no point in contemplating this," he thought – it was something he could never know. What he did know was that by the use of their new weapons, he would need to make sure this one humanoid would learn the same lesson as his tribe that night, or all their efforts would be wasted!

Over the next three days, Tony monitored the moon as it appeared in the evening sky. From the first night he'd done this he'd been able to work out that the light coverage was increasing by around one tenth each day, with night visibility increasing as the surface brightened the land between his community and theirs; from this he assumed the attack would most likely come within the next seven days. He could see the light level was not strong enough just yet, but decided that he and the other males would need to start being at the ready after the next three days. With this in mind, he told the males they'd soon need to be sleeping just outside the woods. Knowing that of all the females he could trust Julie to be on lookout for those few nights, to this end he intended she play that important role in the operation.

That same evening, he spoke to her about the plan and how he intended to execute it; of how he had doubts about using these new weapons and why; but of how he thought it would be the best way to prevent any further conflict. He also told her of how he'd tried to train them not to kill or inflict life-threatening injuries; as Julie listened she placed a comforting hand on his shoulder. "It will be for good, I hope," she said with a kind smile.

"Yeah, that's what they say back on Earth, but sometimes it not work out that way," Tony replied.

"Earth, what is Earth?" she said.

Tony quickly turned his head to her, realising he'd let the word slip. "I tell you some time, not now, long story," he said, trying to cover it over. Those next three days passed slowly for Tony as the light of the moon grew stronger with each passing night. To add to this, one day it rained for hours, and when it rained on this planet... it rained! He'd come to realise though, that just as a watched pot finally boils, the time would come for him to set the wheels in motion.

At dusk the next evening, they gathered by the woods, armed themselves and collected together their camouflage. Tony and Zephyr stayed with Julie until it was nearly dark, then as the stars began to appear, they walked her into the dim shade of the trees. Julie had tried to sleep that afternoon, knowing she'd need to stay awake for the whole night until dawn. She knew exactly what she had to do; at the first sight of moving figures in the distance, she'd run out of the woods, wake Tony and quietly say the word 'red', then go on to do the same with the others. She knelt down to say 'good night' to Zephyr, then as she stood back up Tony tenderly kissed her on the cheek. "Night," he uttered before he and Zephyr walked away to take up their position with the others.

As they came out into the open, on the other side night had now fully fallen. Tony signalled to everyone that it was time to get ready; as they all laid down and covered up, taking a final check around he could see the camouflage was working. Now he was satisfied they were now undetectable, Tony and Zephyr got ready for the long night to come.

As they lay there covered in branches, he began to think back to all the strange places and situations he and Zephyr had spent the night in back on Earth when they were on the road, hopping around the country to one hotel or another that he'd been tasked with running, rescuing some of them, putting things right in difficult situations. And here they were now, light years from their own planet and dealing with a situation every bit as difficult. "And this time I'm not even being paid for it!" he thought, laughing to himself. "Still, like old times, hey, boy," he said quietly to Zephyr in the silence of the night.

As he took a deep breath and closed his eyes, the next thing he saw was Julie standing over him. He jumped up with a start, thinking she'd come to give him the early warning, but as he looked around he could see it was dawn! "Everything... all right? he said, looking around in disbelief at the onset of daylight.

"Yes, nothing," she said with a look of relief on her face.

After Zephyr had had his early morning shake, they set about waking the rest of the males. Although he knew they'd have to do this all over again now, Tony realised last night had been good practise in itself; he thanked everyone and told them to be back at the same time that evening. In the meantime, he took Julie back up to the cave for her to get some sleep, ready for the night that again lay ahead, then put one of the other females on day watch, just in case. They were now running short on food, but Tony knew he couldn't risk leaving base at this time, or even send Alpha and Omega out to fish. After all, he could be wrong; the enemy might have planned a surprise attack in daylight, for all he knew. He didn't really think so, but what he did know was that the sooner this was over and done the better, and he was determined for them to stay in readiness, for as long as it took.

The day passed slowly and Tony felt he was just marking time again. "What a waste," he said to himself, thinking he could be putting his energy into the further advancement of the community, and its inhabitants, rather than playing what seemed to him a pointless waiting game. Evening finally drew in and they all once again took up position.

As night fell, Tony could see the moon was now almost full. He had that feeling it was now or never. Pumped with adrenaline, nearly two hours passed and he'd not even thought about sleep, nor had anyone else it seemed as he could hear sounds of restless stirring from the others. Then, finally he heard a sound he'd wanted to hear that night – the sound of Julie emerging from the woods. "Red," she said as she approached.

He sat up as she reached him. "Go to others," he said as he laid back into his camouflage. They all knew what they needed to do; nothing; nothing until they had the enemy within their circle.

More than twenty minutes of total silence passed before Tony could finally hear the all too familiar sound of rustling leaves from the far side of the wooded border. As the sounds got closer, Tony placed his hand on Zephyr's head as a sign for him to hold fast, his eyes trained on their side of the trees. Then, like an apparition in the depths of the night, came the big, shadowy figure of the leader; standing at the edge of the trees, he ushered in his men. Tony counted carefully as they came through in varying numbers. When the last of them had appeared, he'd counted fifteen in total, so again they were outnumbered two to one.

They began stealthily making their way inward, each of them holding a pole up with both hands clenched around one end; Tony could see most of them were walking straight into where he wanted them, with only two or three straying outside of his perimeter. He felt his aggression kicking in. "You sneaky bastards are gonna get something you ain't expecting soon," he thought to himself.

The next thirty seconds were crucial as they moved ever closer. Tony felt they were almost now in the right place, but then, like the crack of a whip, amplified by the blanket of silence which surrounded them, came the sound of a snapping branch under the step of one of the enemy. This caused Zephyr to let out an instinctive growl. "Stand," Tony said as he rose up from the camouflage. As the males revealed themselves, they began to carry out their well-practised plan, moving in on the enemy in a tightening clasp, but the next few minutes didn't go the way Tony had planned.

Rather than standing their ground as he'd expected, spooked by the sudden appearance of he and his men the enemy scattered, splitting off in different directions. In the chaos that followed, Tony's men also broke ranks, fragmenting into groups of two and three. In an attempt to draw them all back together, he quickly went to Alpha and Omega, sending them in two different directions to gather the others back together whilst he picked up the weapons they'd dropped. As he turned to look towards the enemy's direction, he could see and hear the leader calling *his* men back, trying to get them into some kind of order. Tony knew it was now down to which side could re-group first, but knew he had the advantage of there being less of them than the enemy.

Alpha and Omega were fast to bring the other two groups back to him and they all quickly re-armed. Tony gave them all a steadying look and gesture as they were now back in position for the fight. Turning again to look at the enemy, he could see they'd lost around a third of their men, who must have fled back through the woods. He didn't have time to count, but realised that for the first time they were now only barely outnumbered by the other side, and for once he could see a look of fear on the face of the leader.

Having to re-think his strategy almost impossibly quickly, this time Tony placed the men in a V-shaped position, facing the enemy like an arrow, with him standing to the side of them ready to pick out the leader, Zephyr at his side. He could see the leader communicating with his men, before turning back towards their direction. The enemy began to walk slowly towards his side, the leader holding one arm up; they were around twenty metres away when he brought down his arm. In the seconds that followed, they were running towards Tony's tightly formed unit like an angry rabble. He turned his head back to his men and gestured with his hand for them to stay their ground; in the heat of the moment he knew that victory was within their grasp, as long as they all kept their cool.

In the blink of an eye, the two sides finally clashed; like a highly trained military unit against a disorganised band, they stopped and brought down most of the enemy, stabbing and inflicting puncture wounds and severe gashes in all the places he'd taught them. As the blood flowed from their arms, legs and chest areas, most of them retreated, again disappearing through the woods, leaving only the leader, flanked by two loyal followers. Tony looked on at the hatred on the leader's face, his eyes boring into him in an enraged stare, then, in a gesture for them to engage in combat, Tony raised his hand up and beckoned him on.

The leader raised his pole and lunged at him in anger, letting out a shout of rage; Tony stepped to one side and carefully kept his distance as he trained his aim. Making his first move, he stabbed hard into the leader's upper leg, causing him to drop his pole. Realising his first blow had struck home, he knew he had to continue; again and again he viciously stabbed at his legs, arms and chest. For over half a minute, the leader managed to stay on his feet, lunging forward, trying to punch at Tony with his powerful arms. "When is this bastard going down?" Tony began to think to himself, but eventually he slowed, dropping to the ground in a crumpled heap, then finally and completely collapsing face down.

The leader's men both stood there in silence, one of them behind Tony's back. He moved forward to attack Tony from behind, but Zephyr was too quick to leap, knocking him to the ground, giving him a series of vicious bites to the face. As Tony called him off, the other one ran towards Alpha, who also had his back turned; he was running at speed by the time he'd almost reached him. "Alpha, look out! Tony shouted. Alpha quickly turned round to the sound of Tony's voice, just in time for the other humanoid to impale his torso on the spiked end of Alpha's pole. As it entered through his belly and exited through his back, the male immediately froze, before going limp and falling to the floor in a listless heap. "Shit," Tony said as he ran over to them. Alpha just stood, looking over the male in a rigid state of shock. As he knelt over him, Tony knew there was nothing he could do as the life quickly drained away from the humanoid, before finally he stopped breathing... and passed.

He slowly pulled the pole from out of his body; as the blood gushed out from both front and back, Tony stood up and dropped the pole. Seeing that Alpha was distressed by what had happened, Tony knew that, of all the males, he'd most understood the meaning of what he'd tried to teach them. He walked over to him, waving his arms slowly from side to side. "Not you, not you, Alpha. Just happened, nothing you could do," he said as he tried to console him. Alpha looked at Tony with a deep level of understanding, and sadness in his eyes, then nodded to show he'd understood. He put his hand on Tony's arm in a gesture of friendship. Suddenly remembering the leader, Tony looked round to the spot where he'd fallen, but he'd gone, and there was no sign of the other male. They'd disappeared, seemingly back through the woods like the others, and into the night.

In the hours that followed, they stayed in readiness at the outer rim of the trees in case the enemy decided to double back, whilst Tony searched the area to make sure the leader and the other male weren't hiding somewhere. Again, there was no sign of them. As it begun to get light, they stood down, put all weapons back into store, and buried the body of the fallen male at dawn. Tony fetched one of the females down from the caves and put her on lookout for the day. They'd all only sustained minor cuts and bruising, but they were covered in the splattered blood of the enemy and needed to shower, then get some sleep.

Before they returned to their caves after washing, Tony thanked them all and told them how well they'd done by using a mix of broken language and gestures. He knew there was barely enough food left but told them to meet at the lake that evening and he'd make it go round. Upon getting back to his cave, Julie and Zephyr were already asleep. Zephyr raised his head as Tony sat beside him. "Well, it nearly went to plan, Zeph," he said, placing his hand on him.

As he fought off the tiredness, he couldn't help but think about what went wrong at the end of that battle. For all his planning, he could never have accounted for that outcome, he thought, but as that perfect vision of hindsight began to play relentlessly on his mind, he went over and over what had happened, thinking of ways he could have stopped it. His thoughts then turned to the leader, and of how he must have witnessed much of what had happened in those last few moments at the death of one of his men, but of how he'd probably not seen the full event, of how he'd not seen that it was an accident, but instead a deliberate act of killing, and that now, as a result, although the battle had been won and was over and done with, resentment and the desire for retribution would now manifest itself in the minds of his community. "So much for my philosophy," he said to himself, but as the light grew brighter outside, his eyes grew heavier, and finally closed.

When his eyes re-opened it was to the sound of Julie softly calling his name, along with Zephyr's nose touching his face. "No rest for the wicked," he said, putting a hand out to each of them. It was now late afternoon and he felt refreshed as he got to his feet and gave a long stretch. "OK, let's see what's happening out there," he said, grabbing his knife and pole.

As they approached the woods, Tony felt a sense of calm and a return to normality. "If you can call this normality," he thought, laughing to himself as memories of his previous life came flooding back to him. With a now refreshed mind, he realised that although what had happened last night *was* the last thing he'd wanted, it would still, at least for now, deter the enemy from trying to attack again, and that even the leader would now need to consider the consequences of any future hostilities. As they looked out onto the rocky, barren landscape, and over to the other community, there was no activity to be seen. Tony stood down the female on lookout and they made their way back to the caves to start preparing dinner.

Later that night, after they'd all eaten, Tony put someone else on lookout. This was something he knew he would always need to do from now on, but still he was now looking forward to getting back into a productive routine. For the first time in nearly two weeks, he and Zephyr would be able to go for fish tomorrow, and he thought he'd take Alpha with them too; apart from getting his mind off what had happened, they were now completely out of food and would need to bring back a good harvest.

Chapter 12

At the dawn of a new day, Tony, Zephyr and Alpha set out. The sun was still red in the sky by the time they got to the salt lake. As they walked round the edge, Tony marvelled at the sight of its reflective qualities, turning from red to orange as the sun rose higher in the sky. It caused him to stop for a while and think about how much he'd grown to love this planet. It was just as good to see the old giant vegetarian monster munching on the tree branches with its huge jaws as they passed by on the other side of the river; even Alpha had now become used to the sight of it. They stopped and grinned to each other as they watched it disappear into its woods, bending some of the thinner tree trunks like twigs as it passed through them.

It was a productive day at the lake; they'd filled two bags with fish and were now on their way back, only stopping to collect salt from the lake. Dusk had fallen as they arrived back at the community, and it felt good to be bringing in the much-needed food, but as they passed through the inner rim of the wood and into the open, there was something unexpected waiting for them.

Tony could see a group of males standing in a circle by the lake, their backs towards him with three of them holding pointed weapons horizontally inwards to the circle. Sensing something was not right, Zephyr bolted towards the group with a deep growl; Tony and Alpha dropped the bags and followed. Calling Zephyr back to him and running at speed, he slowed as the circle of males parted, turned towards him, and revealed something he'd least expected to see.

There stood two males and two females, all from the other community, clutching each other in an anxious embrace, the males baring fresh puncture wounds from the battle. Tony didn't even have to guess what they were doing there. "More defectors!" he said to the group. The only question on his mind was what he was ultimately going to do with them. "Take them to wash," he said, pointing his finger at the new refugees. He and Alpha then walked back to collect the bags for salting the fish whilst they were still at their freshest.

Back in the cave, as he and Julie wrapped the salted fish in the leaves, Tony couldn't help but think that the least they could do would be to treat the males' wounds. He asked Alpha to gather them by the lake, wanting to find out exactly what had brought them here. He also asked Alpha to communicate with them and interpret. After around half an hour, Tony and Zephyr made their way back down to the lake. Carrying some salt in one of the leaves; Tony placed it on the ground when he'd reached them. He turned to Alpha, who'd been speaking to them, in his own way, that is. "Well, what's their story then?" Tony asked with an air of sarcasm and preconception, but as Alpha began to explain in his broken tongue, there was much more to their tale than he'd been expecting.

From what he was saying, Tony realised the leader was increasingly becoming a ruthless and cruel dictator. Along with a handful of his closest followers, he'd carry out terrible punishments to those who would fail, or try to defy him in any way: beatings, stoning and the withholding of food, all of which would usually result in death. And there was more: anyone who he just took a dislike to would be isolated and made to stay in their cave, with only a bare amount of food to live on.

Alpha went on to explain that many of their community members hadn't wanted the conflict, but were forced into it through fear of suffering the same punishments. Tony understood only too well the regime that Alpha had relayed to him; God knows there'd been enough of them back on Earth, and there still were at the time he'd left. Caught between a sense of moral duty to allow them to stay in the safe confines of the community, and whether to believe or trust these asylum seekers, he asked Alpha to stay with them and watch them, to give him time to think.

More than two hours had passed as Tony tried to strike a balance between the advantages and disadvantages of adding the extra humanoids to the fold, just as he'd done when Alpha and Omega had first arrived. But this time there were no caves left, for one thing, and besides, they were now already a thriving community. He knew his plans for development had become even more ambitious with the passing of time, but the overriding point was the fact he had no good reason to trust them. For all he knew, they themselves could be some of the loyal followers of the leader, sent to infiltrate and spy on their community.

In the end, this was the deciding factor as he made his way back to Alpha to tell him they couldn't stay. It was with a sense of regret that he did so but he felt it would be for the best, besides, only yesterday 'they' were the enemy, he thought to himself. As he caught sight of Alpha, Tony could see him sitting on the ground with the group of four; Omega then joined them and they were smiling as they communicated. He sensed how much they looked like friends talking over old times. "This is going to be difficult," he thought, but as he reached them Alpha and Omega stood up to speak.

In their usual broken English and with the use of gestures, they told him how when they were back in the old community, they were close with them. From what Tony could make out, they were trying to tell him, in so many words, that they were good people, and they had skills that would be useful to this community. For as much as he could understand, Omega was saying that one of the males could make things – structures, like bordering fences – and that the females had good planting and growing skills for vegetation. As much as he trusted his two closest friends, this still didn't really convince him, but Alpha was about to say something that Tony could neither ignore or deny.

As he looked him in the eye, he spoke the words: "You teach us life precious, we hear, we do this." Tony was speechless for a moment as he stood and stared at them both. He realised they thought that if these beings couldn't stay, it would mean almost certain death for them. He also realised that they knew, in one way or another, that if they tried to survive on the outside they'd be hunted down by the leader and his close followers, and even if they went back they'd face the same punishments and fate which many others had before.

After he'd gathered himself, Tony almost felt a prisoner of his own words. "OK, guys," he said, throwing his hands in the air at them. "But they're yours to care for – if any problem, it's fault of you! Remember that," he said, pointing his finger. As they nodded to him, he glanced at the others, then gave Alpha and Omega a fleeting smile in recognition of what they'd said, and done. As he walked away, he felt proud and humbled by the two beings he'd now come to fully know, admire, and respect.

Over the next few days, the community got back into a routine once more, and things began to settle again as everyone started to resume their normal daily duties. Tony could feel a sense of optimism in the air amongst everyone, as if the events of the last two weeks or so had given all the inhabitants a positive boost. He smiled to himself as he thought of something his mother used to say: "It's an ill wind that blows no one any good." Alpha and Omega were as good as their word and were shepherding the new defectors as though they were children, and that wasn't all; apart from making them pull more than their weight in duties, they'd made them start work on building their own homes – two units, one for each couple.

As the days went by, Tony watched in amazement as the construction process for the newcomers' homes progressed. They'd chosen a spot at an almost vertical part of the cliff face; the two males were building out from this with rocks they'd have to fetch from far and wide, ably assisted by Alpha and Omega. In the end, Tony couldn't resist and joined in with them.

They worked long and hard for a few evenings at the end of each day; the process was slow as they had to ensure each layer of rock was balanced and stable on top of the other. As they had to build four walls, two for each unit, it was pretty painstaking at times, but the one which Alpha and Omega had told him was good at making things did seem to have a natural knack for the job, and within around a week or so they had the walls completed. Tony had the idea of narrowing the two open entrances by bringing them in with more rocks from either side, leaving just enough gap to walk through, so as to create a doorway; all that was needed now was an actual door and a roof for each of them. He had no idea how they were going to do this, but the following day, directed by the one good at making things, the two males, the females, and Alpha and Omega all gathered together piles of dead branches from inside the woods, making several trips before also chopping swathes of the long wild grasses down with their cutting tools.

Tony watched on with curious interest; he realised what they were doing, but felt compelled to find out *how* they were actually going do it as he walked over to them. The skilled male went to work, twisting handfuls of the long grasses together, then using them to bind the branches to make natural panels of differing sizes for the doorway and roof. The expertise of the male was impressive to say the least. "This is going to be very useful," Tony thought to himself – he'd long since noticed that some of the plants in the cultivated area would frazzle in the glare of the sun when it hit them at certain angles, and the odd breeze would spoil some of the newly planted young plants.

Over the next two weeks, he got the male to make enough large panels to form a protective wall around the planted area, which they erected by digging strong, thick branches into the ground and tying the panels into them. By this time, he was thanking Alpha and Omega for persuading him to make the right decision about the new people.

As time went on, the relationship between Tony and Julie grew stronger. He was now teaching her more connective words to enhance and refine their conversations. Her beauty now stunned him at times, and he was finding it difficult to fully concentrate as he taught her an ever-increasing and complex use of language. Although they would now routinely sleep together, they hadn't yet consummated this by having sex. This was getting more difficult for Tony as each night passed, but apart from the fact he knew she was, to all intents and purposes, an alien, he still had no idea about her genital anatomy, or how they even made love.

His thoughts had begun to return to the aliens that had brought them here, and again to whether they were still at the place they'd dropped them off. He now felt an almost irresistible urge to make the trip up to where they'd landed, but as he thought on, the revelation dawned on him with a clarity of absolution – he found himself having almost no interest and no desire to return to Earth.

Although these thoughts came as a shock to him to begin with, looking back at everything he'd done here over the months – building a community, sourcing and cultivating enough food to keep its members well-fed, and teaching them how to communicate by the use of proper language – he realised that by putting all of this together, along with his relationship with Julie and how he felt about her, and the friends he had in Alpha and Omega, "my god, they'd have to kidnap and drag me kicking and screaming to get me back there," he thought laughingly. "So we're here to stay, boy, we're here to stay," he said as he looked around the land and then at Zephyr.

From that moment on, all of Tony's actions were done with a true sense of planning and commitment to their new life and future on the planet. Following the successful construction of the living units for the new members, and the protective screens around the cultivated area, he decided to further utilise the talents of the skilled humanoid by building a proper storage area for the vegetables. With all the care and nurturing they were now getting, the mature bushes were yielding far more than when they'd first been planted, and much of their fruits were going to waste. Tony thought that if they could create a cooler environment, out of the glare of the sun, then this would help to preserve them, giving the community the maximum benefit from the harvests. Just as before, they began to build out from the almost vertical rock face close to the newly built homes; Tony and Omega collected and delivered the rocks, whilst the skilled humanoid and Alpha started on the construction.

Late one evening, as they were about to finish for the day, Tony was carrying a pretty large rock over to the site of the build. It was beginning to get dark and he'd not seen a large stone laying on the ground beneath his feet. Immediately tripping over it, he automatically raised his arms as he fell, bringing the rock up to head height; he smashed the side of his head heavily onto it and felt a severe jarring sensation through his skull. To begin with, apart from feeling pretty stupid in front of the others, he began to laugh it off, until he felt a warm sensation trickle down the side of his face. By the time he tried to get to his feet, Alpha and Omega had ran over to him. Omega reached out to touch his head; as he brought his hand away Tony could see it was soaked in blood.

Knowing there weren't exactly any medical facilities around, and how much the head bleeds, he knew he had to act quickly. Staggering to his feet, feeling dizzy and disorientated, with the aid of Alpha and Omega he began to make his way back to his cavern. As they entered the mouth of the cave, Zephyr, instinctively knowing there was something wrong, began to bark and forced Alpha and Omega back outside. "OK, boy, it's OK," Tony said quickly, calming him down. By this time Julie had rushed up to them; she helped him to the back of the cave and sat him down. Zephyr had smelt the blood and began to lick at the gash on his head. Julie then started to wash away the blood with water, but his head was still bleeding heavily.

"The salt, get the salt," Tony said. She quickly grabbed a handful from his bag and placed it at his side; grabbing a good pinch, he put it straight onto the wound, gritting his teeth as the sting began to take effect. As he felt an overwhelming tiredness come over him, he got Julie to bring over a leaf and press it hard onto the source of the blood. "Whatever happens, keep your hand there," he said. Understanding what he meant, she sat beside him and put her other arm around his shoulder, keeping her hand pressed tightly against the cut. Within thirty seconds or so, he lost consciousness.

Out for around an hour, when he woke he felt a sense of well-being at the sight of Zephyr and Julie sitting around him. Julie must have checked the bleeding when he was sleeping as her hand was no longer pressed to his head. He reached up to feel his hair, now matted with dried blood. "Phew, crisis over," he thought to himself, still shaky. But as he felt his strength begin to return, he looked at Zephyr and Julie, who were both visibly relieved to see him awake. "Thanks, guys. Saved my life," he said, putting his hands out to them both.

As Tony looked at Julie, he was filled with a sense of love and trust for her. He placed his hand at the back of her neck and pulled her closer to him, and as they shared a passionate kiss, nature rapidly began to take its course. Tony grabbed the cover they slept under and wrapped it over them; Julie was totally responsive as he placed himself on top of her. Completely forgetting his concerns of compatibility between them, he could wait no longer. Already between her loins, as he thrust himself into her, only then did he realise she was every bit like a human female! As they did that which now felt so natural, so right to them, they shared a night of lovemaking that neither of them… could ever… forget.

Now in full bloom, Tony and Julie's relationship continued to develop, even to the point that they'd begun to have the odd 'domestic', and Tony was becoming jealous and possessive of her. One day, after they'd had a massive argument, he saw her talking to a couple of the males later that evening, which made him storm off back to his cave. As it got dark and she still hadn't come back, he stood waiting outside the entrance. Looking up at the stars, an old pop song came into his head – 'The Night Has a Thousand Eyes'. "What am I doing?" he said, annoyed at himself. Later on, he could see her walking back to the foot of the cliff with two of the females. "What the hell is happening to me?" he thought, laughing to himself.

They made up that night as usual, and Tony told her how he planned to take her over to the canyon, and how he wanted to show her the view from the edge. He also planned to take Alpha and Omega with them, and go down to the ledge so they could explore, to see if there were any different strains of vegetation they could find, and so that she could see everything down there as well.

Many weeks had now passed since the battles; they'd had no sign or sight of any members from the other community so Tony felt it was OK for them all to leave everything for a few hours. He gave Alpha a couple of days' notice of the trip and they all set out early one morning; Tony felt excited for Julie to see the massive spectacle of nature at its most spectacular.

On the way, he kept a keen eye in the direction of enemy territory for most of the time as they crossed the rocky, barren area, and as far as he could tell it was all clear, all silent, and there were no sightings from the other community. But, as they approached the canyon, he and Omega thought they could hear a slight rustling behind the rocks to the left of them. They all stood still for a moment but could see or hear nothing. Tony took hold of Julie's arm as they walked to the edge; Zephyr went ahead of them and he called him back to make sure he didn't get too close.

The breathtaking view finally revealed itself as they stood only a few metres back from the rim; Tony smiled as he saw the look of almost childlike wonder on her face. As they all stood in silence, their attention was taken up by the sound of the massive waterfall in the distance, along with the piercing sound of huge raptors. Tony made the mistake of looking down, and the usual feeling of disorientation came over him; as he pitched forward, they all reached out to steady him.

Distracted by this, no one saw or heard what was now behind them. Suddenly feeling a dull thud to the back of his skull, Tony fell to his knees. As he looked around at ground level, all he could see was a thick and stocky pair of legs, then in a split-second he looked up to see the hate-filled, angry face of the leader. His head still numbed from the blow, and his ears filled with a dull hum, in his peripheral vision Tony could see four of the leader's men attacking Alpha and Omega as they grappled with them.

At that same moment, Zephyr leapt at the leader, sinking his teeth into his arm and trying to pull him to the ground. As the leader listed to one side, he struck Zephyr several times in an attempt to loosen his grip. Julie jumped on his back, gripping one arm as tightly as she could around the leader's throat; this gave Tony just enough time to begin getting to his feet. As he did so, he reached out to grab a hand-sized rock. The leader had managed to force Julie's arm from around his neck and she fell to the ground, but Zephyr still had his other arm in the vice of his teeth.

Still feeling the effects of the blow to his head, Tony swung his arm with all the strength he could manage, smashing the leader full in the face with the rock in his hand. Zephyr let go of his arm, blood pouring from it as he staggered backwards. Knowing how strong the leader was, Tony knew he had to end this while he had the chance.

He lunged forward, gripping the leader's arm with both hands, and pulled as hard as he could, swinging him round in the direction of the canyon. As he let go, the leader staggered backwards; only just able to stop himself in time, he teetered on the edge. Tony quickly grabbed a large rock and ran up to him. Standing no more than a metre away, he lifted it to chest height. "Catch... bastard!" he said as he threw it straight at him. As his arms automatically wrapped around the rock, the leader slowly but finally tipped over the edge, letting out a deep howl that echoed around the whole surrounding area; the sound got fainter as he fell ever further into the depths of the chasm. Tony walked to the cusp and peered over, just in time to hear the sound of a bone-crushing thud from the rocks deep below; he was gone... for good.

There was a silence; as he stood there, Tony began having strange thoughts about what he'd done. Maybe it was the aftermath of the moment, but he couldn't help feel a sense of destiny about the events that had just unfolded. Dismissing this, he stepped back to look round at the sight of Alpha, Omega and the rest of the leader's men, all standing motionless, each and every one of them bruised and bloodied.

Zephyr now stood by his side and Julie just to the left of him. He walked over and picked up the blood-covered rock he'd used on the leader, holding it up in the direction of his followers. "You next, you next!" he shouted, pointing at them with his other hand. They began to walk backwards with fear in their eyes as Alpha and Omega rushed at them and lashed out with a series of vicious blows. They dispersed in the seconds that followed as they ran back behind the rocks where they'd come from, and out of sight, leaving behind only the fading sound of their swift departure.

Tony could see they were all basically OK; after checking Zephyr had no injuries and praising him, he put his arm around Julie and walked over to the males. Although the reality that he'd killed now lay heavy on his mind, he knew it had been a matter of kill or be killed. But as he spoke to Alpha and Omega, the only question he was asking now was, 'how did the enemy know they were going to be here?' He realised that they must have already been there, given that there was only one straight route across the rocks, with nowhere to hide. If the leader and his men had followed them, they'd have been visible, so they must have been lying in wait. Alpha and Omega looked at each other, and then at Tony, before Omega spoke: "New people, one who make things, we tell them, only them, we tell them we come here this day." After a moment of silence, they told him they were sorry, sorry for trusting them.

"No worry, me wrong, me wrong too," Tony said. They all knew what now needed to be done. Tony looked at Julie. "We will come back another time."

As they made their way back over the rocks, he felt his anger growing at being betrayed by those they'd taken in in good faith, the only consolation being that the skills of 'the maker' – as he'd come to call him – had been useful to them. But one light moment came when he looked over at Alpha and Omega; they looked more angry than he was, stomping as they walked ever forward; he almost laughed to himself.

When they got back, the two males headed straight for the weapon store and grabbed a pole each. Making their way to the newcomers' accommodation, as they got there the skilled humanoid was on top of the buildings, working on the rooves. Tony only had to see the look of shock followed by fear in his face to know how guilty he was. He'd never expected to see them... again.

Gesturing to Alpha that he was all theirs, Tony stood there, his arms folded, a grin on his face as they called him down. The male jumped to the ground and tried to run; Omega threw his pole at his legs, tripping him as he fell to the ground; Alpha jumped on him, pinning him down and delivering a series of blows to his face. As Omega placed the pointed end of the pole to his chest, they both looked back at Tony as though to ask for approval, approval to end his life, but he shook his head. "No, they go," he said, pointing towards the wooded border. "Sometimes have to kill," he went on to say, pointing to himself in reference to what had happened back there. "But not now, not you. We do worse to them, we let them go."

They stood the male up and got him to lead them to the other one and the two females. When they'd rounded them up, they took them back through the woods to the edge of the rocks. "Go," Omega said, pointing outwards towards their old home.

As they watched them walk into the distance towards the other community, Tony tried to explain to Alpha and Omega that what they'd done to these traitors this day was a fitting punishment. Not only did they now have no place in Tony's community, they'd now have no place back in their own; they would be outcasts, with no place to be, and no other safe place... to go. Although they said nothing, he hoped they'd understood, and hoped that in time they'd feel a satisfaction, the satisfaction that comes... with justice.

Chapter 13

Over the next few weeks, they made several more journeys to the canyon. They'd managed to find more and different strains of edible vegetables down on the ledge, as they'd hoped, and Tony was able to show Julie all the wonders of the interior. There'd been no real activity detected from the other community, except for the lookouts reporting the sighting of a couple of humanoids appearing in the early morning and late evening, just watching in their direction.

One day, as Tony was working with two other males on the cultivated area, the thought suddenly dawned on him that it must have been nearly a year now since he and Zephyr had first landed on the planet. "Nearly a year revolving round a far distant sun in a far-flung part of the galaxy," he thought to himself. Still, he now felt almost as though he'd been born to be where he was, and doing what he was doing.

He started to think back to those first few weeks, of how they'd had to find their way day by day on an alien planet they'd become so familiar with in time, and which they'd become so much a part of. The memories flooding back to him gave rise to a kind of nostalgic urge for them to trace their steps back, back to those early days which now seemed so distant. Apart from this, he thought it would be useful; he knew the area around the massive river they'd first walked along was lush in vegetation, and there were bound to be other sources of food there. So that was it – they'd go and explore, just the two of them.

Tony spoke to Julie, Alpha and Omega one day and told them that he and Zephyr would be gone for two, maybe even three days. He told them they were going beyond the fishing site to where he'd been before. Julie didn't like it but he told her he thought there could be many things out there that could benefit the community, and that it was important to him that they all stayed behind and looked after things.

In the days that followed, Tony prepared for their trip, making sure everything was running smoothly and there were no problems with or between any members of the fold. He finally packed his bag with pre-cooked wrapped fish and vegetables, and fruits from the bushes – enough to last them three days – then early the next morning, after giving Julie a long kiss and loving embrace, they started out.

As they emerged from the woods, Tony could see the figures of two humanoids standing outside the other community in the early red glow of the sun. "Morning, guys," he said to himself sarcastically. They continued on and made their way in good time, going past the salt lake and on to their fishing area. Walking up to the plateau they'd once thought of as home, Tony pulled out a couple of fish from the bag for them to have for breakfast. He thought about how strange it was going to feel to revisit the route that brought them here, all that time ago.

It was hot by now and they went back down to the river to drink; Tony took Zephyr into the water to cool off as they got ready to set back out. "OK, here we go then," he said as he looked at Zephyr, and on they walked.

The further they went, the more they could hear the torrent of flowing water in the great river; when they reached it, Tony stopped to take in the sheer size. As he looked down in the direction of the flow, he could see no end, just as before. Having more time and opportunity than when they were last here, he took his time to study the plant life: there was much here that he'd not seen before but nothing seemed to be bearing fruit.

They moved on; around another three miles they walked and most of the vegetation remained the same. As they kept moving, Zephyr stopped, growled and barked a couple of times in the direction of the plants and grasses to the right of them. Realising something must be there, Tony went on alert and reached for his knife. Keeping a watchful eye on the vegetation to the right of them, a short time later he suddenly heard the louder sound of rustling bushes a few metres ahead.

Dropping his bag, he quickly turned to look. There they were, standing no more than ten metres away – three humanoid males, each carrying poles, but this time with the same sharpened pointed tips that'd been used in the battles. He recognised them instantly; one was 'the maker', and the others were two of the males that had ambushed them back at the canyon; all were there...for revenge. A split-second later, Zephyr ran and pounced on one of them, knocking him to the ground. The skilled humanoid and the other male then rushed at Tony; he moved aside fast as they thrust the pointed tips at him. As they missed, he lunged forward.

Grabbing hold of the maker's pole, he pulled it from his hands, turned it on him and stabbed several times at his chest plate, piercing the flesh before thrusting a final stab through his neck that sent him to the ground. Tony then felt an excruciating sting as the other male viciously struck, piercing his upper arm to the bone. As the blood flowed from him, he wielded the maker's pole hard down on to the other's head. The male stood in a motionless gaze as Tony continued to strike him in the head until he collapsed, clutching his bloodied skull.

Looking down at them, he could see they'd both lost consciousness. Leaving them incapacitated, he ran over to Zephyr and the other male, who lay on the ground still conscious, with bloodied puncture marks to his face and body. Tony stooped down to pick up the weapon which lay beside him. "Go," he said to him as he pointed back towards the others. "Take them with you, if you can move 'em!"

As the male scurried away, Tony walked to the edge of the riverbank; holding the poles in both hands he angrily threw them down into the rapidly flowing water. He turned to look round at the males, one of them kneeling over the other two, who were still motionless. "And don't bother again, bastards!" he shouted to them. Tony walked over to pick up his bag. "OK, time to move on," he thought to himself, but as he turned around he saw Zephyr just lying on the ground, panting as though in distress. "Oh my god, Zephyr, Zephyr," he said as he ran back over to him.

Kneeling down beside him, his worst fear was confirmed as he noticed a puncture wound just below his loin, around an inch in front of his hind leg – he'd been speared by the male's weapon. Tony could see the wound was deep; as the blood ran from the opening, he knew he could have damage to an organ. He thought hard and fast about what the hell he was going to do, then, in a moment of desperation, it came to him. "The ship, of course, the ship!" he said. "Come on, boy. Let's get you there."

Picking him up and carrying him in the cradle of his arms, he now hoped to God they were still there. He knew the foot of the mountain was now only around a mile away; walking as fast as he could, and occasionally breaking into a jog, he made his way at his best possible speed, but Zephyr was big and heavy and he had to stop for a few seconds at times.

They finally reached the vegetation with the huge canopies reaching high up to the sky, which he remembered only too well. The dense moisture in the air made the going even harder, but as he ploughed through he knew he was on the right route. With his adrenaline pumping, they went through the long, blue, shaded grasses, and Tony remembered the distinctive black rocks he'd left as markers on their way down. He knew all he had to do was find the first one to send him in the right direction. Laying Zephyr down, he ran to the rocks, frantically searching the whole area.

At least five minutes passed and he still hadn't seen it; it was like finding a needle in a haystack and he knew he was fast running out of time. But then, as he was scanning one particular area, he got a break. Remembering that the black rocks were speckled with some kind of shiny granules, he suddenly noticed a glint of light emanate from between the large rocks. Running over to it, he could see he'd finally found the first of them. "Please god," he said to himself as he ran back for Zephyr. Picking him back up, he started on the first leg of the upward hike.

The dense moisture cleared as they got higher, and Tony was helped even more by the strong afternoon sun reflecting onto the shiny specks on the black rocks. Once he'd passed the next few, he increasingly knew the route just from memory. As he climbed ever higher, he began to feel as though his heart would burst, even stumbling and falling to his knees at one point, but as Zephyr grew ever more limp, he somehow found the strength to carry on.

Then, finally, he got to the plateau; he knew in an instant this was where they'd been dropped. The ship wasn't visible, just as they'd left it. Tony took a deep breath. "I need help! I need help!" he shouted to the empty space. A few terrible seconds passed, which felt like a lifetime as he prayed to God. Suddenly, the great ship gradually but surely began to show itself. "Thank God," Tony said. There was a strange hum as the huge doors began to slide open and the ramp slid out from the underbelly. Tony ran in as fast as he could, the doors quickly closing up behind him.

"Put Zephyr down!" a voice said authoritatively. Tony knelt down, placed him on the floor and stood back. Within a few moments, a wide beam of strong, deep ultraviolet light came down from the ceiling onto the area of Zephyr's wound. As he lay there motionless, around two heart-stopping minutes passed, but Tony watched in awe as he witnessed the virtual miracle of the wound slowly beginning to close and heal before his eyes. As the beam gradually and finally faded away, he noticed Zephyr start to move, slowly to begin with; within a few short moments his strength had returned and he was able to stand.

"He will be fine now. You made it in time, just," another voice said. Tony dropped to his knees as Zephyr turned to look at him, giving himself a shake. With tears in his eyes, he embraced him. Close to absolute exhaustion, and having lost a lot of blood himself by now, he laid on his back, and within a few seconds, he passed out.

When Tony came round, after a brief blurred moment his eyes cleared to reveal a modern, high-tech ceiling above him. With the strange feel of a soft couch beneath him, it only took a few seconds to work out he was back in his old accommodation. He turned his head to see Zephyr sitting beside him with a welcoming smile to his face. "How long have I been out?" he said. As he glanced over at the massive window, he could see it was now dark outside. Raising his head to sit up, he instantly felt a dizziness; his upper arm had been cleaned up and bandaged, but still felt tender and slightly stiff. "Looks like you got the five-star treatment, hey, boy," he said laughingly to Zephyr.

As he sat there and his faculties fully returned, he suddenly noticed he was fully naked, realising that they'd taken his animal skin from him. "Maybe they're laundering it?" he joked to himself. Still feeling dizzy, he got to his feet. "My god, this feels strange, being back!" he said to himself as he made his way to the bedroom. He opened the wardrobe to find all his old clothes as he'd left them; things were feeling stranger by the moment as he realised this modern clothing now seemed so alien to him. "Well, can't stay naked all night," he said, looking at Zephyr. But putting them on felt uncomfortable, restrictive.

As they walked back out and stood at the window, Tony's thoughts turned to that first morning he'd looked out onto the alien planet. He thought of all the uncertainty they'd faced; of how they knew nothing of what was out there; and of the richness of life itself they'd come to find. Just at that moment, he heard the all too familiar sound of the one he'd always called 'the voice': "Good to see you up and around, Tony."

"Well, hi," said Tony in a friendly tone.

"Are you feeling well?" replied the voice.

"Fine," he said. "I am more grateful for what you did for Zephyr than anyone could ever know," he went on to say.

"We know, Tony, we know," came the reply. "You and Zephyr will stay here for the night now. You both need rest, and then... in the morning... we need to talk."

"Agreed," he replied. Considering what would have become of Zephyr if not for them, he felt he could hardly turn down their hospitality. Besides, they did both need a good night's sleep. "Dinner... time for dinner, hey, boy," Tony said as he walked over to the refrigeration unit, but as he opened the door he saw something he wasn't expecting, too. "The fish – our fish," he said as he looked at Zephyr. There, on the bottom shelf, was the same fish from the river that they'd lived on for the last year, and on the shelf above, a selection of the vegetable foods he'd cultivated back in the community. Tony looked back at Zephyr. "Considerate, home from home as usual," he said with a laugh in his voice. It felt odd to cook the same food on a modern stove that night, but after a good dinner they bedded down, on the floor of the room.

They woke refreshed just before dawn. Another thing which felt strange to Tony was the smell of the artificial environment that he'd become so oblivious to on the journey that brought them here. He was now so used to the unpolluted, fresh, natural air of the planet, he was missing it already. As they walked over to the window to watch the sun rise over the landscape and trees below, he thought about how much he was looking forward to getting back to the place he now, so much, called home; to Julie; and to the life he'd made his own.

166

He washed in the bathroom, shaved properly for the first time in nearly a year, then dressed. As soon as he'd spoken to the voice, he'd ask for his animal skin back, before leaving, he thought. "Good morning, Tony," said the voice, her tone striking a serious note. "If you are ready, we will come to see you now."

"Come and... see me?" he replied. The room went silent, the dialogue between them stopped. Tony looked at the door, still trying to believe he was actually going see these beings, after all this time. Filled with apprehension, he called Zephyr to his side. As the minutes went by, he tried to imagine what they'd be like, and look like! A thousand times he'd tried to imagine but could never guess. Then, he had time to think no more as a knock on the door struck three times. "Come... come in!" he said.

His heart raced as the latch clicked and the door began to open. Slowly they walked in, five of them, and Tony could not believe that which he could now see... "You're... you're human," he said in a shocked voice.

They walked into the middle of the room and stood before him; five perfectly formed, humans, two male and three female; all in their thirties and forties, he estimated. "Who, or what... are you? he asked them.

A fairly attractive, professional but kind-looking female with long dark hair stepped forward. "I am the one you call 'the voice'," she said. Holding her arm out in a gesture for them to shake hands, Tony cautiously placed his hand into hers to feel a firm and seemingly sincere grip as they shook.

He cast his eyes over to the others, their faces friendly, their expressions revealing a kind of empathy. Looking down at Zephyr, Tony could see his stance was relaxed and non-aggressive, so he knew they meant them no harm. "You and Zephyr have done well, Tony," the female went on to say.

"Done well! Measured against what?" Tony replied.

"Let me introduce ourselves properly," she answered. "My name is Victoria – I am Commander of this ship." "This is Jose – Power, Propulsion and Engineering Officer," she said, pointing to one of the males; "Dendravous, our ship's philosopher," pointing to the other male;

"Sanfona, Head of Quantum and Relative Sciences, and Andrea, our Medical Sciences Officer. And yes, we are, as you say, human." Victoria continued… "After we have spoken, taken enough time to explain matters fully, we will begin the journey that will take you home, Tony."

"No, no, no, hold it right there!" he said, putting his hand up in a blocking gesture. "This *is* my home now, and I'm staying right here."

With a look of inner sadness in her eyes, and dissent on her face, Victoria answered: "That will… not be possible."

"Don't tell me what's possible and what's not," Tony said angrily. Feeling himself getting more annoyed, he went on: "Look: you take us, me and Zephyr, from our life as it was, and against our will. Then you drop us here, where we could have died, for all you knew – but we didn't, we survived. We have a new life now, a life we've earned, and you, nearly one year later, you think your gonna take us back to Earth?"

Victoria quickly stepped in to speak before he could say any more. "But Tony, listen, listen to me 'please'… This is Earth… "What!" Tony began to reply. "But of course it's not, it's…"

"You do not yet understand, Tony," Victoria cut in again, before he could finish. "It is the Earth of ten thousand years ago…"

There was a long silence as Tony stared into her eyes, a frown on his forehead, his mouth open with a mixture of confusion and disbelief. He looked at the others, then around the room, then at the window. Turning back to look at Victoria, he finally spoke. "Huh, really?. How can that be? You're lying, you're lying to me, it's impossible. You must know that as well as I do."

"No, Tony. No, it is true, I would not lie. It is ten thousand years in the past. If the events that brought you back to us had not happened, we would have retrieved you – you now belong back in the twenty-first century… not here."

"Prove it, prove it to me," he said.

Victoria went on: "Please sit down, Tony. Sit down, everything will become clear. It is very important that you understand; understand what we… and you, have done here." Tony walked over to the window and took a deep breath. There was brief silence, then, he began to laugh, a slight snigger to begin with, building up to a laugh out loud sound that echoed round the room. As his laughter died down, he turned sharply to face them.

"Who are you people? Who are you and what do you want from me? Whatever it is, you've had all you're gonna get." As he took another deep breath, he went on. "OK, start talking," he said, pointing his finger at them.

"You might want to sit down, as I suggested, Tony. This will not be easy, or brief," replied Victoria. He reluctantly walked over to the table and took a seat.

"Won't you join me?" he said sarcastically. Victoria nodded to the others and they each approached the table, drew a chair, and sat down. "Well, this is nice," he said with an air of irony.

Victoria began: "Tony – before you hear everything we have to tell you, I speak for all of us around this table when I say that we completely understand and sympathise with your position, which you have strongly asserted. We also do not expect you to fully believe all we are about to reveal to begin with. I can only ask that hear us out, and give matters time, time for you to eventually come to terms with."

"I'm all ears," said Tony.

Victoria continued… "We are from seven hundred years in the future, from the time which you originate, that is. We are the descendants of an elite group of scientists who lived in your era. They were working in a top secret international undersea research facility, deep under what you call, the Pacific Ocean. Set up five years from when we took you, the facility was commissioned by your 'United Nations' to find answers to the world's growing ecology crisis, which by then had begun to reach critical levels."

"So important was the project, it was thought vital that there be no external influence or interventions, so the decision was taken to place the unit in the most remote location possible. They were there to develop new ways of producing energy, food and materials without further damage to the planet; they were the greatest minds of their time; physicists, geneticists, mathematicians, engineers, biologists, and even philosophers. For three years they worked, and were close to a breakthrough in all areas; each discipline produced a different hypothesis not thought possible by the conventions of the day."

"In time, theories were developed and successfully tested. They had created a whole new paradigm in science, but mixed with their excitement there came a daunting prospect; as they brought their sum total of work together, they discovered that the very science that could save the world, could also destroy it, and could be used to create the most terrible destructive weapon."

"Realising that the potential of such a thing should never leave the facility, they worked secretly for months to eliminate the possibility of this instrument of destruction ever being made, but it was too late. Enshrined in our records is the knowledge that one of their number, a male, left the facility with the enabling formulas."

"From what we know, our forefathers alerted the world's most powerful governments in an attempt to have him found, but he had already gone what you in your time would call, 'underground'. We believe he was involved with a powerful criminal organisation; it was they that provided the resources and facilities to develop the weapon, and four were made in total. Placed in strategic areas around the globe, and technically linked up to work spontaneously, the organisation held the world to ransom, demanding not only what you call money, but for their members to occupy the highest positions of all governments on Earth."

"Faced with the prospect of a corrupt and violent new world order, there was an international co-operation between all nations to track down the organisation, and find and destroy the weapons. As the world got closer, the governments called their bluff. Whether he was mentally unstable, we do not know – perhaps it was through panic and fear – but the scientist who built the devices activated the primary weapon, setting off a chain reaction to the other three across the globe."

Victoria stopped for a few moments to draw a deep breath... then continued... "There was a planet-wide destruction, the like of which man could never have imagined. The world, as you know it, was made uninhabitable; mankind, most animal life and vegetation were all wiped out in minutes. Over time, nature itself was poisoned and genetically distorted, permanently."

Tony felt cold and numb as he looked around the table. In truth, he didn't know if he even believed the tale, but it sounded pretty credible, he had to admit that to himself, and they sure didn't look like they were joking!. "Well, that sounds like the world of my time, I'll give you that," he said, in the absence of anything else say. "But this still doesn't answer my questions. If what you say *is* true, how are we here, and why?"

Victoria cut in. "Enough has been said today, Tony. We will now give you time to think on about what has been said here; and to think about the questions you need to ask. We will give you and Zephyr the rest of the day to do as you wish. We will then meet here again tomorrow at this time."

"Yes, OK, but no going anywhere. We stay here... Give me a chance to talk, properly, you owe me that!" he replied.

Victoria looked round at the others, then back at Tony. "Very well, we agree, that is our word, it is done. We will continue tomorrow."

Tony watched as they all passed back through the door. Victoria was the last out; as she glanced back, she gave him a sad, meaningful look, before slowly closing up behind her.

Tony exhaled a long breath before sitting back at the table. "Did I really hear all that?" he said to himself, still stunned and in disbelief at what he'd been told. Staring blankly at the back wall of his room, he quickly snapped himself out of it and flicked his head round to Zephyr – by the look on his face, Tony could swear he'd understood everything that had been said! He slowly walked over to Tony and placed his head over his leg. At that moment, Tony threw his arms around him. Thinking about the world being destroyed made him realise even more how lucky they were to be here, and have the love, trust and companionship of each other.

"The park!" Tony suddenly thought. "Come on, Zeph."

Again, he felt a stark difference between the synthetic corridors of the ship, and the natural environment they'd grown so accustomed to. As they got to the entrance, he remembered to place his hand on the wall. "All working as well as ever, boy," he said to Zephyr as the doors opened and they once again walked onto the grass. "Same old smell like we're in a tent over grass. Still, it'll do for now," he thought. It was good to see Zephyr bouncing around as usual and as though none of this had ever happened. Hearing the birds were still in the trees, Tony

171

looked up, remembering the first time he'd done that. Only nearly a year, but almost a lifetime ago it seemed now. "Guess that's part of the concept of time," he said with a hint of irony after what he'd just been told. Not able to even remotely bring himself believe any of this, he wondered; wondered who these people really were, and what in God's name this was all about. After going a couple of laps around the park, he realised how much he was already missing the outside, the smell of fresh air, the feel of natural earth and rocks beneath his feet. His thoughts then turned to Julie, who he was missing most of all, then of Alpha and Omega.

"Hope you boys are behaving while I'm gone," he said with a wry smile. But he knew he had some serious thinking to do; knew he had to consider everything he wanted to ask these strangers on the ship; knew he needed to argue his case, the case that he should be left here to stay; and knew he'd got just twenty four hours to get his answers.

When they returned to their accommodation, Tony cooked off a couple of fish for them and made himself a strong tea – the one thing he had missed – then, going over to the drawer where he'd kept his natural science study materials, he pulled out a pad and pen, sat back at the table, and began to write...

As dusk fell and the red glow of the sun came through the window, he'd all but done. Over and over, he went back through the words he'd written, rehearsing every line he would relate to, and argue with them. It was a beautiful evening; he and Zephyr walked over to the window. "My god, did man finally wipe himself out?" he said to himself. And if this *was* Earth, where in the world was this place, he thought, or where *would* it be in the future? Then, now, what difference did it make; it was here and now, and it was home to him.

Deciding that he'd do no more for the rest of the night and start with a fresh mind in the morning, "Come on boy, let's take another walk," he said. Up the long corridor they went, until they reached the place he was sure was the entrance of the ship. He stood and thought; thought that if they didn't agree he could stay, the only other option was to try to escape before the ship took off!

He stared at the door, looking for any weakness in its structure. He could see almost nothing, except for a paper-thin slit at the edge where it met the wall. He figured this might be the break he was looking for; if he could force something in there, like a thin knife, it could trigger the opening mechanism. The outer door would probably be much more difficult, but this was at least something to go on, and where there was hope there was a chance, he'd always believed. After all, when they built this ship the last thing they'd have thought of was the security to keep anyone in!

As he smiled to himself, he suddenly remembered that they could be being watched. He looked up at the ceiling and then behind him, trying to give the impression they were lost. Remembering that they would have passed the gym and pool area on their way there, they headed back in an attempt to make it look like that was what they'd been looking for all the time. Tony took a dip in the pool before they returned to their accommodation for the night. Knowing he needed to be at his sharpest the next day, they bedded down soon after they'd eaten, again sleeping on the floor.

They woke well before sunrise. Tony went to the window and looked up at the star-spangled sky, the realisation dawning on him that if this was the Earth of the past, the zero light pollution would account for the thousands of stars that were now so visible to him, but could never have been seen with the naked eye in his time. But there were more things to think about than this right now. He got dressed, slooshed his face in the bathroom, then sat in front of his notes... and waited.

"Come in," Tony said as a knock finally came at the door. Walking into the room, they each looked daunted by the prospect of this meeting. "This could be a good sign. Maybe I've spotted a weakness in them," he thought to himself. Deciding to stay poker-faced, he believed this could be the vantage point he was hoping for. From his life experiences and legal training, he knew that having the upper hand at the start of any argument was always best.

Standing up as they approached the table, he held out his hand and gestured for them to sit down. As they all took their place around the table, Victoria sat just to the right of him. "You have many questions, Tony," she said with a nod and a discreet, almost nervous smile.

"Yes," he replied. "I'll start with the most obvious. You say your ancestors were a group of scientists who lived in my time, when the world was destroyed – how can it be? If that cataclysmic event did ever happen, they'd never have survived it, not any more than anything else, and no more than I believe your story. The technology you possess didn't come from any broken planet either, did it? You can't be who you say you are, so tell me! Tell me who and what you really are."

"Your doubts are understandable, Tony, but they are not well-founded," Victoria said. She continued: "Those men and women we originate from were still in the facility, still deep below the ocean when the 'event', as you call it, occurred. They knew that if the worst happened it was the only place where they would have a chance of survival. Although in time the surface of the seas and oceans became just as toxic as the land, the depths remained, fortunately, largely unaffected. Using their considerable knowledge and skills, they were able to build on and further develop their scientific discoveries. They put all the theories and tests which they had originally been tasked to work on into practice, synthesising the vast range of foods they already had, and creating an almost inexhaustible source of energy, as well as oxygen."

"They were many in number, around fifty in total; in time they increased their number by breeding. As their children grew, they passed on their knowledge, training the next generation to continue and build on the scientific and technical achievements they had so brilliantly brought into being. What started out as a research team became a community; over time, they used their skills to expand the facility; by the time the original team had died out, there existed another three generations. A whole new society had been born, with its own laws, rules and protocols. In the years that followed, the facility continued to be built on, becoming many times its original size, and we, seven hundred years later, are the product of it."

Tony sat speechless for a while. Hardly knowing what to say, he eventually retorted with a short quip: "Well, why didn't you just say so?" Seeing that his humour was lost on them, he continued. "It must have been difficult; never knowing the outside, and never knowing the pleasure and infinite wonder of true nature, to have the freedom to roam a natural world."

"This must have been so for the first generation who had known the Earth as it was, and the memory of what life was like still ran strong through the earlier generations. But we, and many generations before us, were born into what we have. We had never known your world before our journeys brought us back to your time," replied Victoria.

"And that brings me to my next question: this ship, time travel, how?" Tony said as he looked around the table.

As Victoria began to speak, she held the palm of her hand out to the others. "Before I hand over to my fellow officers to explain the basis of their expertise, I will finish by outlining why the ship came into being, and our reasons for embarking on that which we felt so necessary. Around four hundred years ago, our forebears built a craft to take them to the surface. Heavily clad in highly protective equipment, they walked the Earth, the first humans to do so in over three hundred years. What they saw and recorded had a lasting impact on 'them' and the generations which followed; three hundred years had not mitigated the extent of global devastation and poisoning."

"Incredibly, some animal and plant life did still exist, but these were horribly distorted mutations of nature, with any sentient life living in agony, only to die in the toxic environment long before their time. After witnessing this, they made a decision which they thought would make the community's existence worthwhile, to give hope and purpose to all future generations. From that time onwards, they embarked on the project of interstellar space travel, to reach out to far distances in an attempt to find a new inhabitable world." Victoria stopped there... "I will now hand you over to my officers. Jose, please continue."

A semi-bald man with a neatly trimmed beard, Tony thought he looked like a man who really enjoyed his work. Jose stood up, leaned over the table and held out his arm; Tony did the same and they shook hands. "Good to finally meet, Tony," Jose said as he sat back down and began to explain in basic terms the nature of the ship, and the principles on which it was based.

"This ship is the third to be built in the last four centuries. Our science, first conceived by those people from your time, as Victoria has explained, turns on a completely different axis to those which you will be familiar with. Rather than forging things from nature, turning differing forms of matter into energy only to convert these into unwanted by-products, which is the big problem of the day in your era, those scientists developed a way to achieve a one hundred percent efficient ratio, to harness and work *with nature* to create forces infinitely more powerful."

"It was a revelation; a means of producing almost limitless power and resources; a means to re-create and duplicate substances from creation, apart from sentient life itself, that is, all completely naturally, with no waste, no pollution, and no distortion of the integral order of the elements. It would have saved your world from all its problems of ecology, poverty and starvation."

"Wait! Wait just a minute!" Tony said. "I think 'could' is the operative word here, and a very big 'could' at that. You forget greed, the lust for power, and fear of not having it. It wouldn't have solved *those* problems, and if all I've heard is true, it didn't."

Jose looked around the table as his colleagues all gave a saddening nod. "Yes. Point taken," he replied. "And now, if I may continue... Our ancestors took these sciences to explore the idea of adapting them to the forces of the universe itself, initially by sending probes into orbit around the planet. Finding the same principles were compatible, they began their endeavours to build the first ship. The materials were produced to work with the known forces of the cosmos, the logic being that, instead of trying to resist the cosmic elements, the ship is able to use them to produce a powerful protective force field as it is propelled at speeds which far exceed the speed of light."

"How do you do that? How do you travel faster than light? We've been out there, out there in deep space. I've seen it, so at least I know *that* to be true," Tony said.

Jose paused for a moment and took a deep breath as he once again looked around the table. Casting his eye at them all for a moment, Tony noticed something – they were all starting to look tired, fatigued.

"There has been much said, and there is much more to be said. I would suggest we leave you to catch up with your thoughts for a while, Tony. We will return in four hours; do as you wish in the meantime. We will see you back here."

"Four hours," Victoria told them all as she ended the meeting.

"OK," Tony said with a hint of confusion in his voice. As they left the room, he stood up, went over to the kitchen and drew out a couple of fish from the fridge for him and Zephyr. "OK, we'll eat and then go to the park, boy," he said as he expertly topped and tailed the fish and began to cook them.

Later on, as they were taking their walk in the park area, everything he'd heard that morning lay heavily on his mind. He was finding it difficult to grasp the reality of everything they'd told him, and in any case, the fact was he still didn't trust these people. He sat down on the grass next to Zephyr and began to think; to think about the horrors he'd been told only an hour ago. "Was Earth really destroyed only a few years from when I'd left it?" he thought to himself. "Are these people really who they say they are? And if they are, then how are us *and* them now both here, occupying the same time, a time they say is ten thousand years before I was even born? Ha, you could go crazy Just thinking about it." Although he now felt almost caught between reality and fantasy, he knew there were two things, two things about their whole terrible account of the future that he could not deny; the existence of these people – these seemingly human beings – and the existence of this ship.

Walking back to their accommodation, Tony started to think about Alpha and Omega, and that he'd always thought of them as being part of an alien race on a new world, but if everything *were* true, all this time they've been ancient humans. But the most important question on his mind was Julie: "What had they really done to her?" he thought. Whatever it was, and why, he wanted to get to the truth on that as much as anything else. "Well, here we go, round two," he said to Zephyr as they walked through the door and back into the room.

Ten minutes passed before Victoria and the others returned; Tony couldn't help but notice they all looked rejuvenated in a strange way. As they sat down, Victoria immediately asked Jose to continue where he'd left off. "So I will now approach the subject of propulsion," he started by saying. Tony waited in anticipation, his mind completely focused on everything Jose was about to say. This was really interesting stuff for him; since a child he'd been fascinated by science fiction and space travel, but now the ever-increasing realisation that this was scientific fact had him on the edge of his seat.

Jose began: I am sure you remember seeing the entity which powers our ship, Tony. I call it an entity because, in many ways, it is alive. Fashioned by us, it has an existence of its own, in the same sense as an atom or an electron does. Fuelled by the high-energy protons and ions which exist in space, it has an almost limitless source of energy. It can generate an endless amount of natural power, which is not only safe, but even has many beneficial properties to organic life. I am sure you experienced the effects of that on your visit to the power chamber that day."

"Yes… yes I did. We remember well," Tony said as he looked over at Zephyr with a discreet smile.

Jose went on: "This also explains one of the most fundamental concepts on which our science is based, but we needed to adapt those principles in order to tap into the colossal source of energy out there in space. It was not easy; it took our ancestors more than one hundred years to develop and build the first ship. The first space exploration was launched nearly three hundred years ago. Taking into account Einstein's theory, those men and woman of the first crew knew there would be a significant time difference between their time on board and that which they had left behind on Earth."

"Where did they go? I mean, where did they look? How did they even know where to look?" Tony said with an air of scepticism.

"Our facility has data banks and archives, from the early days before Earth was destroyed," Jose continued. "They contained almost the sum total of human knowledge as it was then; this included star charts and detailed maps of our galaxy. From these, with the use of our powerful quantum computers, they were able to calculate and detect the stars in our quarter of the galaxy which have Earth-like planets of the right size, including those which orbit their sun at the right distance, which would have a chance of supporting complex organic life."

Jose continued to lay out the history of their explorations. "The first test flight was successful, travelling to our nearest star, Alpha Centauri, just over four light-years from our solar system. The outward journey took just over six weeks' duration. Arriving back at the facility just over three months later, in their time, but almost two years had passed on Earth; Einstein's theory had truly been proven."

"In the two centuries that followed, many voyages were completed. Another ship was eventually built and our exploration of the galaxy had doubled. Reaching ever-further distant stars and taking many months, time periods of ten to fifteen years would pass on Earth between the departure and return of the ships. But although most of the planets which were detected by our computers had been located and reached, for a diverse number of reasons each one had proved to be uninhabitable to us."

"Did they find any life though, on those planets? Was there life?" Tony asked.

"Yes, yes, they found life," Jose replied with an understanding smile, but the smile left his face as he went on to say that none of them seemed to contain any complex sentient life, the highest life form being vegetation, the lowest just single-celled organisms. "Maybe these were the beginnings of life on those planets, but nevertheless, there was… life." As he continued, he went on to tell of how they'd discovered something else which was to take them in a completely different direction, and give them a new hope for the future. "It was the purpose that gave rise to the building of this ship. I will now, though, hand over to Sanfona," Jose ended by saying.

As he glanced over at her, Tony thought Sanfona looked like a very ordinary middle-aged person. With a wavy hairstyle and a strangely old-fashioned quality to her face, she seemed like someone who belonged more in the 1950s, rather than a quantum scientist from the future. But as she began to speak, he could almost feel the depth of her intellect and the understanding of the subject. "Over a century ago now, as our journeys to the stars were coming to an end, our final explorations took us to an area near to the closest black hole of our quarter of the galaxy. You remember the black hole, Tony?"

"How could I forget?" he replied.

She continued: "This was when some of our crews of that time began to experience certain anomalies, anomalies in space time. When the first of these happened, the homeward-bound ship arrived back at Earth several weeks before it was due, and nearly a year by Earth time. You have heard of wormholes?" Sanfona asked knowingly as she looked him in the eye. Tony nodded. "It appeared the crew had travelled through an Einstein-Rosen bridge, a corridor, a shortcut through space and time, if you will," she said as she continued to explain.

"Beyond our scientific knowledge at the time, this was the only conclusion we could come to. We had no proof, but the same phenomenon continued with varying outcomes on subsequent voyages as our ships passed back through the same area. We began to investigate, and many exploratory expeditions were sent out. In over a century of research, we still do not know how the phenomena occur, but we do know they only develop in the region of the black hole. We did though go on to discover the existence of negative particle masses, which are produced and thrown out by the singularity. We were then able to detect certain fluctuations between these particles and the natural positive particles which exist in normal space; once we had established this, we went on to trace and locate several wormholes around the vast area."

"After many years of studying these phenomena, our understanding of their nature increased. We discovered the wormholes to have a dormant end, the point from which they emanate; and a transient end, the point which travels outwardly at nearly the speed of light. Depending on the distance travelled, the two ends become separated by many years of real time. By entering through the transient end, it is possible to pass through the corridor in no more than a few instants; technically, you come through the dormant end of the wormhole at an earlier time than which you entered it."

"Time travel; my god, you did it. You really did discover a way of travelling back through time," Tony said as he cut in.

Sanfona went on: "Albert Einstein's genius continues to astound us to this day. We have now been able to test every part of his theory of general relativity; it all works perfectly, except around the area of the edge of black holes – the event horizon. There, for reasons which are still unknown to us, the science changes, works differently. In order for us to actually be able to utilise a wormhole as a means of transport, to adjust, manipulate and expand the wormholes to travel back through a specific time period, it was necessary for us to apply quantum mechanics. To do this, we needed to solve the age-old problem of making quantum science compatible with general relativity – 'the string theory'."

"More than ten years had passed and we had not managed to do this, but then, almost by accident, as the science team were working on an area of relativity, they found an answer to one problem. Everything else fell into place like the cogs of a wheel; just one formula of Einstein's hypothesis and subsequent theory had shown us the way. It was so simple, and to a scientist... so beautiful."

"Realising the importance and possibilities of this new-found capability, the generations of the time knew there needed to be much serious thinking and debate. Decisions needed to be made, decisions of such magnitude that they knew could alter the whole future course of the Earth, and even more importantly... the past."

"'If I see further than other men it's because I have stood on the shoulders of giants', as the saying goes," Tony said as he interrupted. "I know where this is going." He felt cold as an air of silence now filled the room. "For all your intellect, massively advanced technology and skills, you stood on the shoulders of Einstein and thought you could damn near see everything, but what the hell have you done? What have you done here? Do you know the consequences? Do you!"

Victoria stepped in again. "We have much more to explain, Tony. I say again that it is very important to us that you know everything, and have a full understanding, before you judge us. It is getting late now and we tire; will you hear us again tomorrow?" Tony nodded in agreement. As much as he wanted to get off the ship and back to where he belonged, he knew he couldn't leave it there. He knew he still had many questions, of which he wanted answers, and knew he now had an even better chance to argue his case to stay – and for them to leave him be. He could see for himself that they looked fatigued again, and he wondered why. Staying silent and in his chair, he watched as they once again left the room.

Looking round at Zephyr, who'd been sitting there beside him the whole time, Tony was struck by the knowing look in his eyes as they met his; it was somehow all-knowing, profound and beyond his understanding. He placed his hand on Zephyr's head. "What do you know, boy, huh? What do you know that the rest of us don't?" he said with a wry smile. "Come on, let's get out of here." It was now early evening and Tony felt like he needed to clear his head. The realisation that all they had said was possibly true now hung over him like a shadow, his only distraction being that he had to take Zephyr to the park.

After they'd walked around a couple of times, they went to the gym and pool area; Tony swam a few lengths and tried to forget it all for a while. When they got back to the accommodation, he felt as though he was on autopilot as he cooked off another couple of fish for them. He'd started to wear his watch again and a glance told him it was nearly midnight; with a daunting feeling of uneasiness as they bedded down, he did not sleep well that night.

The next morning, as a bright stream of sunlight hit his face, aside from feeling pretty ropey Tony woke with a sense of hope and determination. "Well, Zeph, another new day, for now at least. Let's get ready for our 'guests' and argue the case with our usual vigour." After he'd showered and done breakfast for them, he took his seat and cast his eye back over his notes, re-writing some of them in the light of what he now knew.

When a knock at the door told him they'd arrived, this time he got up, went to the door and ushered them over to the seating area. "Well, you've talked, I've listened, and yes, I've understood, but now, now it's my turn. Questions I have, answers I need," he said as they all sat.

"That is fair, Tony. We understand – go ahead. You now know enough to ask your questions; we will listen, we will answer," Victoria told him.

"I see now what you've done, or tried to do; turn back the clock, change history to alter the future. I know why, God knows if all you've told me is true, I know why," Tony continued. "But how... how can you know what you're doing, or whatever it is you *think* you've done here will change anything, let alone even make things worse? And there's a moral question, a question even beyond anything you've told me so far; I assume you know of the grandfather paradox, the butterfly effect! You, me, what we've done here might have altered, or even wiped out the existence of future generations of people in the thousands of years to come, including yours, mine and anyone else we've ever known. You don't know what you've done, you can't! And then you might not even have stopped what eventually happened to Earth anyway."

"It is not like that, Tony. It is not like that," Victoria said as she slowly shook her head before continuing. "Because of the events which led to the devastation of our world, and since our society was formed, it has been our primary law to do no harm. All our protocols are based around this. We would neither ask for nor deprive anyone of that which is theirs, let alone a life, 'unless absolutely necessary', the one exception being that which is for the good of the macro. This is the maxim of our laws and principles; in other words, the good of 'all' of life or existence, and the environment by which these are supported. Our scientists and philosophers considered, worked on and finally tested theories before we even embarked on what we had set out to do. I will now handover to Dendravous, our philosopher, to speak in more detail."

A serious looking man with a mop of dark hair and short, trimmed beard, he cleared his throat before he spoke. "Well, Tony. Yes, we are fully aware of the train of thought which concludes with the butterfly effect, by which a wisp of air from the flap of a delicate wing in the present can ripple through time to create a tidal wave of events over the centuries," he said as he looked at Tony with an understanding expression to his face. "It is for this reason that for over ten years we have carried out meticulous trials, using countless scenarios to prove our theories, so that we could be sure, absolutely certain of the cause and effect of everything we did."

"How did you manage that? Unless you'd done before what you have done here, you couldn't know!" Tony cut in.

"You are aware of the Large Hadron Collider, which exists in 'your' time," Dendravous replied as he continued. "With science and equipment infinitely more complex and advanced, housed in a colossal chamber built onto our facility below the ocean we were able to carry out laboratory experiments. We were eventually able to create, in some small and basic way, the synthetic qualities and conditions to that of a wormhole."

"With a limited period of less than one day, we sent subjects back in time; inanimate objects to begin with, then plant life, and finally, when we knew it was safe, members of our community. After thousands of exhaustive trials, our experiments were finally proven. Although beyond our knowledge of how, or why, we were able to determine beyond doubt that, regardless of any disruption or interference, time itself is able to correct any anomaly, just as though it has its own purpose. In other words, an action or event which would, or has already happened, *still* happens."

"Put in the most simple terms, it is as though you are walking along a pathway, from one point to another for instance. When you have completed this, you walk back to the starting point and begin again. This time, something pushes you from the path, but you regain your balance, and continue to complete the same course. Regardless of the scenario, this happened every time we tried to alter an event, except when – and this is the most crucial point –the subject matter, the focal point, or the thing from which the specific event emanates, is taken away. Only then does history 'not' repeat itself. You see, Tony, we found that it is possible to pinpoint, with absolute accuracy, that which you change, and that which you do not."

"How the hell can you can be so sure? My god, these were experiments, experiments in controlled conditions. This is real life for God's sake – there are millions of possibilities and permutations," Tony said as he looked Dendravous in the eye.

"I know it is not easy to accept, but I have said all I can," he replied.

"So what do you think you've done here? Why ten thousand years in the past, and what am I here for? I finally want answers to all this, so start talking," Tony said as he looked around the table. Victoria took a long, deep breath before she began to speak.

"This ship, on which construction began before my crew and I were born, was designed and built to do all that has been explained to you. From our early years, each of us around this table was selected for this mission. Five years ago, we carried out our first test flight. Being the first time, and knowing the great risk we faced by having to encounter the black hole directly at the event horizon, we parted from our loved ones, our families, as though it would be for the last time. Fortunately it was not: all our theories, calculations and technology worked perfectly. As planned, we were able to utilise the awesome energy of the black hole to break free from it, then, and most importantly, to manipulate the size of a wormhole to take us back to a specific point in time, by two years on that first experimental flight."

"To prove we had been successful, we set our speed and travel course in order for two more years to pass in Earth time than would normally have done on that journey. Our calculations were almost perfect; allowing for every time differential, we arrived back on Earth at the same time we would have done on a normal journey to and from the black hole. We had proven the science by real application."

"Question: why do you need to do that? I mean.... go right to the edge of the black hole?" Tony asked.

She continued: "Put basically, our early experiments revealed a form of energy, a dense proton mix which only exists at the inner rim of the horizon. These are essential elements for our interaction with a wormhole; they are absorbed into our propulsion entity, but this can only be done by flying directly into where these elements exist."

"Having completed the test flight, we went on to carry out a series of subsequent successful flights, then, able to proceed to the next stage, we set our calculations to travel back to your time, to the time before Earth was destroyed. When we arrived... to see the world as it was, for us it was a revelation. We had seen all the footage from our archives, seen how our planet once was, but had never imagined such beauty. The smell, the feel, you have been lucky, Tony, lucky to have grown up when you did."

"Yes, yes I have. But what did you do back there?" Tony asked.

"Our initiative was to find the man from the original science team, the man who stole the formulas. We placed ourselves into wide orbit around the planet, where we remained undetectable. For us, tapping into your information technology was simple; we already knew his name and where he came from; he was not hard to find."

"So surely all you really needed to do was kill him? When you found him I mean – right at that point in time, so he was no longer able to do what he did," Tony said.

"No, no, there is much more to it than this," Victoria replied. "Before I hand back to Dendravous, I should say that when we found this man it was necessary that we track his movements and find out more about his background, his associations, his motivations. I have much more to say, but will continue after Dendravous has spoken."

"What was his name anyway, this man?" Tony asked.

Victoria nodded to Dendravous and he began to speak. "His name was... Enrico... Enrico de Silva. A scientist in the field of electrochemistry, nearly twenty years had not seen he or his work advance. This could have been his chance, an opportunity to progress when he was asked to join the undersea project as a junior member. Although a hard-working assistant to the senior members, reports in our archives tell us that he eventually revealed himself to have a flawed character, harbouring a grudge for the years his work he felt had gone unrewarded. The team began to notice that he had been working in secret on projects for his own benefit, and so realised the dangers in having him as a team member."

"By the time he was finally expelled from the facility, he had already become aware of the processes and formulas which could pervert the new science into an instrument of destruction. From the time we had traced him, our surveillance revealed that, long before becoming a member of the facility, he had been associated with a powerful and violent organisation. A family member to some of their hierarchy, they would eventually come to harbour him, and fund the building of those terrible devices."

"So my question again: why did you not kill him?" Tony repeated as he interrupted.

"As Victoria has already indicated, there are far more factors to the situation than just that," Dendravous replied as he continued to explain. "The organisation, of which this man was only a part, were constantly looking, waiting for the opportunity to change the world order in their favour. Having learned of the project through De Silva, this was something they had long since hoped for. The events which occurred were all pre-planned; if we had killed him, we knew there were others to take his place. Our philosophy concluded that the event, in one way or another, would still have eventually taken place; as in our experiments, time would have corrected itself."

"It was not possible to take away the point of emanation in the twenty-first century – it was already too late. The organisation had been run by a particularly long line of kinship. Little known until the latter part of the twentieth century, and then only to a certain few of the world's governmental authorities, it had been the hub of many corrupt regimes and other powerful criminal organisations. Their genetic bloodline had run strong through the centuries. We were able to trace this line back to when records began, so we finally needed to make several more journeys back through time."

"The further we travelled back, the stronger the bloodline became at times, always following the same pattern of subversiveness; never any of the great figures through history, but always there, always the purveyors of crime and disruption, always waiting for the chance to emerge. We needed to continue still further to find the true genetic origin; eventually we were led here, to this time, at the dawn of human civilisation, the true point... of emanation."

After a few moments of silence, Tony got up from his chair. His eyes in a fixed stare, he slowly walked over to the window. Looking out onto the landscape, "Where are we anyway? Where are we in the world?" he said, before turning back to look at them.

Victoria stood up to reply. "We are in the country you know as Ecuador, on the continent of South America."

"I see," said Tony as he walked back to the table. "You're all crazy: you know that, don't you?" he said as he continued on. "What you call the point of emanation; that was the man I killed, wasn't it?"

Victoria nodded. "Yes, yes, Tony. It was the one you called 'the leader'," she replied.

"And yes, as I believe you had realised, he was some kind of physical – and to some extent intellectual – advancement for the time. We do not know how, or why, but it is so," Dendravous said as he interjected.

"So you brought me all the way back here just to be your surrogate assassin? This just doesn't make sense," Tony replied as he went on. "Again, if you wanted to kill him, why did you not do this yourselves? And... and how do you know I called him 'the leader', and know my thoughts about what he was?"

"All of this will be explained," Victoria said before she continued. She looked around the table at her fellow officers for a few brief moments. Nothing was said; there was just a shared expression of agreement between them before she looked back at Tony.

"We could not have done that which you have," she began. "There were many more factors to consider. It was not just 'he' who was the point of emanation, it was also that which he had created and presided over; his community and his loyal followers were almost as important. Had he just been anonymously killed, disappeared, he would have left a legacy, and with nothing to replace it, that legacy would have continued. His followers, some of who were the same bloodline, would have carried his regime forwards. His legend would have grown in the minds of those followers and been passed on to future generations not yet born. He would have eventually become even stronger than ever."

"But what have I done any differently than you would have?" Tony interrupted.

"Seven hundred years have taken their toll on our breed, Tony," Victoria replied. "For all we can do, for all the environments, food, water and all else we can manufacture, they are no substitute for nature, no substitute for living in the natural world from which our life on Earth evolved, be it for all the pains and the dangers. Though our intellect has grown, equally our bodies have grown weak. We lack immunity and have lost most of our natural resistance to disease. When we arrived in your time, we needed to immunise ourselves to almost dangerous levels, but even then this does not last; only around eight hours could we spend in the beauty of your era before it would kill us."

"But, I've seen what you can you do, what you did for Zephyr, for which, whatever happens, I will be eternally in your debt. So surely you can correct your deficiencies?" Tony said. Just then, Andrea, the one who Victoria had introduced as the Medical Officer, spoke.

"We can cure, regenerate and repair almost any medical problem in that which exists Tony, but we can do nothing for that which does not – we are not God." She continued: "Had we known what was to happen so suddenly, and without warning, we might have been able to act and reverse the process. With some of the first generation being born with these deficiencies during the last century, only then did we discover the strength of our genes had begun to diminish at an ever-increasing rate. In the last fifty years, we have found it ever more difficult to pro-create.

The building of this ship, the success of this mission, is all we continue for; we ourselves... are dying."

"But what about your hopes for the future? The hopes you told me about? Surely you've not done all you have done, for nothing?" Tony said as he looked at them all.

"There are many crew members, and other inhabitants which are now aboard this ship, but we are all that is left of our society. Those hopes are now for the future of our planet, nature and all of the life we hope will live in it, not... us."

There was an ensuing momentary silence. "I don't know what to say. I don't know what I can say to you. I'm sorry," Tony replied.

"It is a fact we have come to accept. We try to make the most of our remaining lives, though that is through our work, mainly," Andrea replied.

Feeling that he wanted to change the subject at that point, Tony thought this a good time to ask about Julie. "The female, the one I call 'Julie' – you changed her?" Tony asked.

"We enhanced her," Andrea went on to tell him. "We enhanced that which was already there. What would have eventually emerged through generations of her line, we accelerated in a matter of hours, albeit a gradual development to final completion. I am sure you noticed."

"But why?" Tony asked.

"Victoria must now continue," she said.

Seeing they were once more looking tired, and now knowing why, "Would you like to break for an hour?" Tony asked them.

Victoria nodded with a slight smile of acknowledgement. As they got up to walk to the door, "One hour," she said, looking back round at him.

Although by now he did feel some sympathy for them, he also felt like he needed some time to himself, time to think. The full knowledge of them and what this was really all about, although devastating in its magnitude, had given him an even better platform for his final argument, he thought. It was the only glimmer of light he was able to see in this dark tunnel, but he also wanted a back-up plan.

Standing up to stretch his legs, he began to pace around the room a few times. Zephyr looked at him as though he'd gone crazy and Tony started to laugh, eventually to the point that he had to sit back down. "Boy, what would I do without you in these moments of darkness?" he said as his laughter subsided. He only had another twenty minutes, by now, so he had to think fast.

Walking over and opening one of the kitchen drawers, he pulled out a six-inch sharp kitchen knife. "This has gotta be the only alternative to get off this ship," he thought to himself. As much as he didn't like the idea of doing it, knowing they were weak, he also knew it was getting close to zero hour, and desperate situations call for desperate measures, he thought. So, failing all else, if they didn't see it his way he'd hold one of the males hostage. "They'll let me go then – a knife to the throat will always do it!" he said to himself. He actually had no intention of killing any one of them in cold blood, but they wouldn't know that, he also thought as he tucked the knife handle down the back of his jeans.

One hour to the minute had passed and a quick knock saw them come back through the door, all appearing refreshed as they sat down. Looking directly at him, Victoria began to speak. "Once we knew this was our final destination, we travelled back to your time in an attempt to find the right subject."

"Hold on, 'right subject'? I take it you mean person!" Tony interrupted.

"Yes, the person we would finally bring back with us," Victoria replied as she continued. "We scoured all of Earth's information databases, everything they held on every recorded member of the population. There were several of you spread throughout the world, several who were mentally and physically suitable." Tony began to feel himself getting pretty annoyed at the thought of having been looked on as some kind of experiment in a lab, but was compelled to hear all she had to say. He held his tongue and listened as she went on.

"Finally, you were chosen. The main and overriding reason for our decision was essentially because… you were completely alone. Aside from Zephyr, who we know to be just as important to you as any family member could ever be, you were entirely without any close human associations: no one who would miss you, even for a short time period, and in turn, no one you would miss or feel any conscience or loyalties towards. We also knew that Zephyr would be every bit the valuable asset that he has been to you. He is highly impressive; we are all very fond of him; you are right to think of him as you do. It is beyond our comprehension too, but he does have extraordinary qualities." Her face wore a curious smile as she looked at him.

"So we were all pretty convenient for you then!" Tony said sarcastically with an anger in his voice.

"Believe me when I say that this is as difficult for us to tell as it is for you to hear, Tony. We are not without conscience, but we owe you the truth at least," Victoria replied with a hint of frustration. "So, for the answer to the question we know has been on your mind since first you were on the ship – 'How we know so much about you?' – long before that day you first stepped aboard…

"The day we were captured, held against our will, you mean. Let's get it right!" Tony interrupted.

Victoria took another deep breath before she continued: "… we had probed your uppermost thoughts, your emotions, what you cared about, your likes and your dislikes. We had to be absolutely certain you were psychologically suitable and capable in every way of doing what we hoped you would do; all that you *have* done."

"All you set me up to do, you mean," Tony retorted.

"No, no, not like that," Victoria quickly replied. "It is true we set the stage, but all else you have done here has happened entirely naturally – it had to. This was the big risk we had to take, and rely on."

"Tell me, though, how did you do it, without me even knowing, probe my thoughts and whatever else?" Tony asked.

"The closest thing I can relate to you are what you would call drones," Victoria continued. "Completely silent, so small they are almost invisible to the naked eye. We have been able to remotely see, hear and track you wherever you have been. For months, we placed them into where you live, your car and your place of work. Except for respecting your privacy and your innermost thoughts, we knew nearly all there was to know about you and your life. We have, as you most probably realise by now, tracked you at every stage of your time spent here."

"You say you set the stage for what you hoped would happen –

how?" Tony asked.

"The female, the one you call Julie," Victoria replied. "At the right time, we brought her here, to the ship. Knowing that you would not rest until you knew all that was out there, we waited until just before you had discovered her community. Having already found she was a suitable subject... 'person' when we were first here, we studied her in the same way as we were to eventually study you. She appeared to have particularly advanced thought patterns for the era, and a deep love and appreciation for nature."

"Not feeling as though she really belonged, she would go walking outside the community by herself at roughly the same time each day. Our drones administered a mild sleeping formula into her system; using an obscured shuttle we retrieved her, brought her here. She regained consciousness for a short time, after the course of enhancements. Frightened to begin with, we made her feel at ease; she adjusted well to our environment. I assure you she was not harmed or mistreated in any way."

"What did you do with her, after that?" Tony asked.

At that point, Victoria indicated for Dendravous to continue. He began by explaining how they'd lightly tranquilized her, and taken her back in the shuttle to the outer edge of the community, waking her just before they left. "We did this at the exact time you were about to enter her community that day. Realising she was now different to her fellow members, the fear of this made them hostile, which is why they were chasing her out, and that is where you stepped in – it had worked. This was all we needed to do; everything from that point was entirely in your hands."

"So why was this so important? That we met that day, I mean," Tony interrupted.

Dendravous continued: "The female was the catalyst that began the whole process, the start of everything which was to unfold. We knew from your sense of morality and fairness that you would offer her protection and safe harbour; the fact she appeared different to the others, more like you than they, would give you a sense of kindred association. She had family who would search for her."

"The ones you have called Alpha and Omega are closely related;

after they had found her you began to organise and create order; we were sure they would communicate with other members from their community. Wanting to escape for good reason, those others would follow. We knew you had the skills needed to build a new community, which you surely did. We also knew, as did you, that this would create conflict with their place of origin, and most importantly, with the leader."

"Yes, OK I've got it," Tony said as he cut in. "You knew; you knew everything I knew could happen, and you knew me well enough to know that it *would* happen. So, cut to the future, what happens from now?" Tony ended by saying.

But Dendravous went on: "The community which you did not even set out to create will continue. Knowing the leader died in the way he did, his legacy will die with him. Many more from the original community will defect, and the new community will diminish the original in favour of its own matrix. The ultimate power of social cohesion will establish new values and principles, built on those which you instilled in Alpha and Omega. The point of emanation will have been completely removed, and, just as importantly, there will be a new and productive society, with no room for the culture of the old regime... to re-emerge."

"I feel like I ought to kill you all right now; for what you've done; for what you did to Julie; for playing with my life. As Andrea said, you're not God. Did it ever occur to you that you shouldn't try 'playing God'?" Tony said as he pointed at them all around the table.

"Let us remember why we have done this, Tony," Victoria replied determinedly as she continued. "We know of your love for nature and the importance of it, and your love for animals and wildlife – we have hopefully saved it."

"I can't argue with that, it's the only thing that makes sense in this whole crazy story, this whole insane situation," Tony answered. "But have you saved it? For all you say, you still don't know, you can't know absolutely what could still happen. I mean, just look at what *did* happen: man finally found a way to solve almost all of Earth's problems, and some maniac found a way to destroy it with the same thing that was supposed to save it!" he finished by saying.

"Of course we don't really know might happen in the future, Tony, but we do know we have stopped that which did happen; we have given the future a chance at least," Dendravous said.

"OK, OK, I've listened; I've heard you out. Now hear me out," Tony told them. "If it is true that I've played an essential part in all of this, then let us agree that I stay here, you owe me that, I can"..

"Out of the question, Tony," Victoria interrupted before he could finish. "It is too dangerous. You will advance the community too far for this time, you will cause an imbalance of history, and this will disrupt the timeline. We must now leave things the way they are, and let the future and integral events within it unfold, naturally."

"Like you have, you mean!" he answered angrily.

"Tony, there is no more to be said on this," she replied. "Except for one thing... The female, she has surprised us, as all things genetic can do at times. She continued to develop her enhancement far more than we had planned or expected, intellectually and physically. We are aware of the relationship that has developed between you; this was not intended to happen, and for this we are truly sorry, but you know all you can know about matters now."

"There is no more room for discussion, we must leave it there. We will now prepare to take you back to where you belong. The journey will take just over four of your weeks. We will have you back within a two-day time differential from after the time you left. I am sorry," Victoria said as she bowed her head. "Now, please excuse us," she finished by saying as they all stood to leave the table.

Tony was having none of this. "Time for plan B," he thought to himself. He placed his hand on the blade of the knife behind his back. Waiting for them to separate and get half way across the room, he picked off Jose as being in the best position. Suddenly Zephyr let out a soft growl at Tony, as though to give some kind of warning, but he took no heed as he quickly stood up and rushed at Jose, his left arm outstretched to grab his hostage, and the knife in his right hand. Apart from Jose, they were all nearly at the door, and Tony was just two metres away from his victim.

In a split-second after Jose had noticed him fast approaching, Victoria, her back towards them, turned sharply around and held up the palm of her left hand to reveal a round silver disc. There was a sudden burst of energy, and a flash of blinding white light hit Tony like a hard rubber wall, sending him reeling to the other side of the room in a fleeting moment.

The next thing he knew, he was opening his eyes, still flat on the floor with Zephyr standing over him. "Should have listened to you, boy, as ever," he said as he slowly regained his faculties. His head still pounding and dizzy as he pulled himself from the floor, a glance at the window told him night had fallen. "My god, how long have I been out, Zeph?" he said as he tried to keep his balance. Zephyr began to walk towards the window, stopping halfway to look round at Tony, as though to guide him in that direction. Knowing there had to be a reason for this and filled with curiosity, he staggered over. Not four paces away before a sudden and sinking realisation hit him, he placed his hands on the window. "No," he said to himself. Taking a deep breath, he repeated, "No." Night had not fallen – they were back... in the depths, of space. "No! No!" he shouted as he turned to look up at the ceiling.

Collapsing back down to the floor in a sitting position, he put his arm around Zephyr. Laying over his legs, Zephyr gave him a look as though to say 'no more, do no more but rest for now'. There on the floor, they fell into a sleep.

Chapter 14

As they woke to a dark room, all Tony had was his body clock to tell him it was daytime. His thoughts recounting all that had been told to him over the last three days, he had a sinking feeling he'd never before known. "Well, no point just sitting here, Zeph," he said as Zephyr stood up, shook himself and had a long stretch. "Tea – we definitely need a good strong one, boy," Tony said to himself. Standing up to feel he was still slightly light-headed, he balanced himself to walk over to the kitchen area. Pouring some of the tea from his cup into a bowl, he placed it on the floor for Zephyr, then leaned backwards against the worktop and took a reviving gulp. Not one minute had passed before a knock at the door disturbed their peaceful moment.

"Uh shit, what do 'they' want now?" he said as Zephyr let out a deep bark. "What is it?" Tony shouted angrily.

"May I come in?" It was Victoria.

"It's your ship," he replied as though he didn't care less.

She walked through the door hesitantly, her facial expression a mix of anxiety and regret. "Are you all right?" she asked from halfway across the room.

"Some kick, that thing of yours has got," he said.

"I am sorry that was necessary," Victoria quickly replied.

"And no, no I'm not all right," Tony said sharply.

"Tony, we are not without understanding or regret for that which has passed, and that which has now come to be for you," she told him.

"All that I did… I survived with only what you dropped us there with," Tony began by saying. "On what I thought was some alien planet, which it might just as well have been. From that, from those beginnings, I build a new life, a life surrounded by people I came to like and respect, and one which I came to love. No, no you don't understand. You have no idea… you can't. Now go, leave me to get on with it." Victoria gave him a sympathetic smile and a look of sadness, and then turned to walk back through the door.

Tony and Zephyr spent the rest of the day in the usual way; despite feeling how he did, he knew he had to adjust, to adapt to what now lay before him, whatever that might be. The more he contemplated, the more he felt his anger grow towards 'them'; the crew of this ship; these people who were now once again his capturers as they sailed back through the stars and into the future. "The future – my god what will that look like now?" he thought to himself.

Over the next few days, they got back into a routine. His thoughts were never far from Julie and the land he'd come to love, or the community and his two friends Alpha and Omega. Many times each day he would wonder how they all were. By now they'd have realised something was wrong as he hadn't returned; it made him feel sad to think they were probably out looking for him now. Whenever he thought about all his time spent back there, one thing puzzled him. By now, most of everything had fallen into place: the vegetation; the fish he didn't recognise, which were native to that part of the world, or that period in time at least; the constant heat; the equal periods of day and night; and the moon so high in the sky; all because they were so close to the equator. But the strange creatures; the huge vegetarian of the woods; the ferocious birdlike creature in the canyon; these were still a mystery to him.

As time went by, the only contact he had with anyone on the ship was when he had to grudgingly ask Victoria for provisions over the speaker system. He'd kept to fish as their main source of food, but had gradually begun to vary the diet as he knew they'd need to get used to the food back on Earth, in their time, that is. And so they carried on, travelling through the light-years and waiting for their journey to come to its inevitable conclusion.

One day, unexpectedly, Victoria asked to see Tony in person. She said she wanted to talk, and with curiosity having got the best of him he agreed for them to meet later that evening, with one exception – this time he wanted neutral ground. So, to tie in with their last walk of the day, he arranged to meet at the park area.

As they walked the corridor around the curved wall to approach the entrance, he eventually saw Victoria and Dendravous waiting for them.

"I see you've brought your high priest of thought with you," Tony said sarcastically, but this was lost on them as they turned to look strangely at each other. "Shall we?" he said with an equal air of sarcasm as his hand opened the doors to let them through. "How did you do all this?" Tony said as he looked out onto the park.

"We produced the trees, bushes and grass ourselves, from our bank of samples we collected from your time, from your part of the world. The birds are from your time also. We wanted to make this as real as possible, so you would feel more at home. The birds have bred whilst they have been with us; we had never seen this, it is… pleasing. We will let them go when we land," Victoria told him.

"Yes, so what's this meeting for?" Tony asked.

"We are concerned. We want to make sure you are adjusting – to the ways of your old life, that is – before we get you back," Victoria replied.

"I have this in hand, why would you care? You've got what you wanted. Job done," Tony retorted.

"We want to know if there is anything we can do, any way we can help," Dendravous cut in.

"Yes, we do care, Tony," Victoria followed by saying.

He looked up at the trees for a few moments. "It's a shame, you know, a shame you won't live," Tony said as he looked back at them.

"We are not here to talk about us, Tony," Victoria answered.

"No? Well let's talk about you for now," Tony continued. "You're not bad people. As angry as I am about everything, I know that. I know that what you've done, you've done with the very best intention, but for all you say, I do believe you have somehow broken the laws of God, and time.

"We believe in God, Tony, just as we know you do," Dendravous said as he continued. "We try to live by his ways, just as in the Bible. We still have multifaiths, which have continued from the days of the first generation, from 'your time', but ask yourself this: if God has given us all our abilities, allowed us to survive for all of this time, do all that we have accomplished throughout our generations; would he not have wanted us to stop that terrible thing, that chain of events which led to the end of nature on our planet?"

"We could debate this for as long as it has taken you to get this far," Tony answered as he went on. "But for me, I can't help but think as I do, it's a feeling I have. I hope I'm wrong. We'll have to find out, won't we, but now, you must go back to your time, just as I must go back to mine." Victoria and Dendravous both gave him a subtle nod. "And the answer is 'no' by the way. There is nothing you can do for me. I had already asked it back then, two weeks ago now – you gave me your answer," Tony ended by saying.

As they parted company that night, he knew it would probably be the last time he would see them until he and Zephyr finally got off the ship. When they got back to the accommodation, he walked over to the window. Looking out at the stars, he began to think, not just in terms of distance, but of the history they were now passing through.

Assuming they were halfway through the journey, they'd now be five thousand years from his time. "Around the era of the Pharaohs," he said to himself. If his calculations were right, they should soon be turning to head back for Earth. He thought about all the empires that would rise and fall as they hurtled back through space over the next two weeks, and he wondered what kind of world he'd now find back there, in his and Zephyr's time.

Tony grew impatient for the voyage to end during the next week. He was spending more time in the gym and pool to expend the excess energy he was now building up, and trying to occupy himself on the information station. "My god," he said, laughing to himself one day as he was looking back through his natural science module he'd studied, and looking up relevant information on the downloaded internet. There it was, almost by accident, the answer to the question which had been sticking in his mind. He'd inadvertently stumbled across the huge vegetarian creature he'd come to know so well back there. It was a giant prehistoric ground sloth, native to South America.

A further search didn't take too long to reveal the fierce birdlike creature. Both breeds were actually meant to be long since extinct by ten thousand years ago, but Tony knew he'd seen them in the flesh, larger than life. "So much for historical information. Life does survive against the odds sometimes, uh," he said to himself. Sad to think they actually both must have been one of the last of their line, it made him feel homesick.

The rest of the journey passed quickly. Tony knew they must be no more than two or three days from their final destination. Making sure he'd got on the same clothes that he'd had on when they first boarded the ship, and gathering together his personal belongings, he spent the final days in anticipation of their return to Earth. He'd noticed from the window a far distant star getting larger by the hour, and believed it could be their own Sun; his suspicion was confirmed as he saw the star grow to the size of a football in just twenty-four hours.

The following day, the voice of Victoria came over the speaker. "We have slowed and will be landing in less than an hour, Tony," were her first words before she continued. "I need to inform you that in the next minutes which pass you will experience an opaque blanket of light envelop the window. Do not be alarmed: this is the shrouding device which allows for us to be undetectable, not only to the naked eye but to all of Earth's sensors. Just two days, almost to the hour, have elapsed since you left. You will depart at the same location as when you boarded. I must now tell you that we had sent a message in your name to your place of work, to inform them that you needed to travel north to visit a close friend, who had suddenly fallen ill. You were to be away for one week; this will give you another five days to adjust before you have to return... I will say now that we wish you and Zephyr a good life, with health and happiness."

Tony looked at Zephyr as he continued to stand in silence. He had a final check around the accommodation, before Victoria spoke again: "We have now landed. Please make your way to the ship's main doors." Taking a last look at the room as they left, they then walked along the corridor for the final time. Stark memories of that first evening, that first encounter with the ship, over a year ago, now came flooding back to him.

Standing in front of the inner doors for a brief moment before they opened, Tony and Zephyr stepped into the outer chamber as the doors closed behind them. Taking a deep breath in the muffled silence of the void, in the seconds that ticked by Tony anxiously waited to see his old world.

Chapter 15

As the huge doors opened and the ramp extended outwards, Tony was met with an almost identical evening to the one when they'd left there. Walking tentatively from the ship, they were now as free as he'd first been promised. They stepped off the ramp and took their first few paces back on their native grass. Everything looked the same, and a few breaths of air told Tony they were truly back in the twenty-first century.

Even in the relatively rural environment that surrounded them, after a year of living in a completely natural ecosystem the presence of fuel and other pollutants in the atmosphere hit his senses hard. It took a few minutes for him to completely get his bearings, but as the landscape fell into place, they took a brief look back towards the ship, which remained shrouded, then made their way into the woods which they'd come through that evening – a year but only two days ago.

Emerging out on the other side, Tony could see their car in the distance. Pulling the keys from his pocket as they walked back over the grass bank, a sudden and strange feeling came over him; a sense of differential between last being there, and all that had happened since, hit him like a train. It was as though time was physically and latently catching up with him, like a concertina effect, causing him to stop and finally drop to his knees with a strange dizziness.

Zephyr stopped in his tracks and turned to run back to him. "OK, boy, I'm OK," Tony said, putting his hand out to steady himself. The sight of Zephyr looking as though he'd been completely unaffected by their arrival back helped him to regain a grip on reality. They sat on the grass for a while, just the two of them in a peaceful moment. Within a few minutes, the strange effects of that which he could not understand began to pass; a wave of relief washed over him as he began to regain his senses. "Guess that's what you'd call time lag," he said jokingly to Zephyr.

Now feeling more back to normal, Tony got to his feet and they carried on walking towards the car. As they reached it, the thought occurred to him that after not having driven for over a year, he needed to give himself a memory check. "Time to adjust, they got that right!" he said to himself. After unlocking the car and opening the back door, Zephyr jumped in and assumed his usual position. Tony shook his head in amazement. He placed himself in the driver's seat and almost felt like a novice driver.

Before they started out, he took a long look over to the woods. He sensed that they were watching him; watching to make sure he and Zephyr were both OK; watching to see that they were making their way home, so everything they'd planned would now reach its final conclusion. A quick turn of the key saw them on their way, sailing back into their old life, and into a world as yet unknown to them; a world which could be as they'd left it; or a world in which the direction of the future could have radically and unrecognisably changed; he had to find out.

Driving back to the house, Tony observed the roads, buildings and other cars as they got closer to the outskirts of the urban town. Everything looked and seemed the same, 'as far as he could remember', but there was just one thing he couldn't help but notice. As he got ever closer to the built-up areas, there were less cars on the road; less traffic. Even at this time in the early evening there'd usually be more vehicles on the road: people going home from working late, lorries making their way back to the ferry after making deliveries, the odd boy racer and speeding motor bike; but this was more like an early Sunday morning. He couldn't exactly put his finger on it, but there seemed a strange air of sedation in the atmosphere.

Finally arriving back at their part of town, Tony held his breath as they turned the corner into his road. Again looking exactly the same as when they left, he exhaled as he caught sight of the house, and parked in his usual place at the end of the street. As they stepped from the car and walked up the road, memories of their old place in the rocks back there, and of Julie and the community, came flooding back to him. He felt a profound sadness. After stopping in his tracks for a brief moment, a few more paces and they were through the gate and at the door.

As Tony unlocked it and they stepped in, he caught a rush of household scents. Realising his senses were now so heightened, he knew it was going to take some time to get used to what he *couldn't* see, just as much as to that which he could. Right at that moment, the clock struck a half-hour chime, breaking the peace like the sound of a cannon. "Jesus," he said loudly, looking at Zephyr before managing a snigger of irony.

Realising it was now past Zephyr's time for dinner, he went to the cupboard to get out a can and his biscuits; Zephyr quickly devoured its contents as though he'd not eaten in days. "Tea, the second most important thing," Tony thought to himself. Opening the fridge door and reaching for the milk, he felt a slight disorientation when he saw it was still in date!

Later that night as they sat in the living room, Tony felt a series of strange episodes; a kind of numbness, directly followed by a stark reality of all that had happened in the last thirteen months, washed over him with a relentless regularity. "We really need a good night's sleep, boy," he said to Zephyr, who was resting his head on his knee and staring at him with that knowing look, as though he was fully aware of what he was going through. Tony smiled at him, then looked at the wall and had more than a few minutes of deep reflection.

Another strike of the clock broke his chain of thoughts, telling him it was now ten. "The news," he suddenly remembered. "Let's get a look at the world tonight," he said to himself. After turning on the TV and switching to his usual news channel, the first thing he noticed was a presenter he'd never seen before. The second and most curious thing was that a series of topical national and international events that had been building up during the last week before they'd left were not even mentioned.

These issues were important, one being the escalating trade war between America and China, causing chaos in the global stock markets. The other was a more domestic story, but no less serious; an undercover journalist had exposed a ring of corruption at the heart of the British government, which in turn had wide-reaching consequences for other constitutional bodies.

As he sat there, it only took a couple of minutes to realise that something was different. What had been one of the biggest stories of the time had seemingly faded out of existence. It was like a slow news day, with just the inane smile on the face of the presenter reporting on a variety of largely benign issues throughout the country.

Switching off the TV and looking back at the wall, an overwhelming tiredness suddenly came over him. He got up from the chair and switched off the light. Leaving on the clothes he stood in, they bedded down for the night, on the floor.

It had been a deep but uneasy night's sleep by the time they woke at five a.m. For a few brief seconds, Tony didn't even know where he was; not until the sound of an early passing truck broke the silence did everything come rushing back to him. "OK, time to get on with things," he said to Zephyr, who shook himself and headed to his water bowl. They needed food and provisions, so Tony decided they'd take an early trip to the twenty four-hour supermarket. Apart from anything else, he knew this would go some way towards the ongoing process of integration back into his own time, which he was becoming ever more aware of the need to do. Besides, as he didn't need to work today, they could take a walk on the beach afterwards.

Only just remembering to put Zephyr's collar and lead on as they got to the door, he made his way out on his first day back in the modern world. Driving into the huge area of the store, the first thing to hit him was the sight of a stark, empty car park. It was now only around six a.m., but he'd still have expected to see at least a few cars, people milling around – either on their way to work on an early shift, or night workers on their way home – and the odd member of staff shifting trolleys around. But nothing; nothing and no one were in sight.

After parking up and leaving Zephyr in the car, he walked across the ghostly area to the entrance of the building, only to find it was closed, with a sign on the door giving the opening times: 8.00 a.m. to 8.00 p.m. "Stranger and stranger," he said to himself as he looked back out onto the deserted open space. "Right, let's get down to the beach first then… if it's still there, that is!" he said to Zephyr as he got back into the car.

Finally getting back home, after what had seemed like a pretty surreal experience of actually having to shop for food, rather than catching it or sourcing it naturally from the ground and bushes, Tony was already beginning to get a feeling of being cooped up, claustrophobic. He felt restricted, constrained by the civilised society he was once so a part of, but he knew this was just something else he needed to adjust and get used to, if not for himself but for Zephyr at least, who he could see was sensing his pent-up frustration. "I should go back to work tomorrow," he thought to himself, but eventually thought better of it, knowing it might look strange as they weren't expecting him back until next week.

He did them a breakfast of kippers that he'd bought frozen from the supermarket. Apart from the fact the place would normally have been open when they got there, as he'd walked around the store, something else had felt odd, but he still couldn't put his finger on it. It was in the atmosphere and the people; everything and everyone were somehow, different.

After they'd eaten, he had an idea. Going to his laptop, he began to look up and search for some of the most significant figures and events through history. Trawling the net, it didn't take long to get his answers. Alexander the Great and Genghis Khan, these giants of ancient history had still existed, and had still seemingly brought to bear their huge influence on Earth's future; the Roman Empire had dominated the known world of their time; and in more recent history, the Second World War, Hitler, fascism, Churchill, and the allied forces – everything of that time had played out in the same way to ultimately produce the same outcome. John F. Kennedy was still shot in the November of 1963, and man had landed on the Moon in '69 due to his initiative to kick start America's space program.

After another hour or so of surfing the net, Tony drew a deep breath as he finally shut the computer. As far as he could see, the course of mankind had unfolded through time with no change, so why did things seem so different now? Although he knew there had to be a reason, there was nothing obvious. Leaning back in his chair, the nagging thought occurred to him that even if he did find out how or why there were any changes to the world, what could be done about it? After all, what had been done, was now done!

That evening, they went back down to the river for their usual walk. Tony looked over at the woods to where they'd arrived back only yesterday, which by now felt more like a week to him, but uppermost in his mind were the ship and its crew. He assumed they were long gone by now, and wondered what kind of world they'd find back in their time. "Well, I hope they find it's all been worth it," he said to Zephyr as they both stood in front of the opening to the woods on a sultry summer evening.

Over the next few days, they got back into a normal routine. Tony was anxiously waiting to get back to work, wondering what the hell he was going to find there, but he'd decided to make the most of their last couple of days and not think too much about it. What he did do was to keep an eye on the main news channels. Constantly amazed at the relatively calm state of the world, he could sense an air of general apathy running through every story. Nobody really seemed to care, even though most of the topics *were* fairly trivial. The presenters, the people who the stories centred around, and all others who were in any way involved had almost no emotion about them, no passion. It was as though if the world were to end in the next few minutes, unless something was done, everyone would just sit, wait… and watch it happen.

The day had finally arrived for him to return to work. As he left the house in the morning, memories of that last day he went in – that day when it all began – were at the forefront of his mind, but he knew he had to leave these thoughts behind, at least for the next eight hours, anyway.

He approached the practice from the other side of the road to check it out first and see who was there and what it might now look like through the large double-fronted windows, before he himself could be seen. "My god, some things never change," he thought as he smiled to himself. There she was, Mrs Calthorpe, leaning over the desk, going through the appointments sheet, loyally assisted by Sophia. "OK, let's get this done," he thought as he crossed the road and headed for the building.

"Morning, Tony," Mrs Calthorpe said as he walked through the entrance.

"Morning," he replied.

"So sorry to hear about your friend. I hope they're better now," she continued. "You've had a lot of work build up in the week you've been away, but still, I'm sure you'll catch up," she said, handing him his appointment list.

As he walked to his office, Tony felt taken aback by her comments; normally she'd have gloated at the fact he'd got work to catch up on, instead she'd been completely indifferent. "Well, it's not all bad then!" he joked to himself. Going through his workload, it didn't take long for him to see the issues he was dealing with had changed. Although each one corresponded to the same area of law as they had before he'd gone away, they had all altered, only subtly, but nevertheless they were different.

As he began to deal with each case in turn, he went into his legal databases on the computer. Browsing through the latest relevant legislation and case decisions which he'd been all too familiar with, it was immediately noticeable that these had also changed. Initially, only a glance told him that the legislation was relatively, and unusually, less complicated. The text in the sections was more based on trust and honesty, rather than trying to take into account the infinite complexities which human nature can throw up.

An internal call from Sophia told him that his first appointment had arrived. A new client, Jeff Knowles was a local businessman who'd come to talk about employment contracts. Before he went out to greet him, Tony thought he'd better check one of their standard contract templates. "Don't need to guess these have changed too. Yep, right first time," he said to himself. After quickly studying the document, he shook his head and went out to usher his client in.

It was a casual session, and Mr Knowles seemed to be disproportionately concerned with staff welfare, rather than how much productivity he could squeeze out of them; he also accepted everything Tony had to say, with none of the usual questions Tony had grown used to from any shrewd businessman.

After seeing a couple more clients, the morning fast became lunchtime. Tony got ready to get back to Zephyr, who'd been constantly on his mind all morning. After all, this had been the first time they'd been parted for more than an hour in over a year now, in their real time, that is.

When he got back in the afternoon, he spent the rest of the day partially catching up on his backlog. It had been a bloody strange experience to say the least, being back on this first day, he thought. It was with a sense of relief, mixed with heightened curiosity, that he left the building that evening.

In the time that followed, each day began to pass more quickly than the last as the weeks went by, and he gradually began to reorientate himself into a world and it's people that he would struggle to understand at times. As the nights started to draw in, each evening on their walk he'd look up at the stars and think of Julie, still there, living out her life ten thousand years in the past or, put another way, on the other side of that wormhole.

With Zephyr there to help him keep a grip on reality, they sailed through a seemingly unreal society. At one point, he felt as though he was going to hit the next person who smiled blankly at him; or one of his colleagues that he'd tried to have a meaningful conversation with, only to be met by a wall of almost indefinable lethargy. It seemed to him that the world was falling off a cliff-edge, and nobody was even noticing. "What in God's name have those people from the future done?" he'd say to Zephyr.

The months passed by, and Christmas and New Year came and went. It felt a cold winter after a year in the heat of what was now Ecuador. "What a beautiful country that must still be," he'd think to himself as he longed to go back there some day. But the Isle of Wight was also so beautiful, even in winter, and he and Zephyr continued to make the most of any spare time they'd get. By now, he would only watch the news a couple of times a week, mainly for the fact there was hardly anything else to bother watching! But one night, Tony caught something that really did grab his attention.

During the usual boring, monotone broadcasts by an equally bland news presenter, there was a brief and fleeting article on a subject he recognised all too well. There'd been a gathering of so-called 'world leaders' about the worsening state of Earth's natural environment, and climate change. A proposal had been put forward by an association of the world's leading scientists, calling for an international collaboration on the matter; proposals to build some kind of unparalleled facility in order to develop new forms of energy, power and ways of producing food for Earth's ever-increasing population.

The proposal had been... refused; voted down unanimously in favour of putting more resources into conventional methods, citing the fact that the expense of such a project would not outweigh its benefits. It was thought that the general well-being of 'people' should take priority for now, in the short term at least. It was also widely thought that, with slight improvements, the ecology of the planet would recover, and 'sort itself out'!

Then, as he continued to watch with fascination, the report switched to a clip of a member of the scientific association being interviewed about the decision. "This verdict by the world council is a tragedy, a tragedy for future world populations to come," he said as the interviewer blankly listened. That member's name... was 'Enrico de Silva'.

Tony sat frozen in his seat, his eyes wide open as he continued to listen to the interview. There he was; the man who *would* destroy the world was a small, insignificant-looking 'geek'. He turned the TV off. "Oh my god," he said as he looked at Zephyr. "The undersea facility, the thing never gets built, none of it happens. They stopped it; they really did alter that part of history," he continued to say to himself. "But what now? What now that man has decided not even to worry about his own environment, or its long-term condition on which the future of human life depends? Will the world really be such a better place?"

As winter turned to early spring, Tony's frustrations with the world grew. Determined to try to do something about it, he'd decided to go back into politics, thinking that at least he could try to be a voice in this great sea of indifference. "They might not wanna listen to what I've got to say, but they're bloody well gonna hear me," he'd think to himself.

He planned to start by standing for local council again in the coming elections that year, but this time as an independent. Then, if he got elected, he'd look at the main political parties and see which would be the best one to join to suit his purposes, and then work his way in. Knowing only too well how politics worked, deep down he knew he would only be one voice, but he had to try at least. Apart from anything else, he thought it would give him a purpose, something which he hadn't felt since he'd left the community back there.

As he sat at home thinking about it all one night, he realised it was the first time he'd felt excited about anything since they got back to their own time. Although there *had* been a couple of high points which he'd sometimes reflected on in the last few months.

The infamous Urskin-Brown had come to see him one day; this time though, instead of wanting to acquire another broken-down, neglected old property, he was actually looking to sell off some of his estate. If there was one thing about the government of the day, they were now taking a softer and more generous approach to people who were out of work, or had temporally fallen on hard times, in fact they were providing for them pretty well. New properties had been built for that specific purpose, which was putting the Urskin-Browns of the world out of business.

That day, Tony sat there, barely able to mask his delight. He had a smile in his mind as the old git listed two of the worst properties he needed to be sold, which Tony knew wouldn't exactly be fetching the market price, if he were able to sell at all in their current state. "Well *that* serves you right, bastard," he said out loud after his 'client' had left the office.

Another highlight was when the eccentric Mrs Lattimer came to see him. Still out there trying to save every stray or animal in trouble or need, she seemed the only thing in the world that hadn't changed. "Please god and more power to her," Tony thought many times after their last meeting. But other than that, there wasn't a lot to shout about. The world was dying on its feet, and no one was even aware of it.

As spring wore on, Tony prepared to put himself forward to stand for election in his ward. He'd done all the paperwork, submitted his application and drawn up a draft of pledges for his leaflets.

By early April, his application had been granted and he was now ready to begin campaigning. Each evening he'd drive to a different area of streets and leave Zephyr in the car while he did his leaflet drop, before going down to the river for their walk. It made him laugh to himself to think of the last time he stood for election. The furthest things he'd thought of putting on his agenda were climate change and animal welfare. "Well, some things have changed for the better then," he said to Zephyr as they walked past the woods.

Now fully engaged and enjoying the campaign process as he always did, he finished his leaflet drop over a weekend and was preparing to begin the door knocking stage in the coming week. Increasingly looking forward to the cut and thrust of the final stages of the campaign, he was completely unaware of the events which were to shortly and unexpectedly unfold on him.

Walking home from work one evening, he began to get a strange feeling of being watched, followed by someone, or something. It was nothing definite, and he couldn't see anything, but it was as though he could feel a presence, above all. Once and then twice, he stopped in the street and took a good look around, but still nothing.

There was a shortcut through the buildings which separated one main street from another; he decided to take it. If he was being followed, he'd try to filter out whatever it was from the traffic of cars and people. Up the narrow, winding passageway he walked. As the noise from the main street began to subside, he tried to hone in on any tangible sound. It was only when he'd got around halfway up, and could hear a pin drop, that he heard what he thought were a couple of very soft footsteps.

Stopping suddenly, he heard a definite shuffle. Looking behind, he could almost feel something was there, behind the bend he'd just walked round. Silently and slowly, he walked back through his tracks until he'd almost got there. Dropping his suitcase, with two quick steps he leapt to the other side. The shock of what was revealed to him caused more than a brief moment of silence, before what he could now see fully sunk in. "You... you!" he said in disbelief.

"We need to talk, Tony," were Victoria's first words as they continued to stare at each other.

"My god, I never thought I'd be pleased to see you again!" he uttered. "What are *you* doing here?"

"Is there somewhere we can speak?" she replied. Tony had a quick look around, sighed and shook his head.

"This way," he said, grabbing her arm and guiding her up through the passage. "Well this is weird," he said to her as they walked along the high street towards his house.

No more words had passed between them as they reached the front door, but as they entered, "Hello, Zephyr," she said as he came towards them and gave her a look of recognition.

"OK, boy," Tony said with a reassuring tone.

"May I sit down?" Victoria quickly followed by saying.

He sat her at the dining room table and took a seat himself. As he looked at her, he could see how weak and vulnerable she seemed in this environment. "We do not have much time, Tony. I am immunised to the limit and the effects will not last more than another two hours," she said with a sense of urgency.

"OK, so what's this about?" he replied, still half-shocked that she was actually here.

"I think you might have already guessed that. Although we were successful in stopping what we set out to stop, things are still... not right."

"You can say that again!" Tony interrupted.

"Please let me continue," Victoria said as she went on. "When you left us, we went into wide orbit again to observe your time as it is now. Seeing, as you must have, the strange changes and distortions, we travelled forward another one hundred years, only to find a dying world. Mankind had progressed selfishly, with no regard to the natural environment, or their fellow creatures."

"Victoria, I don't mean to keep interrupting, but I've already seen this," Tony cut in as he went on. "It doesn't take much to predict what the world ends up like, but the real point is, why are you here? What's done is done, isn't it? I've realised that... I am here and it is now. All I can do is try to change things, and that's what I'm about to do, try at least, for all the good it might do," he ended by saying.

"Please just hear me out, Tony," Victoria said as she began to tell him why they'd come back. "We then travelled a further two hundred years forward. The surface of the planet and its oceans were completely toxic; natural life was all but wiped out, with just a few pockets of human society existing in highly protected artificial environments."

As Tony listened, the conversation he'd had with them back on the ship echoed through his mind. "Well, what's that about time seemingly to have its own will? Things have ended up just about the same as they did anyway – tell that to Dendravous," Tony said regretfully.

Victoria nodded and continued. "We have considered the matter many times over, and yes, it is distressing to think that Earth is to only eventually suffer all but a similar fate. But... we think there *is* something which can be done, something which could correct the timeline, and make the course of history unfold as it should."

"I'm all ears," he said with an air of irony. But he listened intently as Victoria began to lay out their reasoning as to why things were the way they were, what went wrong, and what could be done to try to put it right.

"We believe there could have been what our philosophers would call a 'circumstantial paradox'."

"Meaning what?" Tony asked as she continued.

"We think we could have been wrong in one sense, wrong about you. In taking you back there, by doing all that you did, and more, albeit unwittingly, we know this became the primary cause for alteration in that period, but it went further than we had expected."

"In our conversations on the ship, you spoke of the laws of time; maybe such a thing does exist; maybe when one thing has gone, the thing which has directly caused that ending must take its place. This did not happen ten thousand years ago. The one you called 'the leader'; he, his regime, and all that emanated from him, had gone; and so... had you. We believe this left a void, a void in time which was not filled. It would appear that void still exists now, although to a far greater extent – this is the only reason we can think of why the world is the way it is."

"The ripple from the wings of that butterfly," Tony said sedately as he stared blankly at the wall. "You know what a court of law would make of this in a trial, Victoria? Speculation, even 'hearsay'. You have no evidence to support it, to support *anything* you've said."

"With one exception, Tony," Victoria quickly replied. "We know you have researched the past since being back here, just as we did, except we have had the time and resources to delve more deeply. You will have noticed that all the major events in history had unfolded in exactly the same way as they did, until a more recent point, the point when the world began to be as it is now. That point... is from the date of your birth. We are here to take you back, Tony, if you wish."

"We know you are adjusting to your life back here now and making plans – the decision is yours. It would though be what you call, a 'one-way ticket', and, for obvious reasons, you must not progress the community any further than you already have. We will leave you there, and interfere with time no more. I know we may not be right, but think on this. What is there to lose?" Victoria ended by saying.

Stunned for a moment by what she'd said, he finally spoke. "Ya know, Victoria, it's strange, the human condition, that is. In some ways this is a better world than the one I'd left, but without that drive, that interest, aggression even, we can still end up destroying ourselves, as well as all that's around us." But when he turned to look back over to her, he noticed a thin film of sweat forming on her face. She was beginning to look drawn and pale. "Are you… OK?" he asked.

"It is time for me to go. I know my way back to the ship," she replied.

Tony could see she was looking worse as the moments passed. "I don't think so, Victoria. We'll take you," he said.

"Give me one minute," she replied as she placed her forefingers and thumb onto the frontal lobes of her head and closed her eyes. Breathing deeply and remaining like this for around thirty seconds, she finally dropped her hand down and opened her eyes. "They are expecting us now," she said.

"You're telepathic, you people, you're telepathic, aren't you!" Tony retorted.

"Another trait of living in close proximity for seven hundred years," she replied.

"Come on, Zeph," he said as he stood up and grabbed Victoria's arm.

As they walked to the car, Tony smiled discreetly to himself as the prospect of having to take her to the A&E department of the local hospital occurred to him. "My god, I'd have a job explaining who she was when they'd ask for her details!" he thought.

She was already having trouble walking as they reached the car; he quickly placed her in the passenger seat before he and Zephyr got in. "I take it you're at the usual place?" Tony asked. She nodded. Keeping a close eye on her, he broke the speed limit until pulling up just outside the woods. By the way she was deteriorating, he could see this was now a race against time.

Weak but still conscious, he pulled her out of the car and let Zephyr out, then placed her arm around his shoulder and put his arm around her middle as they all headed fast through the woods. Coming through the other side, they faced the sight of the deserted empty field, before the ship quickly revealed itself.

He stood once again, his breath taken by the sight and size of it, until the doors opened and the ramp extended outwards. Andrea and Jose came rushing out as Tony and Zephyr walked Victoria, now very limp, halfway up the ramp towards the entrance. "Thank you, Tony," Andrea said.

"Will she be OK?" he asked. Andrea nodded as she and Jose each took hold of one arm and began to walk her into the ship. As they got to the entrance, Tony called out "Victoria!" They stopped for a moment to allow her to turn her head towards him. "The answer is yes. Give me one month, one month from this day. I'll be here, at the same time," he said with conviction as he looked at his watch.

Driving home that evening, he was almost in disbelief at what had happened in the last three hours. All he could do now was try to let things sink in, and contemplate what Victoria had said to him. He knew no more than they did if this was right, who would? Although he'd agreed to their proposals without really thinking things through, he found himself with no regrets. After all, and as Victoria had hinted at, with the world the way it was, and the way it would become, what was there to lose?

As they arrived home, he started to form plans in his mind of how he was going to do this, tie his affairs up, prepare for the long journey back. As he glanced at Zephyr, he thought he saw a look in his eyes which told him that this was all meant to be. He could tell from his body language and expression that he felt good about it. "Well that's good enough for me," he thought, smiling to himself. Later that night, as he bedded down on the floor of the living room he still slept on, he had the soundest night's sleep since they'd been back.

The next day, it was with a sense of relief, like waking from a nightmare, that he began the day. It had felt a heavy few months that they'd had, in one way or another. Tony felt his frustrations had rubbed off on Zephyr, as much as he'd tried to hide them from him, but now he was glad to think of things being better for them.

The thought that he would actually be seeing Julie again filled him with a happiness he'd not felt since leaving her. Of all the women he'd seen with their make-up, clothed in the fashions of the day, none of them could match her natural beauty, dressed in no more than a basic covering. He knew exactly what to do. He started with making a will, which, for the sake of discretion, he enlisted a solicitor from a different law firm.

The next thing was to arrange the sale of his house, and he used the same solicitor to handle the conveyance. After the sale, all that would be left would be money in a secure, interest-bearing bank account which he'd now opened. Nearly seventy per cent of his mortgage was paid so there'd be plenty of equity. Half he would leave to Barnardo's, the other half to the eccentric Mrs Lattimer's animal charity trust fund. "That'll give her finances a boost," he thought with a sense of satisfaction, but this would not be available for another seven years, after he'd been missing for that long; in law it was called 'declared death in absentia'.

Knowing he needed a quick sale on the property, he approached the council. Apart from specifically building more social housing these days, they were also now in the business of buying up decent private properties for the same purpose, a little under market price, but this had lately become popular with private sellers for speed and convenience. Although he'd like to have taken some of his furniture with him – his chair and his modern grandfather clock – he knew these weren't exactly going to look right among the backdrop of ten thousand years in the past! But he was pleased to get a slightly better offer from the council for the inclusion of the contents.

The sale was now set to go through in just two weeks' time. Time was passing quickly, and with everything almost set for their departure, Tony arranged to take a couple of days off to finalise matters, and for him and Zephyr just to spend a bit of free time. He'd already stopped campaigning, which was the one thing he didn't feel too happy about, but he'd be long gone by the time of the election.

One day, after a couple of days' break from everything, and just before they went for their evening walk, he had a moment of what felt to him like absolute clarity as to all that was happening, to everything he was doing, and to the difference between his life as it was now and as it was soon to be. As he looked around the room, it was the first time he'd felt any doubt about things, but just at that moment, something made him think of his mother and father, Sam and Diana. He thought about how they would feel about all this, knowing them as he did.

He put his thoughts aside and went to grab Zephyr's lead; as he did this, he had a strange and unprompted feeling that his mother was smiling with approval, giving him a sign of guidance to continue on. With that, he was now absolutely sure that he was on the right path, and he spent their walk and the rest of the evening with a sense of contentment he'd rarely before known.

Tony had returned back to work in that last week, but as he locked his office one evening, it was a strange feeling to know it would be the last. Contracts for the sale of the house would be exchanged the next day, and he'd taken the last two days in holiday entitlement – that way work wouldn't miss him immediately. He'd have to be out of the property by midday, and hand his keys into the relevant department of the council offices, so he'd booked a room at a local hotel for them to stay for two nights, feeling a slight melancholy at how he would never do this again. They spent that evening in the usual way: they had their dinner, the walk, and then slept in the house for the final time.

The next morning, Tony packed just one large leather bag with all his family photos and other precious items, some personal effects, and two days of food for Zephyr. As they left the house, he felt the normal sadness of doing this for the final time, said his goodbyes, and turned the key.

Walking to the car, he began to feel the momentum of heading towards their new life, and the journey they would soon embark on. He drove to the beach and they spent an hour down there. It was now just past midday, and he checked the banking app on his phone to see that the money for the sale had just been paid into his new account, then made his way to the council buildings and dropped off the keys.

Checking into the hotel that afternoon felt like old times for them, and the realisation that they were really on their way had now begun to sink in. Feeling like they were on a short holiday, Tony decided they'd visit some of the beautiful island's most popular spots: Sandown and Shanklin seafront, The Needles at Alum Bay, Blackgang Chine, and Ventnor Botanic Gardens.

Their forty-eight hours passed quickly, though, and the time had come for them to make the final journey down to the river. Parking up in the usual place outside the woods, they got out and he locked the car. It was to be a mysterious disappearance; anyone who knew him was well aware that they'd take their walk down there every evening. When the car eventually got found, there'd be nothing suspicious; it would look like they were just carrying out their normal routine.

Chapter 16

As they once again walked through the opening to the woods, Tony turned to take a last look at everything. It was a light evening in the first week of May, and all of nature had now sprung to life. The spring and early summer were always his favourite times of year, and he hoped to God there'd be many more over the centuries and beyond.

Walking through to the other side of the woods, he again looked out onto the empty field. "Christ, they'd better be there now," he said to Zephyr in an anxious joke, but within a few moments the ship had revealed itself. As the ramp extended and they slowly began to walk up towards the entrance, the door opened to the empty chamber. They stepped aboard as it quickly closed behind them.

Standing for a few seconds in complete silence, before being bathed in the strange ultraviolet light again; when the inner doors finally opened, the crew he'd come to know were all standing in the corridor. "A welcoming committee?' Tony asked.

"Yes. Welcome back, Tony," Victoria said as she stepped forward to shake his hand.

After the formal welcome, they all made a big thing about Zephyr and he was the star of the show as usual. "Well, you both know your way around this section of the ship well enough," Dendravous said to them.

"Yes, thanks. Come on, boy," Tony said as they began to walk down the corridor to their accommodation. He looked back at them all and found it strange to remember the first time they'd walked this way, and how he'd now come to know and trust these people, at least this far, anyway.

Upon entering the room, he placed his bag down, had a brief look around the place to re-familiarise himself, then walked to the window. Victoria's voice suddenly came over the communication system. "We will be launching in a moment, Tony."

He called Zephyr over. "Here we go again, boy," he said as they took a last look from the window. At that point, he felt the now familiar tremor as the room began to vibrate to a deep powerful hum, and a brief moment of motion as they began to lift off. Rising at an ever-increasing rate, they could see the circumference of the Earth within seconds, before again breaching the thin blue line where the sky meets space.

Within another few seconds, as they went into what he remembered as the revolving motion, Tony watched as the Earth disappeared and the Sun once again became a speck in the vastness of space. And so, for the third time in just under two years, they sailed amongst the stars.

In the initial few days, they settled straight back into life on the ship. On their first visit to the park, Tony noticed that the crew had been as good as their word; there were no birds – they'd let them go, back in his time, as they said they would. Other than that, everything was the same as he'd recalled, and by now was so familiar with, that was until one day, when he experienced something worrying as he was taking a swim in the pool.

Without warning, the lights suddenly blacked out. He could hear a strange sound, like the groan of a huge machine winding down. Zephyr began to bark loudly and Tony quickly jumped from out of the pool. Only able to see under what he realised must be emergency lighting, he dried himself off and shouted to Victoria: "Any problem?"

There was just a deathly silence as he went over to Zephyr. Then, suddenly and to his relief, the lights came back on and the hum powered up to a reassuring norm. At that moment, the voice of Victoria came over the system. "Sorry about that, Tony."

"Any problems?" he repeated.

"We are investigating, but just to assure you, there is nothing to worry about," she ended by saying.

"Jesus, I hope not!" he thought to himself as he looked around suspiciously. It hadn't even occurred to him before now, but deep space was definitely the wrong place to break down, or experience *any* technical problems, for that matter.

Over the next few weeks, Tony got back into his natural science studies, particularly the science of horticulture, thinking that knowing exactly how and why plant growth actually happened would help him to increase cultivation productivity at the other end. Apart from this, there was nothing much else to do but get himself and Zephyr ready for when they landed.

He was building up his fitness again and making sure Zephyr was getting plenty of exercise. This was no substitute for living in the natural environment, but with the benefit of previous experience, he knew they needed to be as prepared as possible before they had to reacclimatise. It felt good to know exactly where he was going, and what he was actually going to, for once; for the first time in two years, he felt he knew exactly where his life was headed.

He was also spending some time with the crew, getting to know them better. He'd now met many more of them, as well as some of the other inhabitants, around thirty in total; each of them seemed to be much like the head officers – intelligent, decent people. He found himself increasingly sorry to think that they were a dying breed, and that they didn't have much time left. Whatever they would be going back to in their real time, only God knows, but one thing was for sure, he knew what an important contribution any one of them would make to any society.

The other things that bothered him were the sudden losses of power and subsequent blackouts that were still occurring from time to time. Victoria had again assured him, saying these were no more than just technical glitches, but whenever he'd ask her whether they'd had them before, she would avoid giving him any kind of answer.

One day, there was a knock at the door; it was Sanfona from quantum sciences. "Would you like to see the bridge, Tony?" she asked. "You can bring Zephyr."

"Yes I would!" was his immediate reply. Filled with excitement, he and Zephyr followed her down the corridor, past the doors of the entrance and on to what must have been the other side of the ship, until they reached what looked like a large panel in the wall. As she held the palm of her hand out, the panel silently opened to reveal a cylindrical chamber. Sanfona ushering them through, they all stepped in.

As the door closed behind them, the chamber began to move. Unlike any ordinary lift, apart from moving upwards, he could also feel they were travelling in a number of different directions. "I take it *my* hand wouldn't work on this thing?" Tony asked. She nodded with a smile and they began to slow down to an eventual stop.

As they stood for a second or two, Tony could not even imagine what he was about to see as he waited in anticipation. The door silently opened and they all stepped forward, but as he quickly looked around, he was more than a little surprised to see what was, in effect, an empty room.

It was big, the whole area bathed in a strange blue light which emanated from the walls. They were obviously right at the top of the ship. As he looked above, he could see the stars through the transparent roof dome, which extended all the way down to the walls, around six feet from the floor. "Welcome to the bridge, Tony," said Victoria.

"Let me give you a tour," said Jose, who was standing beside her.

"But... but there's nothing here," he replied.

"No, really, let me show you," Jose replied as he walked towards him across the large floor space. He continued: "With our technology, we can select that which we require to work on at any time, it is all here." Tony was astonished as he watched Jose direct a device attached to his hand over various areas of the wall and floor, bringing up consoles, whole workstations from below, and panels from the sides, the like of which he could never have imagined.

"They look, what in my time we would call, virtual, not real," Tony said.

"Yes, yes, I am aware of this," Jose replied. "But touch them." As his hand reached out to these things, he was reminded of the doors and walls in the outer chamber of the entrance to the ship. They had the same feel: like silk to the touch, though at the same time stronger than a mix of steel and concrete.

As fascinating as this was, in the time he'd been there he couldn't help but have noticed the odd flicker of the lighting and some slight surges of power. "Impressive, very impressive," Tony said as he continued to look around the area, but as he glanced over at Victoria and Jose, he could also detect a slight look of worry about them, as though they were pre-occupied in some way. "Well, that's been fantastic. Thank you. Thank you, everyone. I'll leave you to get on now," Tony said as he walked back to the door of the bridge.

As Sanfona took him back down to the lower part of the ship, there was an uneasy silence until they got back out into the corridor. He thanked her as she walked back into the chamber, but as he and Zephyr walked back to the accommodation, he knew for definite that something was wrong.

The weeks began to pass more slowly, and their routine, although necessary, was beginning to feel monotonous. The crew had told Tony they were almost halfway through the journey. Still having technical problems – almost on a daily basis – and knowing they were coming up to the point of the black hole, he'd voiced his concerns to Victoria. She'd told him that they had found the source of the problems and would have this corrected before they entered that stage, and that, although she understood his concerns, they had carried out the procedure enough times to the point that it was almost routine. But for all this, whilst he now had the greatest respect for them all, he couldn't help but reserve a degree of scepticism.

In the meantime, he took his mind off the subject and concentrated on his studies. Eventually, to the relief of them all, the problems began to subside, until he'd not noticed any glitches or losses of power in nearly a week.

When the time finally came, Victoria informed him that they had begun their approach towards the direction of the event horizon. Tony would check at the window from time to time, but they were still so far away; it took nearly two days before he could detect that small black speck in the fabric of space.

Another day passed and the black hole by now appeared much larger. Their encounter must now only be a short time away, he thought, and he was waiting for the word from one of the crew as to when it was imminent, thinking that, unlike the first time, as he now knew what this was all about they'd give him fair warning, so they could at least prepare themselves. At that point, a series of flickers and intermittent power cuts started. He could tell this was worse than any of the episodes that had gone before, and called to Victoria.

"Tony, could you and Zephyr come to the bridge immediately, please. I will ensure your hand will open the door to the transporter" she said.

"Come on, boy, let's go," he said urgently to Zephyr as they rushed through the door. Running up the corridor, he knew this must be serious; there was an urgency to Victoria's voice that he'd not heard before.

Once they were in the transporter, the first thing Tony hoped was that the power wouldn't cut out and they'd get stuck in there. If there was a big problem, he at least wanted to see and know what was happening.

Relieved when they'd stopped and the door to the bridge had opened, he and Zephyr quickly walked in. The crew looked frantic at their workstations as they were clearly dealing with a serious crisis. Victoria looked around and walked over as soon as she saw him. "What's wrong?" Tony asked.

She took him by the arm and they walked over to a vacant area of the wall. "We have lost all power to the propulsion system," she told him.

"Well, that *is* a problem," he said.

"It is worse than just 'a problem', Tony," she continued. "We have now passed the point of no return as we head to the black hole. Even if we had all the ship's power, we could not pull away now. We could buy ourselves some time, but without it, we will reach the horizon within two hours, with no way of stopping us being pulled in. We don't even know what has caused the power loss."

"Jesus," was the only thing Tony could think to say.

Victoria seemed to be unusually at a loss for what to do at that moment. He was no stranger to having to think on his feet, but there was not one thing he could think of to help the situation. Victoria left him and rushed over to Jose, obviously to consult with him in some way, but Tony could see by the expression on their faces that the news was looking no better.

As he continued to observe the rest of the crew, he felt a growing frustration of not knowing what they were doing, and of not being able to help in any way. But then, one single thought struck him like a bolt of lightning. "Victoria," he shouted. She walked back over to him, a frown on her forehead showing the strain she was under. "Have you ever actually tried turning everything off, disconnecting the whole thing and leaving it like that for a couple of minutes?" Victoria looked at him as though he'd gone crazy.

"Why would I do that?" she replied.

"Look, I know nothing about your technology, I admit, but in *my* time, if we can't find a technical problem, if there seems to be no reason why something isn't working, that's what *we* do. It works at least ninety per cent of the time, trust me, and to quote something you said to me back on Earth, 'what do you have to lose'?".

She stared at him strangely for a few moments, then quickly looked round at Jose. "Jose – disconnect the power from the drive matrix, then cut *all* power."

"But… but that will…"

"Just do it," Victoria snapped before he had time to finish. She looked back at Tony as Jose began the procedure. There was a sudden draining sound as the power wound down and a shroud of darkness enveloped the bridge. They all stood in a deathly silence. Two minutes passed, which felt like two hours as they drifted in the ocean of stars.

Tony held his breath as Victoria gave the word to re-engage power. First, the lights came seamlessly back on, before a powerful jolt preceded a huge surge of upward-rising energy. There was a continuing silence between them as each crew member checked their stations.

Victoria and Jose were shaking their heads in discussion as they moved around the bridge to check the overall instrumentation. As they walked over to Tony, it was with an air of confusion mixed with relief that they revealed full power had now been restored. "But we are by no means out of trouble," Victoria told him as she hurriedly continued. "We are now approaching the black hole at the wrong altitude, and we have just under one hour to make the best adjustments we can. Whatever we do now, it will not be perfect, but it is the only option we have."

"Will we make it?" Tony replied.

"We cannot say with any certainty, all we can do now is try," Jose interrupted.

"Stay on the bridge, Tony. We need to move fast," Victoria ended by saying.

He watched and listened for the next thirty minutes as each crew member played their part. From what he could make out of the highly complex technical language, they were trying to recalculate the ship's best speed and angle, but his biggest concern was how close to the awesome sight of the event horizon they now were.

Even with the prospect of these being the last minutes of his life, Tony couldn't help but stand almost spellbound as he once again gazed at the phenomenon. Having a more panoramic view this time, this thing was like looking at Niagara Falls times a billion; even more spectacular was the clearer sight he now had of it seemingly to even draw the actual fabric of space into its depths. "Tony, we are four minutes away from contact. This is going to be rough; we need to secure ourselves," Victoria said as she guided him back to the wall.

As he watched the crew each standing flat against the wall, facing outwardly as a kind of hard virtual bar wrapped itself around their chest areas, he knew what she meant, but there was one problem – he realised immediately that it was going to be nigh on impossible to secure Zephyr's anatomy. After some quick thinking, he spoke to her. "Can you secure me if I sit on the floor? That way, I can hold Zephyr myself."

Just a look from her told him she realised what he meant. "Yes, sit down," she quickly replied. As she placed her hand on the wall to the side of him, the securing bar wrapped tightly around his chest. Victoria then ran back over to stand at the wall opposite Jose, grabbing some kind of handset on her way. She shouted over to Jose, who was also holding a handset. "Nearly ready!" she said. As he nodded in acknowledgement, she quickly looked over at Tony to indicate it was time.

Grabbing Zephyr and holding him tight, he spoke for the last time. "OK, boy, whatever happens we'll always be together."

"Now!" Victoria shouted. She and Jose both simultaneously hit something on their handsets. As he looked back over at them, it seemed as though they were now communicating telepathically.

A split-second later, the ship took a sharp turn to the left, before there was a massively powerful pull forward and the whole ship shuddered. From where Tony was sitting, as they hit the edge of the black hole, it looked like they were coming up on the biggest tidal wave imaginable, full of matter and illuminated by a strange source of light.

As they began to circle round at an ever-increasing rate, the ship and everything on the bridge began to vibrate heavily. He could feel the skin on his face ripple with the g-force; by now they were travelling so fast he felt as though the pressure would push him through the wall.

More than another minute passed like this, and it felt like they were on the precipice of destruction. Then, a sudden jolt tried to pull him forward as he clung even tighter to Zephyr. He could now feel that they were moving in an upward direction as the pressure of gravity pressed him hard to the floor. As they gradually rose back to the top of the event horizon, they slowed almost to a stop. Tony remembered this point well, but unlike last time, they began to get pulled backwards. He thought this was it.

"Game over," he said to himself as he looked at Zephyr, placing his hand on his head. At that moment, he heard a deep, grinding hum as the ship managed to pull slowly forward, only to come to an eventual stop. The hum then turned into a high-pitched shriek as they were catapulted back out into space, the force once more pinning them to the wall.

He looked over at Victoria and Jose, who were still intently looking at each other and working in unison. "Now!" Victoria shouted.

Tony again remembered well as he began to see strange spectrums of light appear, before they became enveloped in a completely black 'nothingness'. He realised that they must now be going through the wormhole. Looking back at Zephyr again, "My god, I think we've made it," he said to him as they continued to travel through the silent darkness, broken only by a few intermittent strings of light. Then, as suddenly as the blink of an eye, they finally re-entered normal space. It felt as though they'd come out from the darkest night to emerge into a bright summer's day as they saw the stars and fabric of the cosmos again.

Tony exhaled as he loosened his grip on Zephyr, who shook himself before sitting back next to him. Victoria, Jose and the rest of the crew all released themselves from the wall before Jose walked over to release Tony. As he got up, he, Jose and Zephyr walked over to Victoria. "We made it?" Tony asked.

She nodded. "Yes... yes, we made it," she replied.

"Phew! Well done… very well done!" Tony said as he shook their hands. "I guess I can leave you guys to it now then?" he joked.

As he and Zephyr turned and walked towards the transporter, Victoria called to him. "Just a moment," she said as she got to them. "I do not know what the turning off did back there, Tony. But yes, it did seem to work. We do not understand it but we thank you for the idea."

"Don't mention it. I don't understand it any more than you do!" he said with a smile as he continued to make his way to the door.

Victoria stopped them again. "But there is one other thing I think I should tell you. Back then, when we began to be pulled backwards, we knew it was the end – there was nothing else we could have done. The thing that saved us was a sudden burst of energy, so powerful that even the ship would not normally be capable of producing it. We do not know how, or where… this came from."

"Let's just call it a celestial intervention, Victoria," Tony replied with a look of curiosity on his face as he took a last look around the bridge.

In the days that followed, no one really spoke much about the events of that night, but Tony couldn't help but run through the whole episode time and time again, thinking of how they'd survived, and of how so easily they might not have. But this was no time for hindsight, he thought: they were now on the journey home and he needed to think of what was going to be the rest of their lives. He couldn't wait to see Julie, it would bring a smile to his face each time he thought of her, and he was looking forward to showing Alpha and Omega some of the new growing techniques he'd learned on this last voyage.

The crew had told him that they'd calculated their speed to get him back just two to three days from the time he'd left. He very much looked forward to getting back to a natural environment. There was one thing he'd become aware of in the last two days, though. Zephyr had been constantly giving him one of his 'looks', a look that was somehow telling him to 'remember', to remember all that had happened over this last two-year period of their latest adventure. Profoundly struck by this, he was determined to keep every detail at the forefront of his mind… for life.

Over the next few weeks, he'd finished his studies in natural horticulture. Although the materials had given him more than a few ideas on planting and cultivation, he knew he couldn't interfere with history or disrupt the timeline in any way by advancing the community too far. He thought about how tough this was going to be, and how it really went against his nature, but consoled himself to think it would be a job in itself just keeping things on the straight and narrow.

His thoughts would turn to the crew of the ship; what was to become of them at the other end of the timescale? What kind of world or society would they find back there? Whatever it was, it would be a world they were unable to inhabit, and would eventually die out in a relatively short space of time. One thing was for sure, the world would be a poorer place for it; for the kind of people they are; the principles and values they hold; the sheer scientific and medical knowledge; even their methods of philosophy they'd evolved. A poorer place indeed, he thought.

The next couple of weeks passed with no incident, and their routine remained unchanged. Knowing that they only had a few more weeks to go until they got back made everything seem less monotonous now.

Tony felt he'd got to know the head officers well enough now to invite them to his accommodation one night for dinner. He was interested in learning more of their culture: how they lived, what they liked and disliked. He'd asked them what each of their favourite dishes were, and got them to provide the ingredients. A couple of the dishes were a bit weird, he thought, but he was willing to give them a go. It was nearly two years since he used to have those couple of glasses of whisky in the evening, but now they were sailing in calmer seas and, assuming they could produce it, he thought a couple of bottles of wine would go down well.

They all turned up at seven that evening, and Tony was up to his neck with trying to produce different meals for each of them. When he'd finished, he placed the food in a hot holding cupboard, opened the wine and poured a glass for them all. As they all took a seat at the table, Tony proposed a toast. "To better times," he said with a hint of irony. He wasn't sure whether they really got that, but they each took a sip from their glasses anyway.

As the night wore on, with a glass or two more wine and a good meal they all began to loosen up. Tony talked more about things from his original time and regaled them with some stories and episodes from his life. He in turn listened with fascination as they explained more about their own society; how, in more detail, it had evolved over the centuries; and how they governed themselves.

It seemed to him as though, after that terrible apocalypse, their ancestors had based their culture on everything the world *hadn't* been; based on fairness and honesty, giving instead of taking. Just as Victoria had intimated to him once before, it was considered one of the greatest crimes to covet something which wasn't yours, or even ask for it for selfish benefit. They were a true collective, where each member contributed equally towards the society – depending on their abilities and talents – and not the other way round; and yet everyone's individual beliefs were respected and strictly protected, unless they proved harmful. Their telepathy was selective; each of them could turn it on or off at will. It had developed over time after around three hundred years. When their predecessors realised what they were evolving, they made it a crime for anyone to communicate in that way without permission.

Of all the things they'd told Tony that night, there was one more question he had to ask them. "Tell me, the way you speak, you don't shorten your words, like you must have heard me do; and sometimes, your speech sounds what my society would have considered to be old-fashioned, or even Shakespearean. Why?"

Dendravous carefully explained that many of them spoke different languages, left over from their distant ancestors' origins. English being the universal tongue of that time, they'd used it as their main source of communication throughout the generations, so the decision was taken long ago to use the language in textbook classical.

"Really? And I thought there was something more sinister to it," Tony said jokingly. It had been a good evening and he thought they'd all enjoyed it. He certainly had and so had Zephyr – they'd been giving him samples of their different dishes and he'd been the star attraction.

"My friends, I've so enjoyed your company tonight, learned much from you and it's been a privilege, but if there's one thing 'I' could advise 'you' on; develop a sense of humour, it's important, particularly in times of crises, I've always found." To this they nodded, and even raised a smile. They were now looking tired and excused themselves. As he saw them out that evening, he realised how much he was going to miss them when they dropped him off.

Things carried on in the same way after that night. They were now only two weeks from the end of their journey, and Tony was nearing the end of his science studies. He was re-reading a section on the treatment of plant life and other vegetation, when he came across a paragraph which reminded him of something Andrea had said about their own terminal condition: "You can't treat or put right something which is no longer there."

Something about the phrase rang through his mind like a loud bell. "No... longer there," he thought. "No longer there – that's it!" he said, getting to his feet immediately. "Victoria! Victoria!" he shouted urgently.

"Yes, Tony, what is it?" she replied with equal urgency.

"Come to my place. Bring Andrea with you," he ended by saying.

As a knock came at the door, he quickly invited them in. Standing there face-to-face with him, their expressions clearly showed their curiosity as to what this was about. Tony spoke as he looked them intently in the eye. "My blood, my blood... do you want it?"

The two crew members looked at each other, then back at him. "Can we sit down?" Victoria asked. There was a silence, before Andrea spoke.

"Are you saying what I think you are, Tony?"

"Yes, yes, of course. My blood has what you lack; that which your forefathers once had; that which you no longer have." Andrea nodded and there was a silence again.

"Are you sure you want to give this?" Victoria asked.

"It all makes sense now," Tony replied as he continued. "Because of your principles, you wouldn't have asked, taken it from me or taken it from anyone else. But now I'm offering it – my antibodies, my genetic codes – you could copy them, couldn't you? Manufacture them, integrate them into *your* system; it could be all you need! You already know this but would never ask."

They turned their heads to look at each other, then eventually nodded. Victoria drew a deep breath before speaking. "I do not know what to say. Thank you. Andrea will now prepare her laboratory. Can she come back to you in two hours? She should be ready by then." Tony nodded and they both quickly left.

As promised, Andrea returned just over two hours later, and they made their way to her lab. Feeling as excited as he hoped they'd be, he walked with her to the transporter. From what he could make out, they were now on a level just below the top of the ship.

As they entered the lab, Tony noticed how similar it looked to the bridge: it had the same technology and same lighting, but with different equipment and consoles. Andrea sat him down, placed what looked like a probe to the area of his lower chest, close to the heart, then pressed on the device. After a few regular beeps, which lasted just five seconds, it was quick and painless. "There we are, all done," she told him.

"That's it?" he asked.

"Yes, a small sample directly from the aortic artery. It will be more than enough, and... thank you again! You do not know what this means to us," she ended by saying.

On his way back to his accommodation, he hoped to God this would help them. He'd probably never know for definite before he finally left the ship, but his hopes would always continue.

Chapter 17

The final two weeks had almost passed and they were now only two days away from their final destination. They'd given Tony his old animal skin back to wear, as well as another bag, pole and knife to replace the ones he'd left behind on that final day, just in case they weren't where he'd left them; he'd even remembered not to shave for the last few days. Other than that, there was nothing to do now but wait until they'd landed. Each of the head officers had come to him individually over the last few days, to say their goodbyes and wish him well, which he in turn did to them.

On the last morning before landing, it was with an air of excitement – tinged with some sadness at leaving his new-found friends behind – that he discarded his modern clothes, slipped the animal skin over his head, transferred his precious items he'd brought with him into his new bag, and stood by the window in anticipation. Zephyr *always* somehow knew when they were coming to the end of a journey, no matter where they'd been going, so it was no surprise to Tony that he was acting excitedly. They'd now been to places and in situations they could never have imagined, but it was going to feel good getting settled again.

After a short while, Victoria's voice came over the system to tell him they were approaching Earth and would be landing shortly. With no need for the ship to obscure itself, over the next thirty minutes he watched as the world came into view, getting larger by the minute. He could now make out what were to become the named continents and countries of his time. It was fascinating to eventually see the whole landscape of his home from high in the sky; it gradually got clearer and more detailed until they finally touched down on the plateau. Victoria spoke again: "Ready, Tony?"

"Yes, ready," he replied. He grabbed his bag and pole and took a last look around the room before they walked down the corridor for that final time. When they approached the exit, he was taken aback to see the whole crew were there, lined up along either side of the walls to see them off. While he walked past, they all said their farewells, until he got to the head officers. "Take care, Tony, from us all," Victoria said.

Tony asked whether they were having any results from the treatment yet. "It is too early to tell yet, but it is looking promising!" Andrea replied.

"Well, remember, if something doesn't work, turn it off... and then back on again," Tony said as they all shook hands and warmly embraced for the final time. "I hope you find a world worthy of you all back there," he ended by saying.

As the doors opened and the ramp extended, Victoria told him that they would need to be at least one hundred metres from the ship before it took off. Tony nodded and they made their way down.

As they stepped back onto the natural earth, the scent of fresh, sweet air hit him like a shot of nectar. He turned to look back at the ship. All five officers were standing at the edge of the entrance. As they looked on at him and he at them for that last time, there was a recognition in their eyes; a recognition of all that had gone before them; of what they were trying to do and their hopes for the outcome of their actions; and of how their paths had come to cross in this extraordinary way over their separated time periods. Better than a thousand words were said between them before the doors of the ship, finally closed. "Godspeed, my friends," Tony said as he and Zephyr turned to make their way down.

Walking through the familiar terrain, they suddenly heard a deep, muffled hum. A few seconds later, Tony stopped to stare up at the sky to see what looked like a silver disc, rising and growing ever smaller with each moment. "There they go, boy. Next stop: ten thousand years," he said to Zephyr.

They were now nearing the huge vegetation at the foot of the cliffs and began to feel the wet humidity. Soaked once again as they walked through the huge canopies, they came out on the other side to reach the mighty Amazon River. They were on their way home, and Tony felt free and excited as they walked along the bank.

Suddenly though, Zephyr turned to him, then quickly bolted.

Running after him in hot pursuit and shouting his name, Tony got to the other side of a bend and slowed as he caught sight of him. Now knowing what this was all about, he walked slowly up towards him – he was standing by the now dead body of 'the maker'. "OK, boy. It's OK now, stand down," he said.

The second male was nowhere to be seen. He'd probably survived and gone back his community with the other male, or whatever was left of it, Tony thought. He must have taken his old pole, but his bag was still there, as was the knife laying at the side where he'd dropped them that day. Although he felt no remorse for this guy, he knew he couldn't just leave him there.

Looking around, he had no tools to bury him, and it didn't feel right somehow to just take him into the bushes and leave him there, even though the wildlife would benefit. But there was another option. Zephyr moved aside as Tony picked up the corpse and walked to the edge of the grasses, raised him up to head height, and threw him down the steep, high bank into the raging river. "Fish have gotta eat as well, Zeph," he said as he watched the strong, rapid current wash him away in seconds.

He picked up his old bag and knife and onward they went until turning left to walk back along their part of the river. Tony smiled as he got to the well. They stopped to drink and take a dip to cool off. As they carried on towards the salt lake, Tony knew they were truly home when he heard the deep roar of what he now knew was the giant ground sloth. "Good to see you too," he shouted with a wry smile.

The sun was beginning to set when they got to the wooded border of the community. Tony suddenly stopped; he'd been so excited to be back, but now had to remind himself of what he'd thought about back on the ship. They'd now been away for over a year, but to Julie and everyone else, only two or three days had elapsed. He had to think about acting more normally, and not make this look like a long-awaited reunion – just a normal return. It also occurred to him that, unlike when he returned to his own time, he'd had no effects from the journey through time when they landed, just as he hadn't the first time, and he wondered why.

All was calm as they entered the woods. The first person they saw was the night lookout, who'd come over to greet them. When they came out on the other side, Tony stopped to look at everything. It was a sight he'd long missed, but he would now really need to re-familiarise himself with things. Walking towards the lake, he heard a shout from behind him.

Upon turning round, the sight of Alpha and Omega running over to him raised a smile. "How are you, boys?" he said as they approached him.

"We good, all is good," Alpha replied.

"Julie... is she there?" Tony asked as he pointed up to the caves. Omega nodded. "See you both later then," he said as he headed to the cliff.

It was with a measure of anticipation to say the least that he walked up to his place. "Just keep remembering it's been only two days," he kept saying to himself. Zephyr ran straight in as they got to the entrance; with almost instant recognition, he began to sniff and re-mark his territory.

Tony took a first step in. Julie was already welcoming Zephyr as she left the fire she'd lit for the night. "Hello, Julie," he said after taking a deep breath. As he spoke to her, the realisation that he was actually seeing her in the flesh after all this time, after everything, hit him like a sledgehammer, but to her, it was a normal day.

She walked over to him and put her hands on his shoulders. "You all right?" she said.

With that he held her in his arms and gave her a lasting kiss. "Yes, I'm fine," he told her.

"Did you find anything out there?" she asked.

"No, no, nothing really. We have everything we need here," he replied with a sense of irony. If anything, she'd grown even more beautiful over those few days, and he still couldn't believe that, all being well, she'd be a part of his life for good now.

It was getting dark, and they began to cook their dinner as he and Zephyr settled back in. His thoughts turned to them being together later that night, a night he'd long been looking forward to, and later on, he was not to be disappointed!

Over the next few days, Tony picked up where he'd left off and